ARCHITECTS

The Project Collusion Series: Book 2

M.K. Williams

Copyright © 2020 by Mary K. Williams

All rights reserved. This book or any portion thereof may not be reproduced or used in any manner whatsoever without the express written permission of the publisher except for the use of brief quotations in a book review. The use of any of my works in AI learning or NFT is prohibited.

First Printing, 2020

Publisher: MK Williams Publishing, LLC

Library of Congress Control Number: 2020911597

ISBN:
978-1-7333929-5-2
978-1-952084-18-8

Mary K. Williams

1mkwilliamsauthor@gmail.com
1mkwilliams.com

All Persons Fictitious Disclaimer:
This book is a work of fiction. Any similarity between the characters, companies, and situations within its pages and places or persons, living or dead, is unintentional and co-incidental.

DEDICATION

For JMW

OTHER WORKS BY M.K. WILLIAMS

FICTION
The Project Collusion Series:
Architects

The Feminina Series:
The Infinite-Infinite
The Alpha-Nina

Other Fiction:
The Games You Cannot Win
Escaping Avila Chase
Enemies of Peace
Interview with a #Vanlifer

NON-FICTION
Self-Publishing for the First-Time Author
Book Marketing for the First-Time Author
How To Write Your First Novel: A Guide For Aspiring Fiction Authors
Going Wide: Self-Publishing Your Books Outside The Amazon Ecosystem
Author Your Ambition: The Complete Self-Publishing Workbook for First-Time Authors

TABLE OF CONTENTS

PART ONE

The Sit In

I can't tell you; *this is how it all started.* I don't believe any person, dead or alive, can. But I can tell you how I got here. This whole thing started from so many different places and the root cause has existed as long as mankind. This path is towards nihilism, creating our own ultimate destruction. But you're not here for the philosophical theories about the why. You want to know the how, the when, and the who behind the destruction. I can tell you what I know.

Let's just say that I didn't know everything that had been going on. Not until recently. An assignment from the captain, a suicide mission, sparked off this whole thing.

"Hunter," I heard Captain Gomes bark at me through the intercom that made his voice sound nasal and distorted. "Get up here now."

No need to explain where 'here' was, no need to clarify further. The ship had maybe one hundred people aboard and I was the lone Hunter. I didn't appreciate the accusatory glances of my shipmates as I passed by. Each wondering what I did, what I was about to be told. I recalled one similar trip to the principal's office in elementary school. The mortification and unease mounted with each step as I approached the bridge of the ship, high above the deck with a view of nothing except dark blue below and pale gray above.

I hesitated for a moment before opening the door and stepping over the knee-knocker. Once I was there, in that room, I would know what new crisis would be thrown at me. But for those few seconds, I was in the glorious unknowing; the time when this could still be something positive, maybe even welcome news. I took a quick breath and went in.

"Captain," I greeted him briefly when I spotted Gomes hunched over one of the monitors towards the back of the bridge, closest to his private office.

"Hunter," he started in immediately, standing up firmly and squaring his shoulders, a habit drilled into him by years of procedure. At an impressive six-foot-ten inches Captain Hector Gomes was one of few people who managed to make me feel short at six-foot-five. "Another supply shipment was attacked, never arrived at the depot on land, nothing for Roz to fly back."

Roz was our helicopter pilot on the ship, and she was also the only one who regularly went to shore. We all looked at her with a mixture of fear and reverence. She was brave enough to go there, but she could also be carrying some pathogen with her.

Gomes continued, "We need to figure out what is causing the disruption. It's happened too many times in the past three months for this to be anything unorganized. We need to find out who is behind it and eliminate the problem."

"I did notice our rations were getting rather bland," I offered in my own particular brand of speaking. I wasn't military. I wasn't part of his crew. I was a refugee on this vessel, and I had resisted the vernacular that was foreign to me for the three years I'd been aboard.

Captain Gomes had been upset with my non-compliance at the outset, but I think he either got used to it or he was told by Peec that my particular skill set afforded certain exceptions. Or maybe we were so far removed from people and procedure that it didn't seem to matter much anymore. But with everything that happened, it felt as though procedure was what would keep us all sane. Either way, he had softened to me and what would have earned one of his soldiers a quick rebuke for being so informal was met with, "Yeah, tell me about it."

"So, what do you need me to do?" Aside from my observation regarding meals, I didn't know the extent of the problem. With this new information and the rations that had been issued in the past two weeks, I inferred that we hadn't received a new shipment for at least a month. But I'm the biomedical engineer; I'm the science guy, the tech nerd. I don't touch the logistics. If what the captain had just said was true, the situation was likely more dire than I could have imagined. Even with a small population of about one hundred on the ship, The Pricus Capricorn, without new supplies more intense measures were likely on the horizon.

"Well, the crew is dwindling," Gomes started. My mind flashed on the image of something moving quickly in my peripheral vision, a blur of black and gray out of my porthole window, followed by a near-silent splash. I winced at the thought. The crew was indeed dwindling, people losing their minds, the sea looking all the more inviting each day. The captain continued, unphased, "I need as many of my trained team to stay on board to keep this thing afloat." He smirked and leaned up against one of the consoles, relieving some of the weight off of his boots. "Based on who I need on board and who can do the task on shore, you're it."

So, who can you expend in case this goes south? "I don't have the training for that kind of mission." I had this argument with him in the first few months on board. He knew this, sending me ashore was tantamount to a death sentence.

"None of us had any kind of training for this." He shook his head and considered his next words carefully. "We think that the attacks on the shipments can be stopped with your little invention." Gomes didn't notice, but his right hand went to his left forearm.

"And if I am attacked onshore, who will be able to help you with it?" I countered. I knew the power I had; I knew I was the only one left who understood the technology and could interpret the readings.

"If you don't go, we may never get another supply shipment onto this vessel. You want the life of every crew member on your conscience?" He narrowed his gaze at me, willing his mental picture into my own mind of the ship drifting afloat, unmanned, and only inhabited by the corpses of a starved crew.

He knew exactly what button to push to get me to jump. "Fine, I'll go," I turned to leave, my mind was already racing with the violent ends I would meet onshore. Disease, or attack from survivors, now rabid with only their primal instincts to guide them. "We'll do a briefing at 2000 this evening. You leave tomorrow at 0600."

"Meeting at eight. Board at six. See you then," I muttered on my way out, my last defiance as I knew I would likely never return to the ship.

I held it together for as long as it took me to get back to my bunk. I tried to calm myself, turn my inner thoughts from my inevitable demise to the promise of success. *Visualize success, visualize a positive outcome.* I had to have some kind of memory of what that felt like buried somewhere deep in my mind. I ran through the same mental route I had carved over the long months on that ship. My own warped form of meditation. A word association exercise:

The first visual in my mind was from my college days. *Rushing to class, running down historic streets where the upturned bricks in the sidewalk almost tripped me up. Some poking out. Some crammed back down but always jiggling when your foot struck them. You were at risk of twisting your ankle. You had to mind them, unconsciously, you avoided the loose ones. I don't ever remember stumbling, but I recall that I learned to sidestep one nasty section at the exit of my favorite pizza shop.*

If we had to play the game "Desert Island," the food that I could eat every single day is pizza. No toppings, lots of toppings, doesn't matter. Piping hot pizza with cheese melting off it. Piping, why is it called piping? Hot like steam pipes maybe?

Well, now, I've gone and done it. Steam pipes, PVC pipes. The ceilings in every corridor of the Bunker were lined with pipes. They went every which way, following us as we hustled to our laboratories. Sometimes I would picture an invisible cable reaching from one pipe down to the crown of my head, like I was a trolley car and I was being guided along my route.

Bunk to cafeteria to lab. Lab to Rattray's office. Office to cafeteria. Cafeteria to Rec Room, Rec Room to Bunk. It was a fun little mind game I would play sometimes. It doesn't work here. The pipes on the ship are too wide and bulky, too utilitarian to ever play host to my little daydreams.

The little hash marks on the wall next to my berth do play though. They remind me of cave drawings; perhaps I should go back and attach eyes, appendages. Would that help my psyche to make them alive? To give life?

No, they would turn on me in my sleep. They would fashion Clovis point spears and attack me when I least expected it. I cannot animate them. I've already had two nightmares this month, each time I wake up in a sweat. As my eyes adjusted in the dark, I thought the hash marks were really scratch marks, someone clawing at the wall, itching at something beneath it. No, no more little mind games to pass the time.

I had been keeping a journal of these dreams for months. I was in the habit of journaling and writing down my thoughts and experiments, so I added a new practice to include these vivid dreams. Dr. Simmons was the only psychiatrist on board and had been inundated with discreet requests for treatment. I heard through an unofficial network of other passengers that there was an opening. What with all the jumpers, her schedule was clearing up.

The journaling helps a bit. It makes me feel like I am doing something. Survivor's Guilt. She joked during our first session that it had infected everyone on board, but I didn't get the joke until a while after it ended.

She is a reputable doctor, but I'm sure all of the stories that she has heard so far have all been the same. Every person here had to watch from afar as the world burned; the flames not visible on the coastline, but still, we knew what was happening on land.

I thought that perhaps my story would add some new excitement to her routine, or I could just lie, make something up. But the truth is already unbelievable as it is. It's not every day that you meet someone who knows that they are culpable for an apocalypse.

Earlier that week, or was it the previous week, I had been telling Dr. Simmons about my worries, neuroses, guilt. "They called me up to the bridge yesterday," I said to the ceiling as I laid on the empty bunk in her cabin. She had no bunkmate so this served as her makeshift office. On my first visit, she told me that we could just sit and talk facing each other. But I preferred to lay on my back, speaking to the ceiling. She told me every time that this wasn't psycho-analysis. But I couldn't break the habit.

"I heard," she replied without further prompting. Of course, she had. Everyone on the ship could hear those announcements. No way to not hear them. We were referring to the last time I was called to the Bridge to help read the flashes on the screen, the flashes that I created.

"They're going to send me ashore, I just know it, and then I'm dead." I had expressed this exact worry to her multiple times. Every time it felt fresh and new, as though the words still had the potential to explode back at me, finally becoming reality. No amount of saying it out loud dulled the effect.

"Maybe they will send you ashore, but why would that necessarily mean you would die? You've survived this long, haven't you?" Dr. Simmons always answers my worries with questions. She never tells me anything new. I like that though. I don't think my brain could handle anything new.

Now that I have my orders from Captain Gomes all I want to do is pound down her door and say, "I told you so." But that won't change the captain's mind. It will only make me feel slightly better. Validated in my paranoia.

I knew that my time on board would be ending. I could just feel it. My days of staring at the gray walls and finding myself lost within a tangle of passageways would soon be at an end. I always assumed I would find myself overboard, just another one of the mentally weak scientists who went stir crazy without projects to tinker with. Of course, I didn't believe any of the bulletins they gave as the cause of the disappearances of late. People were starting to lose it. Everyone aboard was starting to go stir crazy, agitated. There were strong dividing lines between the soldiers and the refugees. The ones who had earned their spot on the ship and the ones who had earned everyone a one-way ticket to misery.

Our place here, my place here, was based on timing. They weren't going to keep me on the luxurious cruise ship in the middle of the Pacific that I happened to be aboard when the outbreak happened. It was arranged that the top scientists would be picked up so that they would help with the situation. But no specimens were ever provided. Instead of my story being that I took the opportunity so that I could help, I just took the out so that I could live a protected life on this vessel.

The paramilitary team was welcoming at first, but they made it known that they didn't think much of us egg-heads. Where they had physical strength, tactical awareness, and the first priority on the ship, the scientists had theories, and laboratories, and our skills were no longer in high demand. They told us that the disease had already spread too quickly and that at this point every country had entered into a state of martial law. No need to start developing a cure, most of the population was already dead or dying. Best for us to hunker down and wait for the all-clear. But the all-clear hadn't come for three years.

I began to speak out, having the audacity to ask when we could leave. I had indeed lost a small piece of my sanity, but the thing with your mental health is that you can lose a bit here and there, but you don't know which bits are the most important until you've completely unraveled.

"Maybe the team that is supposed to give us the all-clear was infected. We need to send out a search and rescue team!" I remembered my first conversation – or argument – with Gomes.

"Rescue? Rescue them where? You bring them aboard and they could infect us all." The captain made his response clear. I tried to connect with his lieutenant, Nelson Chang, to see if he might harbor the same concerns that I did; see if I could convince him to break rank. I was shut down, and ever since then, I've been awaiting the day that he would try to call me out, to get me off the ship. And that day had arrived.

After wasting idle moments back in my bunk, throwing soft items at the metal walls and feeling no relief, I stormed out and worked through the maze to try and find Dr. Simmons. The last of my colleagues had all found their way over the railings in the past few months, leaving me with no one else to talk to except the good doctor.

I tried to politely knock on her door, but my hand refused and curled into a fist, pounding instead. Demanding an immediate answer. She didn't respond. I pounded again. Did I scream out her name? I can't recall. After I tired myself out, I charged back to my bunk.

I tried to have a conversation with the Doctor in my mind. What questions would she ask, what platitudes would she offer? *Hunter, why don't you tell yourself a new story?* I could try to convince myself that this is what I wanted. I'm going to leave the ship.

That could work. But I would remind her that I knew this was coming all along. There was a conspiracy among the crew to slowly pick off the scientists one by one, to eliminate us, punishment for our crimes, and to save food for the rest of the soldiers. She would tell me that conspiracy theorists are often wrong. I would ask her a question, finally. *"What do you call a conspiracy theory that turned out to be right?"*

My feet thumped against the hallway. Everything about life on the Pricus Capricorn was loud. Every surface was metal. Conversations echoed. Light footsteps sounded like a pounding march. Engines whirred on and off, steam whistled, and then subsided. There was always noise on the ship. I added my fair share to it.

When it was time, I headed to the meeting to learn about my onshore mission. I entered the small conference room off of the command center. Lieutenant Nelson Chang was fiddling with the remote control, trying to set up a visual presentation. He was extremely lean, almost frail, compared to the rest of the crew. All of them were supposed to be ex-special ops soldiers. I never would have figured this guy for that line of work in a million years. But perhaps that was his advantage when he was on the front. The ability to look weak and draw people in was his distinct skill.

I sat down in the seat closest to the exit. I was being forced ashore against my will. I wasn't about to put on my chipper face and pretend that I wanted to be at this briefing. Chang acknowledged me as he reset his computer.

He finally got the display working correctly as two other crew members arrived. Dr. Jordan Michaels and Specialist Ansel Dawes. They didn't appear to be too pleased about being there either. Both men had been on the Pricus when I had arrived three years earlier. They had worked with Captain Gomes for years prior to the outbreak. I was shocked that he would put people I considered to be his most valuable team members on a suicide mission, but I didn't let that show on my face. *Maybe this mission isn't completely doomed*, I thought as Chang began.

He started with aerial shots of the helipad where our supplies were to be picked up. Then another of the supply depot further inland. There were older images as well as fresh ones the Connect glider had taken earlier in the day.

"We have limited information on what has happened to the supply line and limited time to explain, so I'll just dive in. You are not authorized to discuss any of this until you are on the ground tomorrow. Nobody on the ship can know what I am about to tell you. Our supply lines were interrupted three months ago. We've been living off of our reserve store of food and MREs. It's almost empty." He paused for a moment; his mouth twitched. No more food meant starvation. I nodded to signal that I understood the full gravity of the situation. Michaels and Dawes did the same. *Three months.* That was way longer than I had even anticipated.

"The three of you will start out at the helipad depot and work your way inland to the supply depot. It's a good sixty miles, so we expect it to take a few days on foot. We suggest you follow the road but stick to the trees."

"Where do you think the disruption point is?" Dawes cut in with the first question.

"We haven't had any communication with the team at the supply depot for six weeks. Their last contact let us know when the supplies left, part of our routine. After that, nothing. No supplies at the helipad. We think some of the local survivors tracked when the trucks rolled through and set up roadblocks. Our team has gone silent, so it's possible they can't safely communicate with us to establish a new route-"

"Or they're all dead," Michaels interrupted.

Chang took a deep breath. "We don't know for sure. The crew in the supply depot had sent us some of their concerns about the locals."

"You think they were attacked?" I jumped in as well. These onshore headquarters were all secure underground facilities. Buried miles into the earth, they were fortresses. They could wall themselves off and survive for years if they needed to. They'd already been surviving for years, providing us support and shipping food to the coast. Within each of these onshore headquarters were command centers for their region, medical facilities, barracks, and machinery. They could continue to produce plant protein from internal greenhouses for a hundred years. Or, in the case of the facility in question, package it and send it to the crew on the Pricus.

"We're not sure, that's what we need you to find out," Chang said in an exasperated tone.

"Well, what did they report to you about the locals?" Michaels asked.

"Some chatter around vigilante organization," Chang let the anger in his voice show, he was losing control of the briefing. Chang and Gomes were all about maintaining control. I noticed the vein on his temple start to wiggle with tension.

"So, you don't think it could be another strain of the outbreak?" I followed up. Michaels and Dawes looked over at me. Their eyes confirmed it, they were thinking it too. We had been safe on our ship, away from the biochemical weapon, insulated by miles and miles of ocean.

"We don't know." Chang didn't try to sugar coat it.

"But you think it is more likely that they were attacked than infected?" Dawes tried to get him to confirm a theory.

"Yes," Chang said and advanced to another slide. The screen lit up with several clusters of blue dots. "We know there is a small population in the area. Our latest check-ins from other depots around the continent tell us that the infection has died out, all who remain were either quarantined or immune. So now that the world is nearly empty, we've returned to small bands of tribes and wandering groups of nomads."

"Why don't we just go ashore if the virus has died out?" I wondered why the obvious solution to the supply problem wasn't being discussed.

"If the supply depot was attacked, we don't want to have this ship, the crew, and the technology we possess attacked, killed, or stolen," Dawes answered this question and glared at me across the table for daring to ask.

"So, if the coast is clear, we may get to the depot and just tell you guys to come ashore?" Michaels chimed in.

"Your primary mission is to re-establish the existing supply lines. But, to the questions you have all asked, keep us apprised of your position and any contact with survivors," Chang was using his authoritative voice, he wasn't making eye contact with any of us. He needed to deliver his information to us like he was feeding data points into a computer. But we were human; we didn't operate that way.

"How many are there?" Dawes directed the question at Chang, but he was too busy picking at his fingernails to look up.

"Ten thousand," Chang said.

"In all of British Columbia?" I asked.

"On the continent." Chang pursed his lips at this comment. This information caught all of our attentions. I saw Michaels and Dawes look up at him out of the corner of my eye.

"We think there are maybe twenty to thirty survivors total in the region you'll be in. Hunter will have remote access to the Calm program to be able to manage any issues, should they arise."

Now it all made sense.

Dawes. Michaels. Me.

Muscle. Medical. Miracle.

"We haven't had a massive breach since late 2015, about six months after the outbreak," Chang jumped back into his briefing. He advanced his slide to photos of one of the regional headquarters. I remembered them from the first time I saw them. Our regional headquarters near Coeur d'Alene, Idaho was attacked by two survivors. They set off cans of the Cease aerosol and shot up the place. It was a grim day. It was the day I realized that trying to help the world survive wasn't just about stopping the toxin anymore. It was going to be about stopping humanity from ending itself. A grim reminder of why the one hundred members of this crew might not be able to handle thirty hungry and rabid survivors on land.

A shiver ran down my spine as I thought back to the headquarters attack. We had all been working around the clock to stop the riots and insurrections.

Losing a huge staff of trained soldiers and half of our executive team was a big blow. I didn't want to be the one to step in our supply depot and find the grisly scene repeated.

"If this was another breach, we may have no choice but to spray the area," Chang said with a grim face.

I opened my mouth to object, but Michaels beat me to it. "You're telling me there are maybe ten thousand people left on the entire continent of North America, and you want to spray and kill potential survivors if they attacked our supply depot?"

The idea sounded barbaric. An attack on them to even the score? We would lose the rest of the population quickly if that continued. "Do we really want to try to rebuild the world with a bunch of murderers and thieves?" Chang responded sharply.

Isn't that what we already are? I thought to myself, smart enough to not let those words pass my lips.

Michaels crossed his arms and leaned back in his chair. Clearly, he had heard enough. Dawes had resumed his thorough inspection of his cuticles. Chang dismissed us back to our bunks, reiterating his warning that we were not to repeat any of these details while still aboard.

Right, right, I thought. *Keep up the illusion.*

I couldn't sleep that night. I sat with my eyes open, staring at the gray ceiling of my bunk, memorizing the imperfections in the paint, the nicks left by whoever had used this bunk before I moved in three years earlier. The first light of dawn filled the small porthole with a red glow, casting ominous shadows about. The walls were bare; my few items had been stored into my rucksack. Everything I had on that ship had been borrowed. I arrived in the early morning hours, completely unprepared for the emergency evacuation. I had traded out a sport coat and tie for a pair of tee shirts, cotton boxers, a black canvas coat, and thick khaki cargo pants. My wardrobe hadn't increased much since then. An extra set of boxers, a set of running shorts, one extra tee shirt. All pilfered from the bunks of my previous colleagues who had jumped overboard. I felt no guilt for scavenging their clothing. I did feel wrong when I took their journals, but paper was a tough commodity to come by.

As a child, even as a teenager, I would fill volumes of journals from edge to edge, leaving no margins. I would have a journal for my sketches, my little inventions, and ideas. Another for my home experiments on fried electrical circuits I tried to revive, observations of neighbors who passed by on the sidewalk, and chemical mixtures and their smells. I would have a third journal for my thoughts, my ideas. Being stuck on this ship has been intolerable. The confinement, the isolation, the fear, have all weighed on me. But the worst has been the extremely limited supply of paper.

Taking the clothes that fit me from Holtz and Kupper didn't seem like a big deal. Taking their journals did. I needed the paper, I needed the outlet for my ideas and to track my memories of this entire ordeal, my observations, and updates on how the device was helping the remaining population. But it felt like a violation. To pick up a written account of their thoughts, a partially complete excerpt from their brains. To see their writing on one page and to so callously place my own on the next. As though I was hijacking their thoughts, as if I were interrupting the final information from their minds. But I had to do it, I had to make the most of this resource.

But as the captain had so clearly explained the day before, food was truly the scarcest commodity. I pulled on the coat that had started out black, but years of wear and spray of saltwater had weathered and eroded the fabric to a thread-bare charcoal gray. I picked up my rucksack, the stack of journals I had accumulated and filled, making it heavy on the bottom. My few extra articles of clothing were piled on top.

Morning came without any pronouncements or somber music to announce my fate. I was ready to leave within moments of getting out of bed. All this time stuck on this ship and in a matter of minutes, it looked like I had never been there. I shrugged off my self-pity. I left that cramped bunk without a backward glance. The room itself meant nothing to me, my collection of hash marks would be there when I returned. If I returned. And if I was assigned a new bunk at that time, I would be just fine.

Topside, I spotted Dawes and Michaels chatting with Gomes. Our pilot, Kelly "Roz" Rosen, was running through her pre-flight checklist. Completely covered in her flak suit and her thick helmet already secure over her head, I only knew it was her because she was the last pilot remaining. Her dark features and unruly hair were hidden from view.

I looked to my left and saw the sun still battling against the endless horizon of the frigid North Pacific. An endless sea that was at times beautiful and isolating, but most importantly, had been the perfect natural barrier. The biochemical weapon that had been released claimed ninety-nine percent of Earth's population in weeks, and another point five percent in the following months had been unable to span the mighty sea.

I started toward the Sikorsky Black Hawk helicopter to store my small bag beneath the row of seats bolted to the back wall. A few of the crewmen were adding thick boxes and securing them within the fuselage. Gas masks and wearable oxygen tanks for each of us. I had picked up on the technical names and uses for each of these items. You spend enough time around these military types, and their precision, their accuracy in terminology grows on you.

Dawes was my height and had me by at least fifty pounds. He was bulky with muscle. While I stuck to running a track around the ship to clear my head, Dawes was always pumping weights. A man's man through and through. His skin always had a tan glow, even in the dead of winter on the sea when we all hid inside to avoid the bitter cold. His dark skin and pale eyes were arresting. Everything about him said, "don't mess with me." In general, I tried my best to avoid him. He walked over to the chopper with his pack and rifle. "We've all been inoculated, but we haven't had to come into direct contact with the toxin yet. We're taking precautions," Dawes said as he approached me, noticing that my gaze was fixed on the boxes.

It's hard to admit out loud or to yourself when you are terrified. But I had seen the video footage that had been broadcast on the ship after arriving. The bodies splayed out in the streets. When the device was first leveraged as a potential solution to stop the in-fighting that resulted from the complete anarchy, I saw the scurrying of those blue dots. Each dot represented a person, a survivor. But I saw them blink out within months. The world had become a lawless place as the biological weapon spread through the air and stripped society of its leaders, its police, its military. Surviving the disease had put each person in danger. So yes, I was terrified that the inoculation that was given to each of us six months after the outbreak wouldn't be enough. But I was also afraid of who we would find on our route.

I'm not sure what I expected from our abrupt departure. Some prophetic and inspiring words from the captain? A final warning? Something? But that didn't happen. He appeared happy to be rid of us, giving me, Dawes, and Michaels a brief handshake before turning to head back to the bridge. He wouldn't be waving goodbye to us from the deck as the helicopter took off. This was a military operation in his mind. No need to get all emotional. We had a job to do. And the expectation was that we would get the job done and return to the ship.

Strapped into the harness, I found my eyes staring at the horizon. The endless expanse of water would soon end. Roz was relaying a first-hand account of what she had seen on the last supply run to my colleagues. The three of them were all cut from the same cloth, or at least trained in the same regard. Military training and a career moving up the ranks until they had all joined the private sector. Peec, the global technology company, had hired an entire fleet of ex-military to protect their assets around the world. The crew of the Pricus were all that remained.

I had been the fish-out-of-water on the ship because I was the last of the non-security team remaining. I was quite content to be "one of the scientists" that evacuated to the ship, better than being stuck in the Bunker I figured. Until I had become the only scientist left standing.

I caught some of what they were saying over the headsets. Even with the three of them sitting close by and the headset jammed against my ears, the thunder of the helicopter blades still made it near impossible to hear what they were saying. I could ask for a summary once we landed.

Landed.

That's a concept. I hadn't been on the mainland in years, even before the outbreak. I tried to remember what it was like before I left when I spotted a brown line approaching on the horizon.

Shoreline.

I had dreamed of it for so long until my dreams only focused on water and metal. And there it was. It might be barbaric and lawless now, but it was home. I had been longing to get transferred back to the home office on the mainland when everything happened. I had been trying to get there. It was home, and then, it had become quarantined. It had been a place that I couldn't go. Over time it became a place that I dreaded. The lone survivors would be tough and ruthless. Though I had not left the world, I was about to re-enter a world I had once left behind. Only it would be completely different. Like going back to your childhood home after a long time away. The shine is gone because things have changed. And you realize that home was never a place, but a time. So, this landmass may have been the place of my birth, the place I lived and studied and dreamed. But it was not my home anymore. I steeled myself for the transformation I was sure to witness when we landed.

I thought back to my early memories and how I had evolved over time. I started out walking. A boy and the Earth. Boot and ground underfoot. I started out as a human on a path, a hunter. Not actually hunting though. I could never imagine myself working up the will to kill something. Not until now, but especially not now either.

As a child, when I wasn't in the woods, I was inside my room tinkering. Ignoring my sister's pleas to come outside and play with her. Artemis would whine until she tired herself out and went off on her own.

I enjoyed the solitude. I would take apart toys that had robotic components to perform a Frankenstein like surgery on them. Talking teddy bears soon had light-up eyes; the effect on Artemis was entertaining for me, even if it terrified her. As I got older and the camping trips got more involved, so did my time soldering components together. I was either out in the wild making do without any conveniences, or I was in the lab with the robotics club. I didn't join in with sports or parties. I really only read books that would advance my knowledge of current robotics. I wanted to make something now. I wanted to make something that would help.

And then, one day, I happened to be walking through the living room on my way to my bedroom when my mother stopped me to ask about my day. I tried to shrug it off when the images moving behind her caught my eye. The evening news program featured a small child with a device planted on the side of their skull. I turned my focus from my mother's caring attention to the story; I turned the volume up, much to her frustration. Why had I been ignoring the TV for so long? What if I had never seen this story? I likely never would have had my lightbulb moment if I hadn't passed through at just the right time.

I studied everything I could about the Cochlear implant after that news segment finished. How it worked, how scientists were able to marry biochemistry and neurology and mechanics. I knew that I wanted to do this. Not to reinvent this device, but to make something that would help people.

I would take my lifelong passion for robotics and focus on creating a device that would change humanity. Cure some ill. Advance or enhance some trait to give us superhuman abilities.

Many years later, I had the right ill to cure. I'll never forget when Fort Hood happened. (Isn't it weird how we say that the location "happened" instead of the mass shooting at the location?) That single event is when it all coalesced for me. I realized that I could help. I could invent something that could stop the madness; that could stop the terror. And not even for the mass-shootings and larger events that caught headlines. Violence resulting from PTSD and other mental health issues doesn't just manifest in headline-grabbing events. It appears when a soldier, returned from war, sends their fist through the wall over something that should have only elicited a grunt of annoyance. It appears when someone who hasn't taken their medication relapses into mania and lashes out on those closest to them, convinced they are plotting something sinister. But what if I could help them? What if I could develop a technology so that when they are calm and thinking clearly, they could have it implanted to ensure that the next time they lost control, they wouldn't hurt themselves or those around them? What if I could make the dying stop? *What if I could fix it?*

And thus, I began my journey. I spent years studying not only the biomedical advances that would allow for an implanted device to administer such a solution, but searching for the correct solution itself. Adrenaline and nor-adrenaline became my two best friends. Their interaction, the conversation between these two chemicals, became a new language to me. I observed it, I spoke it, I dreamed in it.

After years of loving science, but hating school and the social indignities that it afforded, I signed on to stay in through a doctoral program. Thankfully, after high school, my lot improved and I could elect to spend all my time with equally odd nerds who liked to play video games and build robots and watch reruns of space shows all the time. No need to put ourselves out there and talk to the few girls in our classes. They were too shy to talk to us for the most part as well; it was an amicable truce. Or at least that was what I thought. Until some of my buddies had girlfriends and I was left as the single guy with fewer and fewer friends to hang with on a Friday night. I tried to go to a party, I attended one. But after thirty minutes of standing in the corner watching others having fun and convincing myself that

I wasn't meant to be there, I left.

My fortunes changed slightly when I started my doctoral program because there were girls in the program who seemed to understand that I was painfully shy, so they approached me. Thank goodness for small miracles. But no woman could lure me from my true passion, my need to invent a solution to the violence plaguing our society. I was determined. I was singularly focused. I was also a very inattentive partner or boyfriend or whatever it could have been called. I preferred to spend all my time in the lab, alone. The isolation of life in the Bunker and then at sea wasn't what scared me. It was being dropped back into civilization that did it for me.

As the helicopter began to descend, I thought that the super-human skill I could most benefit from was the ability to levitate or fly. To stay off the ground for a little bit longer. To delay this moment. My palms began to shake as we set down. Dawes and Michaels were cool under pressure, taking specific motions to unbuckle, gear-up, and drop-down. I felt three years' worth of unspoken fear surge to the forefront of my mind.

The water ended at the shoreline of a gray beach covered in rocks, waves pounding into the sand. We flew over a thick patch of trees. I could have sworn that the trees were so tall that they could have scraped the bottom of the chopper. The forest was punctuated only twice by thin strips of road and then again by water as we neared our destination. The landing strip appeared on the next patch of land, just past a large island.

Dawes and Michaels had their gas masks on and their rifles ready. I had been too busy zoning out and staring at the ground below to see how they had done it. My hands felt thick and ineffective as I tried to grab my mask and portable oxygen tank from the thick foam-lined box in between us. I fumbled for my rifle. We each had one and a minuscule amount of ammunition to carry with us. It was not only heavy, but it was becoming increasingly rare. Michaels and Dawes were trained to shoot and wouldn't miss. I was likely to waste any ammo on my shots, but I had to believe I could take action if the time came. I really hoped that it wouldn't. *Just a stroll to the headquarters to knock on the hatch and have those inside tell us that everything is A-Okay.* Or at least that's what I needed to tell myself to get over the fear of how dangerously ill-prepared we were if we did face any issues on the road.

Roz dropped us off, touching down for a few moments as Dawes and Michaels expertly grabbed their gear and jumped to the ground. I held us up, unintentionally, as I fumbled to unstrap my harness. I jumped down and then made for my gear. I could sense that Michaels and Dawes were frustrated. Roz looked over at me, I'm sure she was just doing her job to make sure I was clear of the chopper. But I could have sworn I saw the slightest shake of her head, disapproving of my presence on the mission. I was the least trained; I was the one who would slow the whole thing down and jeopardize the mission. This part isn't paranoia. I knew that the original crew didn't like me or any of the other scientists that had been on the ship. I was the last one left; I felt the disapproval of all of them focus on me. It was acute. The disdain that had been spread among many people now settled resolutely on me.

I tripped over my own feet, heavy inside the steel-toed boots that were supposed to protect me from injury. I was more likely to stumble and land flat on my face in them. Michaels and Dawes had their rifles drawn; the stocks set squarely against their shoulders as they scanned the perimeter. Roz took off after I was clear of the chopper.

It might have been more fuel-efficient for her to stay, but she couldn't do that. Our food supplies had been raided and attacked before we could get to them. The three of us could be expended. But we couldn't lose our pilot and the only functioning helicopter on the ship. I didn't realize just how dire a situation the Pricus was in until I saw Roz flying away. The wind generated by the blades beat against my face as she climbed higher and higher. That was it, the only means of contact that anyone on that ship had with the mainland. We had all survived the outbreak, but we wouldn't survive isolation.

Dawes handed me a gas mask and oxygen tank. I put them on quickly, already worried that I had been exposed for too long. Then my rational brain kicked it, reminding me that I had taken every precaution already. This was just a back-up, a fail-safe. Dawes and Michaels looked identical once their faces were covered. Their uniforms and masks so alike. Michaels started to speak; I could hear his muffled voice through the thick plastic. His heavy midwestern Chicago accent was distinct, even when it was distorted.

"You good?" he asked, gesturing with a thumbs-up sign. I mimicked him, giving him the same signal as I nodded my head. Between Dawes and Michaels, I would pick a mission with Michaels any day of the week and twice on Sunday. Knowing that he was on this expedition gave me a small feeling of relief. Michaels was the least territorial of all the soldiers on the ship. He was the only one who tried to get to know the scientists. Partially because he was a man of science himself, a doctor. When I first arrived, I kept to my group as best as I could. But as the weeks passed by, I knew we had to start to adapt. Michaels was the first to introduce himself to us. "Dr. Jordan Michaels," he said as he extended his hand.

"Wait, your name is Jordan Michaels?" I asked, about to make the obvious joke.

"Yeah, and I grew up in Chicago," he added.

"So, do you play any basketball?" I thought the question was reasonable given his namesake.

"Nah," he shook it off and continued to introduce himself to the rest of the scientists. It had been a good start to our interactions together.

I also liked that Michaels was on this mission because he was the last one remaining with any trauma training. Dr. Simmons could take care of our psyches, but Michaels had been a combat medic. He could work quickly and under duress, if anything happened. I hoped that he wouldn't have to dust off those skills. My own knowledge was limited to basic first aid and what I had to learn to test and develop the Calm implant. Michaels was the one who was the healer, the guardian of our physical well-being.

We started out with a host of scientists from Peec and two doctors aboard when we were evacuated to the ship years ago. The ship would be without their doctor for as long as this trip took, but we were now in treacherous territory. Not only were we risking exposure to the toxin if it remained, but all manner of injury or attack. This mission was too important to risk us not making it back because of something that Michaels could heal in a matter of minutes.

Dawes uttered a muffled, "let's go," to get us all focused on the task at hand. I surveyed the space around us. The depot was a metal structure that used to house small jets, private planes. At the time of the outbreak, all the planes were out, none of them made it back. It happened to be the closest airstrip and helipad to the Peec supply facility that the ship was using. Between Peec and the crew that was based on land, the entire site - the depot, the associated structures, the runway, the helipad, everything within the chain-link fence - became ours. Grass had started to sprout through the cracks in the concrete along the runway, having already conquered the edges of the facility by growing three feet high wherever it could.

This was exactly how I expected it to look. Abandoned, grim, desolate. The overcast sky seemed to accentuate the glum despair, the water stained spots on the concrete stood out more, the rust along the depot walls looked grittier. Dawes had walked over to the entrance, the fence gates swinging open freely with the breeze.

"That should be locked," Michaels muttered to me as I watched Dawes walk away from us. I felt distinctly unsafe. I checked the screen on the tablet I brought with me. I could see three blue dots grouped together tightly, just past land-fall. I zoomed in on the scene and could see the dot that marked Dawes moving away from the ones that indicated Michaels and myself. I didn't see any other active blue dots anywhere near us. The closest appeared to be several miles away, further inland, and they appeared to be static. No one else was around, but I still felt like we were being watched. In a way, we were. I was watching us on my screen, able to see our devices pinging. But I could sense there was someone else, something else, observing us.

I turned to check that no one was behind me. All I saw was the helicopter growing smaller and smaller against the gray sky. The clouds were thick; they had all banded together to completely cover the sky. The imposing trees were staring down at us, aware that we weren't really supposed to be there. I had once loved the bold green of the Pacific Northwest. The entire region had been synonymous with the word "lush." But now, after years of unending sea and sky, I expected to stare at these verdant wonders in silent reverence. Instead, they only proved to disappoint. They weren't as green as I had remembered; they didn't seem to be alive. They were just another feature of a dead continent. The trees had just continued to grow, indifferent to the annihilation of the human race. They only tolerated us before. Now that I was back on land, they didn't look happy to see me.

As Dawes continued towards the depot entrance, Michaels moved towards the hangar. I decided to keep close to the doctor. All I could hear was the sound of our boots and the slight breeze rustling the trees by the far fence line. Until Dawes' voice came in over our headsets.

"Looks like the lock was cut with bolt cutters. Same with the chain. No idea how long ago this happened." I could hear Dawes drop the metal in his hands back onto the ground.

"You think local survivors got hungry?" Michaels asked while he did a visual check to his left and right, his rifle raised to his shoulder.

"Probably," Dawes responded. I could hear his boots through the intercom and saw him walking back towards us.

"You think they stayed in the area?" I asked.

"My guess is they took the food and ran," Dawes said, his words repeating as I heard his muffled voice through his gas mask now that he was closer to me and again through the headset on a short delay.

"No signs of life in the immediate area. Closest survivor looks to be a few miles out," I pointed to the other dot on my screen.

"They might start moving in closer if they saw the helicopter land," Michaels added.

"No movement yet," I confirmed as I showed him the screen as well.

Michaels was silent for a moment, appraising the dot on the screen. "Alright, let's refocus. We know they came through the gate and cut the lock. The last team that tried to land and get our shipment found the place like this. That means our supply trucks haven't been able to get through to deliver our rations."

"Or they knew with the lock cut that the rations wouldn't be secure," Dawes added to Michaels' theory.

"You think they don't have a spare lock they could have used?" Michaels voice, though muffled through the thick plastic, was still noticeably incredulous. "No, I think our suppliers knew to not come back."

As he spoke the words, a strong gust of wind flew down the abandoned runway and shook the large doors of the hangar. The ominous sound of metal scraping against the concrete sent a chill up my spine and made the fillings in my teeth whine. We all looked up towards the noise at the same time.

Back on alert, Dawes and Michaels lifted their rifles. The one I had been provided was still slung across my back. I fumbled to tuck the tablet back into the front pouch of the body armor I'd strapped on as we landed and grabbed for my gun as well. Not nearly as smooth as my colleagues, but I got there eventually. I felt exposed and ill-equipped. I had been given standard issue army body armor. Camouflage green with a heavy plate across my chest and back. Dawes and Michaels had the same, but it looked more effective on them, they knew how to wear it, they knew how to maneuver in it. I wished we had the more advanced suits that I had seen Holtz working on years earlier, but the entire stock had been assigned out during the outbreak.

I followed closely. They carefully stepped one foot in front of the other towards the hangar. The wind blew once more, moving the right door open and then leaving it to slam shut once the gust relented. Michaels entered the hangar first, checking to his left and right, then looking up. Dawes followed and flanked Michaels. It was a carefully orchestrated ballet of movements, the two of them working in harmony without having to say a word. I continued behind him, feeling secure that the coast was clear.

The hangar was empty except for a few packages of rations that appeared to have been ripped open. Particles of the wrapping and dehydrated flakes of food were scattered across the concrete floor. Derelict and deserted, the hangar was supposed to house enough food for the crew of the ship to survive for two weeks when it was at full capacity. Given the population decline aboard, each shipment lasted longer and longer.

But the depot was barren. We had been told prior to leaving that the supply shipment hadn't been restored for at least three months. That was six trips where Roz came back empty-handed. The issue in the supply line went further back than this point. Nothing had been getting to the depot, and we would need to figure out why.

Dawes lowered his weapon; there was no immediate threat, no one lurking in the shadows. He bent down by the discarded wrappers and shook his head. Michaels let down his guard as well, taking in the entire space with his eyes, casting his gaze towards the ceiling. I let my own rifle drop and swung it back over my shoulder.

And then it happened. It was so fast. I heard a muffled "what the-?" coming from Michaels and then the zipping sound of a wire speeding across a pulley. The sounds were so interlinked, I was hearing them at the same time, but I know I heard his voice first. And then I heard the liquid sound of metal slicing into something organic. Dawes heard the same things that I did. We both startled and grabbed our weapons quickly, looking to see what just happened. The flutter of something in my peripheral vision caught my attention. Dawes must have seen it too.

Hanging high above the concrete floor, at least twenty feet off the ground, was Dr. Jordan Michaels. Our only team member with any medical expertise and the one guy of the whole crew who I could get along with.

Strung up by his left foot, he hung upside down with a stream of blood moving like a river down his front and onto the floor below, a small puddle starting to collect. He had stepped into a trap. That speeding wire was the one that was now tight around his ankle. That liquid sound was the jagged piece of metal now sticking through him. And that item that caught my eye: a dirty canvas tarp with three words drawn in uneven letters.

FEAR THE REAPER

This all happened within seconds. My eyes darted quickly from each element trying to make sense of it all. I looked down at my feet, careful that I wasn't about to walk into the same trap. Dawes began to scream frantically into the intercom. He called out for Michaels. Michaels didn't answer. Perhaps he was still alive and his words were too quiet inside the thick plastic of the gas mask. But that didn't seem to be the case. The doctor was dead. I could only hope that it had been quick and relatively painless for him.

"We need to get in touch with the ship now!" These words from Dawes were the first that I processed in my own moment of panic.

"What?" I asked, unsure if I had understood him.

"You have the radio! We need to call this in now!" Dawes had crossed the distance between us in no time at all, his hands already outstretched, expecting the device.

"We should cut him down," I protested.

"No, that could be another trap. We need to call this in. Where is the radio?" Dawes looked as though he was about to shake me. Maybe that would have helped me to snap out of whatever headspace I was in. I felt calm, collected. I felt just fine. And then, I remembered.

I pulled out the tablet from my front pouch and unlocked the idle screen. Three alarm notifications were going off. One confirmed what I had already seen, Michaels was gone. Dawes and I both had dangerously high levels of adrenaline pouring into our systems. I tapped the screen a few times and could sense that Dawes was starting to relax, his motions less reactive, less violent, less angry. The team on the ship would have received the same alerts. I stuffed the tablet away again and removed the pack from my back and set my rifle on the ground. I reached in and grabbed the radio, handing it to Dawes. He took off his gas mask, his face sweaty and red from the material.

"Hello, Pricus Capricorn. Do you copy, Pricus?" Dawes barked into the radio. He took big gulps of air now that his face wasn't covered. I worried that he would be exposed, but I suppose he figured this mission was doomed, given our current predicament. Not even on the ground twenty minutes and a third of our team was gone.

A voice filled the empty hangar. The sound coming from the radio interrupted itself, punishing our ears with harsh stops and starts.

"Team Leader, please confirm your location," the voice demanded. I couldn't tell which of the command center soldiers was speaking to us; the sound was too distorted.

"We are at the supply depot. Michaels stepped on a trap; he is critically wounded!" Dawes shouted the words back into the radio, as though he could force them through the device if he spat right up against the receiver. I wanted to correct him. Michaels was gone, but perhaps Dawes was still in the denial phase. I had accepted that the mission was doomed. I had been thinking it ever since Gomes gave me the assignment not twenty-four hours earlier. This was just confirmation of what I had feared.

Now, Hunter, that kind of thinking won't make the situation that much better. I heard Dr. Simmons' soft voice in my mind. Her calm and even tone reminding me that I needed to take a deep breath. This wasn't my fault; I hadn't willed this mission into failing. I tried to inhale deeply, but I felt restricted, the armor too heavy, the mask too tight. Seeing that Dawes had yet to show symptoms or drop dead, I decided to trust that the air was clear. I pulled my mask up, letting it sit atop my head, and took a deep breath. Then another.

Dawes was continuing to bend over as he hollered into the radio. Pouring all of his effort into each word as though he were straining to finish a deadlift. "The depot is empty. The chain and lock out front are broken!" Dawes looked up at me and shook his head. Was he unhappy with me individually or just displeased that I was all he had left to help him on this mission?

"Copy that, Dawes." The voice responded after a few seconds. There was a delay in time for the messages to transmit. It had already been a minute and the pool of blood below Michaels started to spread, the liquid finding the imperfections in the concrete.

"Michaels is gone, do you copy that?" Dawes retorted hotly. Talking back to his superiors wouldn't help anyone, but he was keyed up and needed to express his frustrations. He wouldn't go into a full fit, that I was sure of. He wouldn't kick my pack or punch the wall or throw the radio. His emotions would continue to level off. His mind would be clear again in a few moments. We both needed to grieve Michaels, we needed to process what we had just witnessed and the severity of the situation. But we would do so when we were out of danger. When we were back on the ship. We would each need to spend hours with Dr. Simmons.

"Confirmed, Dawes. Is Hunter safe?" The voice filled the hangar once more. Dawes shot me a look as he processed the question. He stood up straight and stuck out the radio, forcing me to take it from him.

I pressed down on the button to speak. "Yes, I'm unharmed." I knew better than to say I was fine. Or okay. I had been neither of those things for a long time. I couldn't ever assert that I was safe. This was hostile territory. I was alive. For now.

"You manually adjusted the devices just now?" the voice barked back.

"Yes, sir," I nodded as I spoke. They couldn't see me, but Dawes could. He was staring straight at me as I answered. He shook his head and turned as he walked away. He strode over to where Michaels was hanging.

"Good thinking," the voice sent through their approval.

"Sir, this facility is not secure. There was clearly a trap set that killed Michaels. There could be more." I knew I was speaking out of turn, but I was only repeating what Dawes had been trying to yell through the receiver.

"Copy that, Hunter." the voice was now clipped, short.

Dawes had walked around the growing puddle, now heading toward the far wall. He was inspecting every inch with his eyes, stepping slowing, checking the floor for any additional traps.

"Dawes said there was a message on the wall?" The voice asked for confirmation.

"Yes, it appears to be a handmade sign that was released when the trap was set off," I turned to look at the message again as I spoke into the radio.

Dawes had made it over to the sign without incident. He reached up and pulled the canvas in his left hand. It released with some effort. I wondered how long it had been lying in wait for us. Once it was down, Dawes started to roll it up in his hands. I didn't like that he was touching things, shouldn't we leave it exactly as we found it?

"Fear the Reaper'? That's what it said?" the voice spoke, calling my attention again.

"Yes, sir," I confirmed as I watched Dawes walk back towards me. The person on the other end hadn't disengaged from the radio, so we both heard what was said next. A conversation we weren't supposed to catch.

"This damn Reaper again. These survivors have lost their minds. We should just take 'em out. I can't stand this shit!" That voice I recognized as Captain Gomes. I heard a thud; I pictured that it was his fist hitting the desk.

Dawes ripped the radio from my hand. "Sir, did you know about this?"

There was a long silence. I opened my mouth to speak, to ask Dawes a question, but he held up his finger to silence me just as the radio crackled to life.

"When we picked up our last shipment a few months ago, there was a -" the captain's voice paused. "There was a poster," he resumed, his voice indicated that this was the best word he could select. "It had the same words on it, 'FEAR THE REAPER.'"

"Maybe it's just one person with a twisted mind. I mean anyone who survived probably lost it mentally." I tried to rationalize what had happened.

"They stuffed this sign in the middle of our packaged rations. Which means they opened them up, planted this little note, and then expertly resealed it. We had strong suspicions that the food was poisoned." The captain's words were grim.

I looked over to see Dawes examining my face, checking for my reaction. He looked just as concerned as I felt. Not only was it unsafe on land, but even if we survived and returned to the boat, we would do so in just enough time to watch the crew starve. This mission was life or death for every person on that ship. This knowledge pushed my pessimism aside. I could help, I could fix this, I could undo some of what I had done.

"Sir, the disruption in our supplies is clearly further upstream. We are going to secure this location and then head inland. We will radio-in this evening when we make camp." Dawes appeared to be less pissed off, his own eyes glowing with purpose. I wanted to remind him that we didn't need to call in on our position, they could track us with the same device I was using, but he had his orders and he would follow them to the letter.

"Copy that, Dawes." The radio went silent and it was just the two of us left. I turned to face Michaels.

"What do we do with him?" I asked, nodding towards his body.

"Cut him down. It's mostly concrete out there. I don't think we could bury him in the depot," Dawes said as he walked closer to him again. There was a scaffold on wheels by the entrance. I rolled it over behind Dawes. We cut Michaels down and placed him on top. My heart was pumping heavily in my chest; I worried that this action would result in another trap releasing a metal spike through one of us. I worried that the scaffold would slide on the wet floor and create a loud and violent crash. I worried that a rogue group of insurgents would sneak up on us as we lowered Michaels' body down. None of those things happened. Yet.

We let Michaels lay undisturbed on the top of the scaffold and wheeled it out to the abandoned airstrip. It was easier to carry him this way than sharing his weight with our arms, but that thing was loud as anything. The wheels seemed to be designed to draw the most attention, but then again, the cracked concrete wasn't helping. Blackbirds with widespread wings swooped past us, calling out their displeasure as we disturbed their serene silence. As they flew off, I wondered for a moment what kind of birds they were. Crows? Ravens? I wasn't sure. We probably scared away every bird in a one hundred-mile radius with the noise. Or attracted every predator in the area.

Once we made it to the fence, we took him off the scaffold and laid him in the ditch by the road. Dawes combed through the items in Michaels' pack. He took a pair of clean socks and dry clothes, stuffing them into his own bag. I went for the more a practical acquisition and did my best to shove his medical supplies into my bag, cramming extra gauze wraps, an orange bottle of penicillin, and a pre-filled tube of antiseptic I could into my bag without crushing the delicate instruments. At least I had been required to take advanced biology and anatomy courses for my doctorate, but that had been almost a decade earlier.

We covered him with the canvas, the blank side facing up. It wasn't sufficient, but Dawes reiterated that we needed to get moving. I thought we should say something. A prayer, a memory. Something. It didn't feel right to just leave him on the road. But Dawes had already started walking.

I followed Dawes as we headed east, further inland. I looked back once as we approached the tree line; I could just see the top of the canvas from that distance. I made myself a promise that when we came back through, laden down with supplies for the crew, that I would take the time to bury him as we waited for Roz to pick us up. I really wanted to keep that promise.

The depot looked just as desolate from this perspective, seeing it from outside the fence line. With each step, we would move further from the shoreline, further from the vessel that had insulated us from the outbreak. As we continued down the road, the view ahead became a narrow lane flanked by giant trees. They towered above us, the sentinels watching as we walked into hostile territory.

Dawes walked several feet ahead of me, his rifle cradled in his arms. I could hear the crunch of his boots on the gravel that had found its way across the road. The wind whistled through the trees; I looked up to see if the tips were swaying, I couldn't tell from this far below. I took out the tablet to check for any signs of life nearby. A few miles ahead, there was a bright blue dot on the screen. I walked ahead of Dawes and curved right, making for the tree line along the road. I felt safer with the protection of the few trees. It would give us some cover. Dawes followed without a word of protest or clarification.

I always appreciated the position of observing unseen. Having led several studies during my doctoral program, I had trained myself to watch silently. Able to see the action, but directly removed from it. Peering in through the fishbowl, on the other side of the one-sided mirror. My time on the island was defined by my time behind that mirror. I picture myself there the most. During those trial observations, I was closer to the action. In the room monitoring instruments, confirming that the device was indeed functioning as designed.

For a time, I felt exposed, in danger during those earlier studies in graduate school. I had been in the room with murderers, after all. I had to understand the roots of violence. And that meant I had to learn from those who were successful in their endeavors, those who had killed. Back when I was much younger the knowledge that I would be so close to these murderers made me nervous, *would they try to kill me too?* As Dawes and I walked silently, I almost chuckled out loud as the thought passed through my mind. I had no idea how much danger I had been in on that island. Even my interviews with mass murderers didn't compare to the interactions I had in the Peec research facility.

But I had once been young and naïve. During the first year of my doctoral program, I had been the most anxious for the Clifton study, a notorious mass-murderer. I suppose I was scared because he had that label applied to him.

A man, almost always young, almost always white, sitting in his isolated bedroom and simmering in his frustration. That's how it always starts. He would find a community where his anger and resentment could flourish, grow, and reseed like spores. He would talk a big game about a plan and take steps to show how much of a big man he was: buy a gun, buy another, buy lots of ammo. And he would call it ammo, not ammunition. Because he was tough like that.

And then one day something would snap. All those little things he picked up from others, all those weapons he stockpiled would be at his disposal at just the right moment. And bam. Or more appropriately *clack-clack-clack*. A quiet morning in a church, or a school, or a park would be destroyed. The screaming of pain and the whaling of sirens would put all of that quiet to an end; the noise of tragedy would put silence in its place.

I wanted to make all that noise stop.

Our graduate research team had been granted access to interview Thomas Clifton. The mass murderer who had shot and killed twelve people at a football tailgate in Phoenix, Arizona. What made him do it? What was going on inside his mind, inside his body at the time of the crime?

It was an odd sort of field trip for us to make. My thesis advisor, Professor Raymond Oswelu, had emphasized that we all needed to represent the university well, or this opportunity may not be available to other students. He reminded us in his perfect Queen's English accent as we drove in the university van to the prison. In my own mind, I thought that with this opportunity we would be able to gather data that would make this kind of study, this kind of crime, a thing of the past, and that would negate any future need for research visits. Like I said, I was young and naïve.

We started out with some preliminaries, Sarah, Tyndal, Nardeep, Roy, and myself all took turns with our introductions. What happens when a sociology major, a psychology doctoral student, a chemical engineering student, and two biomedical engineering research fellows walk into a prison? A dream team is what I would have said, no pun intended or feigned.

Thomas Clifton seemed perfectly amiable. His skin was pasty white and flecked with patches of red. His mousy brown hair was thinning on the crown of his head. His eyes revealed his mania though. He may have looked physically defeated by life in prison, but he was still sharp as ever mentally.

The attention that he commanded must have given him a bit of a high. I could still see the anger on him, etched into each worry line, growing out of the follicles on his arms, emanating from him like an aura of hate.

Sarah and Tyndal tried not to let their nerves show. Sarah remained mostly silent as she set up with video recording devices and documented the entire encounter with meticulous precision. Tyndal became more aggressive, trying to show that no one could mess with her. Nardeep, Roy, and I set about the process of hooking up the leads to Clifton's skull and heart. We would measure every possible output as we interviewed this monster, this man who did monstrous things.

After we were all set up, Professor Oswelu conducted the interview. We had all worked on a list of questions for weeks. Each one had a specific purpose in the course of our combined research efforts. Sarah wanted to know what factors would have driven this man to do such a thing. Tyndal wanted to know his frame of mind. Nardeep wanted to know how medical intervention prior to the incident may have impacted his state of mind during the event. Those three were all looking into the past. Roy and I were the only ones looking for a way to stop such a thing from happening ever again.

To start out, Oswelu made small talk, how was Clifton doing on "the inside?" Was he able to interact much with his friends or family on "the outside?" Was the food really all that bad? Those kinds of things before diving into his childhood, his mother, his father, and his personal life. I kept a close eye on the monitors throughout the interview. The hippocampus glowed when he spoke about his family life as a kid. Normal.

As Oswelu began to ask questions about his time in college, Clifton began to shift in his seat. He tried to adjust his hands; to fidget with them, but the ties were keeping his arms in place so that we could take accurate measurements. He began to perspire a little. The patchwork of activity lighting up on our screen indicated that he was preparing to lie, to deceive us. His dorsolateral prefrontal cortex and parietal cortex began to slow on our screen.

This was a moment of discovery. This was where the madness lived in his mind. Monitors were recording his pulse, his breathing, blood-oxygen count, his hormones. Roy and I read through pages and pages of data after the interview, and a hypothesis was born. An idea.

If the rise in adrenaline and noradrenaline in Clifton's system was the first precursor of anger and violence, then all we needed to do was detect when the right variables were present and stop the action. *All we needed to do.* But how could we tell if someone had elevated adrenaline? What if it was something as benign as a dog barking nearby? If someone who had this predisposition to violence wanted to stop themselves before they could harm others, then we would need to have an answer. Maybe, just maybe, we could make a device that would work. Roy and I set to work. We had theories to parse through, thought experiments to elaborate on, and a device to build.

It was almost a year later that I saw a news report that there had been a mass shooting at a mall in my hometown. It was the day after Thanksgiving and people packed in for deals on presents. I texted my mom to make sure that she and Artemis were okay. I was three states away at the time. When I hadn't heard a response twelve hours later, I hopped in my car and started driving.

I didn't drive to my childhood home. I drove straight to the hospital. I fought past the police lines and finally found a doctor who gave me the news I had been dreading. They were both gone. Killed at the hands of a madman. No, not even a man, a child. A seventeen-year-old kid who was mad at the world. And I couldn't even be mad at him; I was too busy blaming myself for what I couldn't even control. I felt inept. I knew I could have stopped it all if I had just worked a bit harder, a bit smarter. I boxed up those emotions though. I had to. If I was too emotional about my work, too irrational, it would never be complete. I often wondered if I had tempted fate. Had my proximity to the violence brought it to my doorstep? I had to avenge them; I had more purpose from that moment on. But I also knew I couldn't let my heart make any decisions on our research; it had to be my brain. Unfortunately, that is an invariably flawed machine as well.

The beep of the tablet broke my memory. Dawes stopped immediately; he heard it as well. Amid the organic sounds of our feet on wet duff and the swish of our clothes as we moved, the distinct technological beep wasn't too quiet to skip our notice. Dawes' rifle was up on his shoulder instantly. I pulled the tablet from my front pouch again. We had been walking at a decent pace, but I didn't think we could have reached the blue dot I had spotted earlier. Apparently, we had done just that.

I took two cautious steps to reach Dawes who was already doing a visual sweep. The road was now about six feet to our left and about ten or fifteen feet down, the line of trees climbing and giving us a raised view of who might be down there.

I showed Dawes the tablet. One blue dot about one hundred feet ahead. I could see an abandoned gas station just down the road. That had to be it, whoever it was had to be hiding in there.

"We continue past, we'll move further east and pass as quickly and quietly as possible," Dawes gestured to our right.

"Why?" I didn't understand. We were here to investigate what happened to our supply lines. We found a living person, there was no guarantee we would come across any more for a few days. Judging by the view on the tablet, this was the only person we would encounter for at least thirty miles.

"Why?" Dawes asked my question again, clearly frustrated that he needed to explain himself.

"Yeah, why? We're here to find out what is happening with our supplies. They might have seen something."

"Yeah, or they might have been the one to set the trap back there." Dawes shook his head as he spoke, as though he were explaining basic concepts to a child. I didn't appreciate his attitude.

I didn't respond right away. Dawes did have a good point. Whoever this person was, friendly or hostile, they had survived the apocalypse. They lived through the biochemical attack that killed billions and the ensuing anarchy. I looked down at the station again. Whoever it was could be sitting there waiting for us, or they could be asleep inside, sheltered from the elements, and insulated from any noise we might make. It seemed that while I was considering his position, Dawes was considering mine as well.

"Can't you knock 'em out? Then we don't have to worry." He gestured down to the tablet. I looked back over to him.

"People who are incapacitated are really difficult to question." I rolled my eyes as I responded.

"Yeah, but you can give 'em a little juice. Take the edge off. Right?" Dawes asked. His crude summary was correct. Heck, he had been feeling the effects of it himself, although I suspected it was starting to wear off.

I nodded. This was our best plan using the resources we had available. I didn't like using the device for this purpose, but we had just seen Michaels murdered by the horror-show booby-trap, so I wasn't above a little manipulation. I selected the blue dot for our stranger and a control window appeared on the screen. I slid my finger up about halfway.

"Is that enough?" Dawes looked over my shoulder. I didn't respond. I only had sarcastic comments about not knowing my own invention and I didn't want to tick him off.

"It'll be enough," I said as I locked the tablet screen.

"Okay, let's go," Dawes headed past me towards the embankment, starting to side-step his way down. As he walked further ahead, I unlocked the tablet one more time and selected the blue dot that corresponded with his implant. I upped the dose on his before stuffing the tablet back in my pouch and following behind him.

My device is pretty cool; I do have to admit that. It has a very sleek design and corresponding application. It was what a nerdy kid like me dreamed of while other kids frolicked outside and played sports. I've always had a fascination with science fiction. My favorite alien species were the Borg, the part human, part machine hive mind that was so often demonized in *Star Trek*. I liked to think of them as pseudo-robots, enhanced humans. I loved the Next Gen movies (that's *Star Trek: Next Generation*, for those who aren't in the know), but what they sparked in me was far more long-standing: a love of science and cool technology.

It was in high school that I first heard of The Living Cyborg Challenge. It was a science-fair on steroids. The P.C. Corporation sponsored a global competition for fourteen to eighteen-year-old students. The challenge was to develop a biomechanical device that would solve for a medical ailment or social ill. I had taken the challenge seriously and poured myself into the project; my grades suffered slightly as I had a tunnel vision on my first invention. Having been inspired by the Cochlear device as a child, I thought I could use a similar device to enhance the eyesight of the color blind. I had designed the external sensor and was ready to present my device to the regional judges so that I could advance to the national stage of the competition.

Then Neil Harbisson went and announced his status as the first living cyborg with, you guessed it, an external device implanted into his skull. The wind had been sucked clean out of my sails. I fumbled through my entire presentation. Everyone interested in the competition had certainly heard the news already. My palms were too sweaty to grasp my note cards. I wanted to run away and hide, but I at least finished the speech I had prepared and lifted the cover off my prototype. I didn't advance to the next level in the competition.

My dreams were crushed, but then it was time to graduate and I decided to focus on my next big idea. One that would be truly unique.

I studied hard. After a biomechanical engineering degree from Drexel University, a doctorate from M.I.T., and then two years working on a project at the Mayo Clinic, Uncle Sam came knocking. I don't mean this literally. I mean Samuel Metz.

Metz was a researcher who I knew in name only at the time. I had read several of his research papers and was keen to meet him one day. But he was never at any of the conferences I attended. It was like he only existed on paper. Until one day, I received an email from him. I couldn't believe my eyes. He had been working on a government contract with P.C. He knew our research would be mutually beneficial and asked would I consider working for their R&D team? All of my research would belong to P.C., but I could at least see my device through to production.

P.C. The same company whose student competition I had completely whiffed on. The combination was perfect; the government contract secured our funding and getting to work with P.C. was a major opportunity to add to my resume.

Yes, I was drawn into the glamor of P.C., the all-powerful and far-reaching technology company with a veritable army of engineers and designers working globally to make the world less evil. I had recently taken to calling them by their new street name "Peec," it was an elongation of the company initials "P.C." What those initials stood for had been long forgotten, a footnote on a corporate page that no one ever visited.

With just a few email exchanges and the public perception of the company to count on, I was recruited, roped-in, signed-up, and shipped-off to the basement research and development labs where the natural light of the sun never-ever shone.

I felt the same wave of nerves that I experienced during that high school competition wash over me as I approached the Peec headquarters in Seattle.

I had my best suit on, cleaned, and pressed for the big day. I had tried to sleep as best as I could, but my anxiety was getting the best of me. I smiled at the acknowledgment of my own anxiety. I could cure it. I had the research. As I was ushered through each checkpoint, I felt the tension build.

I was cleared at the front driveway and instructed to park in a visitor spot. *What if they remembered my failed competition presentation?*

A guard met me at my car and signed me into the front desk. Large metal letters were welded onto the walls reading "Peec on Earth." I smiled at the pun, but it didn't do much to calm my internal worries. *What if they thought my research wasn't fully developed?*

A badge was swiped; I was granted access to the elevator. *What if they ask me questions that I can't answer?*

By the time I reached the tenth-floor, I could feel the sweat pouring down my back, equal parts frustrated with the wool blazer of my suit for causing that sweat and grateful that it concealed the dampness it created. A secretary escorted me to a waiting area. I sat quietly, observing the hubbub around me. The quick pace of the office workers who dashed by, on their way to meetings or off to save the world, fascinated me. The well-decorated hallways and polished wood surfaces screamed money, but Peec was known for having a CEO, Edwin Hurlbert, who dressed in jeans and sweatshirts. He wanted to be the 'everyman' of tech. And every man wanted to work for him. Including me.

"Mr. Rattray will see you now," a delicate voice called for my attention. I hopped up and followed her through a set of doors into the most magnificent office I had ever seen. I spent my career in academic dungeons or claustrophobic labs. Moving to the private sector meant two things: I would be labeled as a sell-out by all my colleagues, and I would get access to all the trappings of a sell-out life. This office represented the promise of both scientific breakthrough and financial status. It was exactly what I needed to see, to experience, to get me to buy in on the idea of switching to the corporate side of the business.

Malcolm Rattray was the head of Research and Development at Peec. As far as I was concerned, this man was God. My life, my career, was in his hands. He could bestow a job offer upon me like a benevolent lord, or he could squash all of my aspirations in one glance. I looked at the degrees and framed photos, the clean desk without a pile of research or cluster of notes visible. This was the big leagues. There was a miniature Ford engine model in a protective case on the desk. A nod to the ingenuity that took us from one mode of humanity to the next? A gift from someone who wanted to inspire greatness? I wasn't sure, but to me, it made him cool.

On the far side of his office was a large whiteboard with lists in different colors. At a glance, I only picked up on a few words, most of them didn't make any sense to me and I only had a fraction of a second to glance at it without looking like a snoop.

"Hunter, right?" he confirmed my name. Rattray had an angular face with pronounced jowls and a slender nose. His stomach ballooned into a paunch that spilled over his belt; a uniform physique for men in the late forties.

"Yes sir, nice to meet you," my right hand quivered as I extended it. If he noticed any physical signs of my nerves, he didn't let on.

"Metz tells me you're the man we need to finish one of our major initiatives," Rattray continued and directed me to sit in a chair across from him. He gently leaned back into the soft sofa and crossed his right leg over his left. (Yeah, he had a sofa in his office. That's how much of a head honcho he was.) As I sat across from him, my mind seized. Based on what I had read about Metz and his work, I needed his research more than he would ever need mine. Had I missed something? Instead of asking the dummy question of what the major initiative was, I decided to dive right in.

My initial research focused on alleviating PTSD in veterans by suppressing their adrenaline response. Because of the military applications, I focused on the PTSD angle. I told him that I believed there could be additional use-cases to help those with mental disorders to keep them from acting out violently. "Gun laws can only do so much. We know that when lucid, most of these men would insist that they would never want to hurt anyone. If we present an effective option to suppress that violent outcry, we can save the lives of others and keep them from destroying their own lives as well."

Rattray nodded along as I spoke. He followed my line of thinking and had clearly researched me thoroughly before our meeting. "You think this could have stopped Clifton?" I thought back to the shell of a man that I had interviewed in Arizona. It was a large assumption to say that I could have prevented those deaths with my invention, but I believed that this device could help people who were in pain and keep them from spreading that pain to others. Could I have stopped Clifton? How would I know? But then, a memory of Artemis flashed in my mind. We were kids; it was one of the rare occasions that she persuaded me to play outside with her. She had been stooping to pick dandelions. This vision, this remembrance, modified my response. It didn't matter what happened before. It only mattered what I could prevent. I had to get this job to continue my work and feel that my loss was not in vain.

It was a gutsy move, but I needed to show him that I was not just a great researcher, but that I was a leader. That I was Peec material.

I looked him square in the eye and answered, "I don't just think it, I know it." I hoped that I portrayed the confidence necessary to back up a claim like that.

That must have sealed the interview for me. After a few more moments of small talk and some perfunctory questions, I was told that I would hear from the team shortly with a decision. I didn't realize just how soon that would be.

A guard met me as I stepped off the elevator in the lobby and escorted me to Human Resources to start my onboarding paperwork. I thought I was taking a huge leap forward, I thought I was agreeing to a life in a private lab.

But I had never signed on for this. I hadn't signed on for the series of events that would lead to the destruction of mankind. Or would lead to me trudging through the mud to interrogate an isolated survivor in an abandoned gas station.

As we made our way down to the road, I could clearly read the sign affixed to the store: Maxine's Mini-Mart. I continued on as Dawes stopped to scan the road again with the sight on his rifle.

"Hey," I heard him whisper and I stopped in my tracks. I turned to look at him, expecting that he would be signaling some new threat. Instead, he just nodded his head and waved me closer to him.

I took a few steps back toward him. "Yeah?" I asked once I was within whisper-shot.

"If there is only one person, if we both go in, it could be perceived as a threat." His logic wasn't unfounded, but I didn't like where this was going. I did not want to split up. Not because I found any comfort in his company, but I distinctly did not want to end up like Michaels.

"I'm sure the rifles would be a clear signal that we're a threat," I tried to point out the other obvious signals.

"Exactly," Dawes nodded. "I think you should go in unarmed."

"Fuck off!" I couldn't keep my voice down. The man might as well have just told me to offer myself as a sacrifice to whoever was inside the shop.

"If this person has been on their own for any amount of time, living in isolation, they're not going to be excited to see either of us." Dawes grabbed my arm, pulling me closer to him. I tried to shake him off. "Their minds have probably twisted," I felt his grip tighten, trying to keep me from making a scene. If we got too loud, we would lose the element of surprise.

"Your mind is twisted if you think I'm going in there without any protection. You saw what just happened!" I broke free from his grip. I may not have been ex-military, but I wasn't a wimp either.

"Yeah, and what good did his rifle do him? If we go in there and spook whoever this person is, they could start firing at both of us. Then we both die here, and everyone on the ship starves." I didn't want to accept his words, but he had a point.

"You've been planning this since we started walking?" I crossed my arms and waited for him to respond.

"I was thinking about it when we were on the chopper. Any groups or individuals we come across won't be nice and polite. They'll be on edge; trying to stay alive tends to reduce their manners." Dawes looked over at the shop, still a good one hundred yards away. The windows appeared to be covered with a film of dust or mildew. Whoever was in there might be able to see us, or they might not. If they were watching, they would see two men talking, trying to figure out a plan. From their perspective, we could be looking to loot their cache or just hoping to find supplies. Either way, we would be enemies.

I let out a deep sigh and handed him my rifle. With a swift motion, I ripped the Velcro flap open and pulled my tablet out and unlocked it. "If you hear me scream, this is the dot for our guest," I pointed to the blue dot that we had seen earlier. I tapped on my dot and changed the color to red. "Don't touch my dot," I instructed him, bluntly uttering my words to emphasize each one. He nodded. I moved my finger back to our unknown stranger's dot. "If you hear me scream tap on this one and you'll see a control option. Crank it up as high as you can, you just swipe your finger up." Dawes nodded and took the tablet with both hands.

I turned to face the shop and began my long march to what seemed like a sure-fire suicide mission. The crunch of gravel under my boots was the only sound I could hear except for the loud pounding of my own heartbeat. The lane widened into a broad shoulder and then the open parking lot of the convenience store. The two gas pumps were rusted, the hoses flaking, and decayed from lack of use. The sun had started to beat down, drying out the loose dirt on the ground, and forcing my skin to sweat through my clothes. The cool spring air had turned humid and muggy, but I had experienced worse.

The clammy air on my skin reminded me of the tropical paradise I had been delivered to years earlier.

I landed in Kailua-Kona, Hawai`i, after a day-long flight. Thankfully, it had been a quiet trip and I had been able to catch up on three movies. They would be the last that I expected to see. I had no idea if the research facility would have any kind of entertainment, and of course, I would not be permitted outside the facility. I had signed on for the opportunity of a lifetime.

I would be able to carry out my research with the top technology company in the world: Peec. After decades of pioneering telecommunications and biotechnology, the world's most visible tech company had silently started its own research arm. The company made more money than anyone could comprehend. They decided to funnel their excess profit into the ultimate R&D.

It wasn't just about making devices that they could sell to people, fueling more profit for another few quarters. They were instead focused on projects that had no apparent financial gain for the company. But if it could benefit humanity, then everyone would win. It also didn't hurt that they had numerous exclusive military contracts. These connections helped to secure funding and support the production of our work.

I could feel the excitement building as I waited to get off the plane. I was as giddy as I had been before every science fair, every report card, every academic accomplishment in my life. This was it. I had made it to the big leagues, and I was on the cusp of a major breakthrough. One that would redefine human history and help mitigate the atrocities that were occurring more frequently.

As I climbed down the stairs and onto the runway, I spotted the little huts that comprised the open-air terminals. I was told that I would be met at the gate by a Peec official. I looked around as I saw the stream of passengers heading straight for the luggage belts.

As my eyes passed over the people who appeared to be waiting for someone, the discrete drivers with their whiteboard signs, I saw one that caught my eye.

"We come in Peec." How very on-brand.

A man who looked as though chauffeuring was his second-career, after a life of heavy weight lifting and bouncing people from clubs, stood before me in khaki shorts and an overtly tropical short-sleeve button-up shirt. His outfit screamed, "Hawai`i dude!" But his haircut and stern face told the story of a security professional, posing as a driver.

"Hello, I'm Hunter. I think you're my ride. I work with -"

"Hunter! Great, come this way," he cut me off as an unnatural smile broke out across his face. It looked like something he had to rehearse, not quite normal for him.

I picked up my bags from the luggage carousel and followed him to a dated white SUV. The windows were rolled down, and the paint was starting to bubble from the spray of the saltwater hitting it. I tossed my luggage and backpack into the vehicle and climbed in. This wasn't what I had expected from Peec, especially after the luxurious headquarters, but then I learned that island cars tended to be beaters. And certainly, no one would expect a new high-profile scientist to be picked up in that rust-bucket.

Only once we were both in the car did the chauffeur speak. "We're heading to your next destination right away." He still hadn't introduced himself, but I started to get a feeling that he wasn't going to. I wondered if I asked his name if he would make one up or just smile and tell me that he couldn't say. We cleared the long road leading out to the highway and I seized the moment to take it all in. I was in Hawai`i, a place I had only ever dreamed of traveling to, and I was here to do the work I loved with a big-name company. I was living my dream. And it felt like a dream, the vibrant blues of the water and sky were brighter than I had imagined. The black of the lava fields captured my gaze, the rock so unbelievably dark and fresh, only a few thatches of wild grass daring to grow on such menacing ground.

We sped along the coast for a few moments before I gained my sense of direction. We were heading north. Not east. While no one had expressly instructed me that my research facility would be on Mauna Kea, it was the obvious location. There were already communities of scientists living on the mountain, my plane ticket had been to Kona, not any of the other islands. So why weren't we headed inland towards the great mountain?

"Uh, where are we headed?" I asked.

"Your transfer to your research facility leaves in a little over an hour. Got to get you there on time." He didn't take his eyes off the road as he drove.

"Oh, I thought my facility would be on this island," I tried to dig for more details.

"Nope. But if you thought your facility was here then anyone thinking of digging into your research would come to the same conclusion." He turned his head briefly and winked at me.

The level of security and secrecy should have concerned me then, but I felt like I was on an adventure. I was an important scientist whose location had to be obscured, people wanted my research. I felt like a big deal. There is no narcotic in the world that could manufacture that feeling, but if it did exist, I could have made a fortune dealing it.

I sat quietly waiting for him to elaborate further. The wayward breeze coming off the Pacific cooled the air in the car a bit. I looked out at the vast plains that led up to the volcanic mountains in the center of the island. After weeks at the Peec headquarters, where I was able to explore the city of Seattle a bit, I had hoped to get some time to see the sights on the Big Island. There was fresh flowing lava pouring into the ocean on the south side of the island. There was olivine green sand that only existed on this patch of land. There were starry skies void of light pollution. I wanted to see more, but I didn't say any of that. I wasn't here to be a tourist; I was here to solve a big problem. I was here to fulfill my destiny. I assured myself that it would all be there for me when I was done. But it never finished.

We arrived at a heliport on the north side of the island. The quiet drive to an unknown destination began to wear on me. It had been a long flight. My neck was stiff from sitting for so long. I was eager to get there, wherever there was. I had worked my whole life to get started, I was impatient to wait any longer. Or perhaps I was just hungry and irritable. We stopped just inside a chain-link fence near the edge of a sheer cliff that dove one thousand feet into the Pacific. The valley below was spectacular, it had real *Jurassic Park* vibes.

A helicopter was waiting, one of the fancy kinds that executives would use, or I imagined that they would use. No idea of the make and model, I only saw it once more and that was years later. I grabbed my items from the SUV and waved at the chauffeur.

"Thanks, Tim!" the helicopter pilot called out.

"No worries, Bruce," my driver responded. Were Tim and Bruce even their real names? I'm convinced now that they weren't. Now that I know everything.

Within a few moments, I was buckled into the helicopter and sinking into the buttery soft leather bench. The exhaustion from the long journey started to hit me, but I was too excited to give in to it. The blades began to spin, the shadows of them whirring past on the ground. We were up and flying over the open Pacific Ocean headed to the next step in the journey.

There were so many stops along the way on that trip to get me to the Bunker. It didn't make sense as I was living it, confused at each new arrival and change over. But looking back it all fit, it was a linear path.

That short walk from where Dawes stood on the side of the road to the entrance of the dilapidated convenience store should have been linear. But I had to play my role. Forrester had given us all lessons in deception, keeping up the illusion. I needed to play my part. Not a scientist sent in from an off-shore vessel to restore the supply lines that would have driven loudly down this road. I needed to be a wanderer, a leather tramp happening by this structure.

I walked up to the first window and peered in with my hands cupped around my eyes to shut out the light. I could see a figure moving around towards the front of the store. I moved over to the side window, passing the door altogether and peered in once more. I was sure that whoever was in there had seen me. I walked back to the front door and opened it; a bell tinkled overhead.

Even after a morning of walking and years living in this hell of a reality, I half-expected a smiling Maxine behind the counter when I walked in. I still expected a casual greeting and a perfunctory conversation upon check-out. I was not adjusting well to this new world.

"Hello?" I called out. I knew full well that someone was in there, but I had to play at being curious.

"You stop right there." I froze. A tired voice, raspy from age or inflammation called out from the front of the store. "State your name and business." I spotted the source of the voice. After years in the Bunker, only ever seeing the same faces over and over, and then the same on the ship, the sight of a new face was jarring. I hadn't encountered someone I didn't know for so long, I forgot that one person could look so different from the people I saw every day. I forgot the stunning beauty in the novelty of seeing a person for the first time.

"Hunter," I barely got the word out in one breath. I lifted my hands to show that I intended no harm.

"Is that your name or your business?" I took a cautious step forward, just one.

"Name," I swallowed, summoning courage. The woman before me was short, her shoulders hunched over. Her hair was greasy and falling in thick locks from beneath a knit cap. Her face was hidden, her features naturally dark and then obscured under layers of dirt and grime. I could smell the musk coming from her even at a distance of a dozen feet away. I noticed that her hands were held low, I expected that she had a shotgun barrel aimed at me from below the counter. "My most pressing business at the moment is food, thirst, and relief."

"Bathroom is in the back, although the water hasn't been working for years so hold your nose while you are in there. I guess some habits break hard. When you're done, you'll come right back here and we'll chat about the other items."

I lowered my shoulders, the tension escaping as it became clear that she didn't see me as a threat. At least not for the moment.

"Thank you. Maxine?"

"No, I'm Paula. Maxine is gone, along with most everybody else."

"Oh," I couldn't think of the right words to say. Should I offer condolences or were they moot at this point? I suddenly felt the fear surge into my mind. What if she is sick? What if she is still carrying the germ and I am now infected? What if I die a painful and slow death to the bio-toxin plague that had been released? What if she shoots me the second I turn towards the restroom? "Well, thank you for your hospitality, Paula, I'll be right back." As a sign of goodwill, I left my small pack on the ground near the entrance.

I followed her advice and took a deep breath before entering the bathroom, it was foul, but I needed to relieve myself and that feeling was worth the stench. I had taken for granted the accommodations aboard the ship. While cramped and economical, they were functioning. On the way out, I did wonder at how long it would take me to lose the habit of using the facilities. To confidently urinate into the wild, into the wind, without a care for manners or society or urinals. I still instinctively turned to wash my hands. No water came out of the spigot. I looked up and saw a fractured reflection; the mirror above the sink had been smashed. I averted my eyes quickly and wiped my hands on my pants.

"Thank you very much, ma'am," I waved as I returned down the aisle towards the counter.

"It's all fine. We've had more and more people coming through the past week or so," she waved her hand as though it was no bother at all. I tucked away these pieces of information. More people coming past here? There were more survivors in this area than there had been previously? Also, the very distinct 'we.' We implied more than one person. We implied that she wasn't alone here. Or Paula had developed a second personality. Either way, 'we' was dangerous. My tablet only showed one person alive in this area.

"I can help you with food and something to drink. All of this here was Maxine's, and money doesn't do me any good, so I won't ask for cash. But I will ask that you help out before you pass on." Paula's request was fair, I nodded.

"Certainly, I'm glad to help where I can," I was eager to get my provisions and be gone, but I couldn't deny that some form of payment would be required. I was so deep into my ruse that I had almost forgotten that I had a full pack of rations by the door. The shelves were threadbare and the waters had been raided, but an air temperature Gatorade and a few bags of chips would be a feast considering the other option was nothing. I didn't see anything that looked remotely like the khaki tear away pouches that all of our ship's rations were packaged in. I wanted to complete my improvisation and get out. For as much as I had relaxed around Paula after she said she would help, I started to get a bad feeling with her last revelation.

Paula pulled a crumpled list from her back pocket. "Can you chop firewood?"

"I haven't done it before, but I'm sure I could learn it," I answered, confident in my strength.

"Eh, last fella who passed through and tried that nearly lost his foot. Better not. How about trapping and hunting?"

"I went through Eagle Scouts, so I can make a trap and see what comes of it. Any game in this region?" I figured if I helped in this regard, I could push the conversation into the territory of the supply trucks that would have passed through here.

"Not that I've seen lately, but good to ask for help when we can. We'll set that as a maybe," she made a mark on her list with a pencil.

"Okay, what else is on your list?" I tried to mask the shaking in my voice, the worry. How many people had come through here? Just what was waiting for us up ahead on the road? And what was happening outside? Was Dawes being captured by the rest of her 'we' while she stalled and kept me in here?

"Just one more thing," her eyes darted quickly to the door, as though she were checking that no one else was about to walk in. She furrowed her brow and nibbled at the stub of a nail left on her thumb, all the tell-tale signs of worry present. She looked down each aisle and behind her. This paranoia seemed comical to me. There was literally no one else for miles, well except for Dawes who was waiting outside in case I gave him the signal. She stooped low to the counter, as though keeping her next question close to the surface would insulate the sound of it, would make it easier to grab the words and push them back where they came from should someone else walk in.

"You have any skills as a doctor or nurse or anything?"

My curiosity was piqued. Why would this need to be such a quiet question? Why would this need to be kept on the down-low? "I have some basic skills in first-aid." Dammit, I thought. Why had it been Michaels who had been killed back there? Not that I would have wished his fate on Dawes, but still. It seemed especially cruel that this was her greatest need. My degree in biomedical engineering gave me enough knowledge to conduct my research, enough information to be dangerous. I was a Ph.D., not an MD.

I would have to recall my knowledge quickly as this seemed to be what she really needed.

"Follow me," she took off through a door behind the counter that led to a small office and then out of the building.

The door opened out onto the back end of the building; I had left Dawes standing one hundred yards away on the opposite side. If he was watching the dots on the screen move, he would know that we had gone out the back, but what if there was a delay? What if we were moving too quickly? The Connect gliders were good, but the internet they provided could run slow at times. Paula's haggard and hunched frame moved with purpose.

I paused as she continued ahead, unsure of what to do now. She could be leading me into a trap. *I knew splitting up was a bad idea.*

The crunch of her boots on top of the dried leaves continued to crackle. She must have sensed that I had stopped moving behind her because she turned around.

"Well, come on," she waved me towards her. I wasn't sure what to do next.

"I, uh-" my brain had frozen.

"I'm not one of those types, there's no trap ahead," she offered in a mothering tone. A reassuring tone. However, my suspicions were equally quelled and supported.

"It's just," I turned to check behind me to see if Dawes was coming around the corner.

Paula cocked her head to the side, curious as to my objection, impatient for me to spit it out.

"We didn't know if anyone was even in your store. So, I walked ahead to check it out. If I don't come out in a few minutes, he'll think something happened and start to worry." I checked behind me again.

Paula put her hands on her hips, her lips pursed as she considered my words.

"Well, I can't blame you. But I don't much like the idea of your man in hiding," her tone was stern. I could see her point of view as well. But still, I didn't like that she was leading me off somewhere to likely connect with the rest of her party. We were both going to have to trust each other a little more, but neither of us were ready to move just yet.

"We mean no harm-" I started.

"Call him out," she interrupted. Her voice was gruff.

"Dawes!" I hollered, not breaking eye contact with her. "Come around to the far side of the store." We hadn't worked out a code word for him to know if I needed him to come out guns blazing or slowly and calmly. I figured he would have assumed the worst, and sure enough, he slowly stepped out from around the side of the building with his rifle high on his shoulder, his right eye staring down the scope.

"Dawes, she's safe. She's going to help us with some supplies if we can get her some first aid help. I think I know enough to be useful." I wanted to lay up the situation before he could say something to betray the ruse. Or start shooting. Because that would leave us with no new information, a potential pack of 'we' after us, and another life on my conscience.

"Dawes, is it?" Paula asked. She stood stock-still, waiting for him to make a sound.

He stood watching her, standing in the sights of his weapon for another moment before he lowered it. "Yeah, I'm Dawes," he nodded.

"Well, just to get all this out of the way while we're all tense and suspicious of each other, I've got three kids in a make-shift bunker. One of 'em really needs some help." She bit at her thumb again, quickly raising and lowering it, a twitchy little tick.

I nodded and looked over at Dawes who did the same.

"Understood," he said.

"You boys must have had it rough down south. A whole bunch of you have been walking through this way for weeks now shell-shocked. Can't say I blame you, but like I told Hunter, I'm not one of those kinds. This region is *protected*, you're safe here." She waited for us to acknowledge her words before she turned and started up the embankment behind the store.

We followed her up the small slope that led to the gathering of thin and spindly trees that would pass for a forest. After about seven minutes, she stopped and kicked away the leaves at her feet, revealing a wide cover that she quickly popped open. "Get in," she commanded, looking behind me to ensure that no one had followed.

I wanted to protest and claim a fear of small enclosed spaces, I wanted to take off running in the other direction, but that wasn't an option. For the second time in my life, I stared into a subterranean hole, not sure of when I would ever come back out of it.

The other Bunker I was thinking of was the one on Ni'ihau. The Forbidden Island. The tiny island in the Hawaiian archipelago that the world had forgotten. The perfect place for a secret R&D project.

The Robinson family leased the land to Peec for an undisclosed amount in an undisclosed agreement. The Bunker rose ten-foot by ten-foot by ten-foot out of the ground on that empty island. It looked like a lone pillbox, a remnant of an earlier time when the island chain was protected by men sitting in these concrete huts and radioing in any activity over the south Pacific.

However, looks are deceiving. The pillbox with the crumbling concrete and rudimentary graffiti was a fortified structure. It was the entrance to a larger facility. Five-year-old me would have loved to work in a fort. Secret, hidden, *who goes there? What's the password?* But adult me, soon realized that there was no risk of attack on this forgotten patch of land, only risk of escape.

When Bruce landed the helicopter on a square patch of ground that had been cleared for such a purpose, I thought he must have been lost. This island was so small that it looked like a high-tide would sweep it away. The motor idled and he hopped down to the ground, I followed his lead. This was hardly the welcome I had expected. We were exactly in the middle of nowhere. The shadow of Kauai was barely visible on the eastern horizon. Otherwise, it was all ocean and scrubland.

Bruce approached the pillbox and waited in the doorframe for me to follow him. I grabbed my bags and scuttled along. I looked around to my left and right as I approached the structure, unsure of what I would find inside. The skeletons of deceived scientists past? A gang of mercenaries about to torture me for top-secret Peec information that I didn't even know yet?

Instead, I walked into the cramped box and waiting for me was another man, a short and stocky guard in full tactical gear. My skin broke out into a sweat just looking at him. My jeans and t-shirt were perfectly suitable in the lazy Hawaiian breeze. But this guy must have been boiling hot, especially in the concrete box with no air conditioning.

"I'll take it from here, thank you," the guard nodded at Bruce. The pilot turned to excuse himself. I was completely confused. Where was the lab?

Where was the cleanroom and bank of computers? Where was Metz who had sold me on this plan and Rattray who was supposed to be my boss? I heard the helicopter roar to life and then saw it take off into the pale blue sky. Only once it was out of sight did the guard address me.

"Hunter," I turned to look at him after he spoke my name. "Welcome to Peec on Earth," he stepped aside as he said this and I saw a small portal in the floor behind him. He unsnapped a cover on his forearm and pressed into a screen. I heard a hydraulic hiss and the portal opened. A man with long salt and pepper hair popped up from the ground with a large smile.

"Ah, fresh sea air!" he said as he looked at both of us. "Hunter, I'm Sam Metz. Come on down and I'll give you the tour," he nodded and ducked back into the ground. He looked about as I expected him to, but I was still surprised to see that the man I had built up in my mind was real, wrinkles and all.

I peered into the dark hole that he had disappeared into. I should have seen the cloak and dagger style of the set up as a warning. I should have been concerned about just how remote we were and how off the grid I now was. No one knew how to find me. No one could reach me. Also, no one was looking for me. I had no family and my only friends were also my competition in the race to scientific discovery. I was the perfect person for their task.

Little by little, small reactions, rationale changes, explanations, and concessions wore at my view of reality. This was a surprise introduction to my new lab; this was a hidden lair. This was somehow cool. Without realizing it, I was led down a tunnel, and at the end it was clear that there were no escape routes. Only one way in and out, through the utilitarian pillbox.

You don't expect that you're being recruited for a sinister purpose, because you believe what people with more experience and knowledge tell you. You accept the quirks of the culture in that environment and before you know it, you are at war with your teammates over perceived slights. You become a product of your environment. People in closed systems, in tight societies, trapped in Bunkers - they change. They adapt in order to survive.

And Paula's band of survivors were no different. I followed her into the tight quarters packed in below the leaves and ground cover. Dawes followed. Once inside, my eyes began to adjust. 'Bunker' was a generous term for this space. It was a dug-in hovel that was maybe five feet tall, seven feet wide, and ten feet long. On the ground were three other survivors. Two were sitting crouched with their legs pulled up to their chests, the arc of their backs a painful sight. They were curled up, trying to make themselves smaller to fit the space. The third was laid-down flat, their head propped on a sweater that had been bunched up to form a pillow. The floor of the hovel was packed-in mud and pinecones, soft and earthy. With all six of us in the space, it was tight.

Paula walked with a hunched back towards the sleeping one, her steps herky-jerky as she tried to move along without bumping her head on the corrugated metal that served as a ceiling. The sun leaked in at the edges, giving the pit just enough light for us to see.

"This one is sick. She's the one who needs medical help," Paula whispered over the girl. As I scooted closer, I could see that she was young. Maybe sixteen or seventeen at most. My eyes glanced back at the other two against the wall, one boy and another girl. Both appeared to be in their early twenties, but with the layers of dirt on them and the rapid aging that life in the wild can bring, they might have been younger.

"What's her name?" I asked Paula.

"Timoney," she whispered. I nodded. *What should I do now? What would Michaels do?*

"When did she get sick?" I mustered all of my courage to ask it. Logically, I knew that she couldn't be suffering from the toxin that decimated the population. Those deaths were swift, people dying faster than they could have even noticed the symptoms. That outbreak had been impressively lethal. Whatever Timoney had, she was still alive. So, I knew it couldn't be the same disease, or at least not the one Dawes and I had been inoculated against. *A mutated variant?* Maybe. *Something equally contagious and deadly?* Probably.

"She's been really pale lately," the boy in the corner spoke. "I mean we've all been a little pale from being in here, but she got this drained look about two weeks ago. She's said she was dizzy and tired."

I nodded. "Any coughing, fever?"

Paula answered, "she's been like this for a few days now, her forehead is clammy. I don't know what to do," she bit at her thumb again.

The next steps I just fumbled my way through. "Timoney, my name is

Hunter. I'm going to try and see if we can help you feel better."

"She can't hear you," the girl in the corner said.

"Rachel!" Paula chided her.

"What? She can't! Jack and I have been trying to get her to wake up. She won't!" Spoken like a true teenager, Rachel gave me a clear idea of what kind of state Timoney was in. She rolled her eyes before returning them to the spot on the dirt in front of her. Like Paula, her hair stuck out at odd angles from beneath a knit cap. Hers was waxy and orange, compared to the gray and black dreadlocks on Paula, but there was a similarity that ran deeper than their overall appearance and trying to stay warm. There was a stubborn resilience, an inability to give up.

I looked back at Timoney. Sweat collected on her cheeks and in the crook of her neck. I pulled down the blankets and maneuvered her right arm so I could check her pulse from her wrist. It was weak but fast. This was clearly an infection. As I moved her arm again, the sleeves of her sweater slunk down. There was a gray bandage wrapped around her forearm.

"What's this?" I asked.

"A group came by a few weeks ago and said to cut 'em out, those things. They helped us," Jack responded.

"Cut what out?" I asked.

"The trackers," Rachel mumbled, I could tell that she had suppressed the urge to add on "duh."

I furrowed my brow. "The kids all had 'em in their arms, so they were able to help cut those out. They weren't too deep. Mines still here," Paula wagged her thumb at me, the one she had been biting. "Said they couldn't cut it out without just cutting the whole thing off. So, I thought we better not."

"You all had devices implanted?" Dawes finally interjected.

"Yeah, like from day one. The people who have been walking up from the south kept telling us to cut 'em out. Finally, one group came through that said they could help." Paula explained. "What, you don't have one?"

"We both have implants," I responded to her. I couldn't be certain, but I was fairly sure we were talking about the same thing. My invention that was intended to help keep the surviving population calm in the wake of the outbreak was being cut out of people. Cut out of them while they lived in the wild, cut out of them without sterile devices.

Carefully, I pulled away at the dirtied gauze from Timoney's arm, unraveling it. I turned and instructed Dawes to go back to the store for my bag. I added that it had fresh bandages for Paula's benefit. As Dawes climbed out of the hole, I reached the end of the wrap. I let the ruined cloth fall on the ground.

The wound was pink and crimson, orange puss wept from the cut. I looked over at Jack and Rachel. "Have you been cleaning your cuts?"

Both nodded silently.

"Let me see them," I instructed. Paula watched silently as they each rolled up their sleeves, exposing their right forearms. Their scars were in the first stages of healing, bright pink with a clean and straight seam. I nodded and set Timoney's arm on the blanket. I rolled up my sleeve and showed them the faded white line on my forearm. The three of them leaned forward.

"Wow, I've never seen one look like that," Rachel shook her head in disbelief.

"I was one of the first to get one," was all I could offer. "Your scars should look like this when you are done, a thin line." Although the incision on my arm was a shade lighter than my pale skin. Jack's would heal as a bright copper, slightly brighter than his skin tone. Rachel's would heal just fine as well.

"How far south did you come from?" Paula asked, her eyes twinkled artificially, she was trying to mask her suspicion as genial curiosity. I rolled my sleeve back down and moved back over to Timoney.

"Far," was all I felt safe offering. I needed to stay alert for the next few moments to ensure that Dawes and I could leave safely. If what Paula said was correct, then our tracking devices were quickly becoming less and less effective. If people all along this route were told to cut out their implants then we would have no way of anticipating any ambushes from nomadic survivors. They were also leaving themselves susceptible to panic and fear-induced violence. *Didn't they know how important the device has been to their own survival?*

"How long ago did the people from the south start walking by?" I tried to dig for more information, no longer weaving my questions into any organic conversation. In our last count, we saw only a handful of people alive on the West Coast. But if people had been cutting out their implants, then there could be way more. More survivors meant a higher chance of rebuilding. But it also meant that they were more likely to create factions, 'us versus them' sects. That would lead to in-fighting and insurrections. Unless they could remain calm.

"The trend really started a month or so ago. But we also had some people from inland come out this way as well."

Inland, further east, closer to the source of our supplies.

"Yeah? What brought them out this way?" I inspected Timoney's wound again as I spoke, trying to mask my naked inquiries.

"Came to see if anyone was alive. I saw 'em in the shop," Paula explained. "They said they had a good community fifteen miles or so inland and that they had protection."

"Protection, like what? Like gas masks?" I wondered if the promise of security had been genuine or not, but Paula was still here so they clearly didn't take offense to her rejecting their offer.

"Naw, they have some guns. Each of them had one with them. But they also have the Reaper." Paula whispered that last word. It sent shivers up my spine.

"What?" I pretended that I had never heard the name before.

"The Reaper," Rachel repeated. "One of their kind, sent to help us. Sent to help us break free."

"Who is they? One of the people from the east?" I asked. Paula looked at me as though I had just spoken in a foreign language.

"One of *them*, of course," she emphasized the word.

"One of the people from the east?" I tried to confirm. The Reaper's name had been on Michaels' pall. This could be another clue.

"No," Paula shook her head, "one of *them*." Her tone was, well there is no better word for it: Reverent. She revered the Reaper, she feared *them*, whoever that was. *One of their kind, sent to help us.* I took this to mean that some faction was threatening people, and they had a mole among them. If there was a faction in the area and they wanted to claim complete power, it would make sense that they embargoed our supply trucks or tried to stop them altogether. But then why would this Reaper, one of them who was trying to help others, set up a trap to kill anyone at the hangar? I couldn't figure it out yet.

I didn't have time to ask her more questions. The heavy footfalls of Dawes alerted us to his return. He ducked down and passed the bag to me.

The foxhole was incredibly cramped. I felt bad for Dawes as he tried his best to make himself small, but he was a big guy and he could only do some much to shrink himself down.

The makeshift bunker felt stuffy and crowded again as I grabbed the medical items from my bag, thankfully still stuffed on the top. The cramped quarters weren't the problem; it was the lack of light.

The Bunker in Hawai`i had been abnormally bright. At least it was light during the day, the team inside the Ni`ihau facility had set the lights to mimic daylight with the sensors increasing and decreasing with the natural rhythm of the sun. I would learn all about that on my tour. But first, I had to descend into the darkness of the tunnel.

I climbed down a narrow ladder for what felt like a ridiculously long time. I kept telling myself not to look down, but I also had to remind myself not to look up. The light was narrow on either end, a cursory glance would give me vertigo and claustrophobia, and I couldn't risk panicking at that moment. I finally felt a cool breeze on my ankles and emerged into a white-walled corridor. I dropped down onto the ground, grateful to be standing on something solid. I hazarded a glance back up. The pin-prick of light that was the opening in the pillbox looked to be an impossible distance away.

"All clear!" Metz hollered with a smile. "Oh, you'll want to step to the side," he said softly to me, gently pulling at my arm.

I took two steps to my right and then heard a whistling sound. A few seconds later, my bags landed with a thud on the ground where I had just been standing.

"Come on, I'll introduce you around to the other Project members." We weren't team members or colleagues. We were Project members, all part of the Human Capital Project. The branding cues were implanted everywhere. In the terms we used, in the design of the labs. Everything was considered. This was all part of my orientation period. I completed a ninety-day on-site training at the Peec headquarters outside of Seattle, WA. The facility had been massive, but I had been restricted to my orientations and back. The rest of the Peec workforce didn't have clearance on the Project. Their non-disclosure agreements were thorough, but mine was air-tight. No need to risk them asking any questions about my new role. Better to be sequestered as

I learned all about the company history, policies, and protocols for the Project. I learned the icons used to represent each sub-project.

I suspected that the standard employee orientations lasted one day, a week at most, with detailed sessions on retirement plans and paid vacation. I would get no vacations, no days-off. 'Shore-leave' was defined in my onboarding paperwork, but after descending that ladder, I didn't have much interest in making another trip for a long time. I didn't want time-off. I wanted to rid the world of violence. I felt the need to solve for this problem; it was urgent. I was racing against a clock and there was no known time limit. It could go off at any second.

I followed Metz down the first series of corridors until we came to a sealed doorway. I had been trying to memorize each step, but the hallways were identical. Each clinically clean, white, devoid of markings except for fire alarms every twenty yards, and because of the uniform nature of those devices it really wasn't any help. The pipes were bolted to the ceilings, and they all looked identical, snaking this way and that.

I heard a slight beep and Metz held open the door for me. "All of the doors require you to swipe your card to enter. We'll get you set up with one today." He waved a plastic rectangle in the air and then pocketed it.

"Should we have something more sophisticated like retinal scans?" I asked, half-joking, half-serious.

"We have a lot of administrative staff here that aren't read-in on our projects. We don't want them to get any ideas about what we are or aren't doing, so we keep the security measures at current industry standards. That way they don't go running to the next tech startup sprouting ideas about eye-scanning technology being used to lock away key secrets at this facility. Also, we're on a desert island in the middle of the South Pacific."

Metz's response was thorough. It made sense to me, but I was slightly confused. Why have people work here at all if Peec didn't fully trust them? I let that thought slip away as Metz led me down another long, featureless corridor until he stopped at another door and opened it. The room he stepped into was tiny. It was smaller than any dorm room I had lived in during my college and graduate school days. I saw a twin bed bolted to the wall with a thin mattress. A metal desk and chair.

Metz must have read my mind when he said, "The bathroom and shower are down the hall."

I dropped my pack on the bed, nodding as I took in the reality of the room. The door was solid metal with a window at eye-level.

"Are we in a mental institution?" I looked up at him as I asked this.

"No one likes the accommodations. They are very utilitarian, but you'll spend most of your time in your lab or the cafeteria. This is just a place to sleep." He brushed off my concerns.

I nodded wordlessly.

"Come on, it's not that bad. I'm personally glad that the rooms are sparse. It means there is more in the budget for food." As Metz spoke the final word, my stomach grumbled audibly. I decided to focus on the positive and gladly accepted the cue to move on to the most important location in the whole Bunker: the cafeteria.

Metz helped me to navigate the social hierarchy of the dining hall. Much hadn't changed since middle school. I needed to avoid sitting with the admin staff; they had their own little clique. The life support and operations teams ate in shifts, as soon as one group finished their meals and stood, the next set was ready to relieve them. As though they had to stand guard over their table, someone always on watch, securing it for their team. And the executives almost never ate there. If they did, they usually sat off to the side at one of the bistro tables, occupying one of the two chairs. The open chair was never an invitation to dine with them. Metz snaked through the labyrinth of tables until he reached the one that we were meant to sit with. The rest of the Human Capital Project team.

"Hey team, this is Hunter," Metz nodded in my direction as he sat down on the bench in front of the table.

"Hi," I waved at the half dozen unfamiliar faces. They would soon become my friends and colleagues; they would soon be the only people I recognized in this facility. But at that moment, they were all strangers.

"Hey, I'm Rita." The lone female of the group extended her hand to me as I sat down. I felt my stomach drop once more, although this time it was not from hunger. I didn't want to wait too long before reacting, so I reached for her outstretched hand. I shook it briefly; her grip was light and affable. She was just extending a social pleasantry, I reminded myself. Her pleasant nature was a stark contrast to the sharp edges of her jaw and the wild spirals of her hair. I looked away from her, realizing I had probably been staring too long.

"I'm Forrester," the man to her left followed the pattern. But his handshake was firm, firmer than it needed to be. He was trying to assert his dominance. He had the appearance of the prototypical alpha-male: white, clean-shaven square-jaw, thick dark hair combed neatly. He had the corporate look about him, too stiff and formal for us scientists.

The rest of the table introduced themselves. Some by first names, some by last names. Kupper. Holtz. Sean. The big scientists. Each of us selected because we were the best in our respective fields. Each of us given the resources of Peec to solve big problems, find solutions that would improve society. We were the best of the best. Or so it had been sold to me that way.

"What's your project?" The man who called himself Holtz at the far end of the table asked as he piled another forkful of his lunch into his mouth. He was hungry, for food, for information.

"Project Calm," I said with a brief smile. I had been working on "Implanted and Wearable Biotechnology to Diffuse and Deescalate PTSD and other Post-Traumatic Outbursts." That was my project title and elevator pitch all rolled into one. Until I had signed on with Peec. The corporate initials were P.C., so our Projects all had to have a "C"-name to match. We were all part of P.C., we all worked on P.C., the corporate propaganda and internal marketing and branding were strong within the organization. My perfectly succinct and detailed name was shortened to "Calm."

"He'll be making good use on my new compound," Metz added in as he salted his mashed potatoes.

"But not too much," I added. It was Metz who had initially nominated me to join the team. I needed his research, or I felt that I needed it, in order to get my device up and running. He had already done years and years of work on the exact chemical compound that would react to spikes in adrenaline and noradrenaline. I would have to recreate his exact results in order to synthesize the same compound, and then I would still have to pay fees to him because it was now under patent by Peec. Now that we were working together, I could make use of his compound in my research without any issues. A lengthy application process, cutting bands upon bands of red tape, and a one-way ticket to The Forbidden Island, and I was finally able to use this formula. I had signed on to a life of seclusion and agreed that Peec would own the intellectual property to all of my findings. But I would be able to finish my work.

It seemed that everyone already knew all about Metz's work on Project Cease. His budget was military-backed as well, most of our projects were directly tied to government contracts. Metz was looking to create an aerosol device that could dispel riots quickly and without any loss of life. The intent was to be able to have a teaming mass of would-be insurrectionists inhale the gas and fall to sleep. The early results were mixed. Sometimes it was too strong and caused brain damage, even death. Sometimes it wasn't strong enough and the hoard was slowed, but not stopped. He knew that if a march turned into a riot, often the police were called on to start shooting or batting at protestors. Both sides were at risk of injury, or worse. With Metz's little canister the madness would end and the group would wake up hours later feeling rested and glad that they hadn't been carried away. That was his vision, that was the part of the idea that Peec had been keen on. But the US Government saw the potential for quelling rebellions and insurgents on the front lines. Metz knew that whoever ended up using his invention would only do so in dire situations. He had to get the aerosol formula just right.

Thankfully, he had already perfected the serum, which is what I needed.

Never underestimate the power of an effective chemical. *The right mixture can cure or kill.* I thought about the many chemicals I used to have at my disposal as I tried to clean Timoney's infected wound.

As I stooped down low in that earthen hovel in the woods off the North Pacific Coast, I knew that a vile of penicillin might have saved Timoney if we had found her sooner. The septic infection looked to be advanced. Michaels would have known exactly what to do; I was just guessing. I had to go through training on preventing infections as part of the research protocol for my device. I knew what to do to sterilize the implant, to ensure a safe procedure, and what the early signs of sepsis looked like to be able to refer a subject to a doctor immediately. I rubbed the antiseptic cream on the cut and handed Paula three of the pills that I had saved from Michaels' gear. I doubted that Timoney would ever wake up to be able to swallow them, but at least now they had one apiece for themselves.

I gently rewrapped her arm and tucked it back inside the blanket. I hadn't been able to administer anything other than hope. I was certain that Timoney would die.

"Ok, we've got a nice clean wrap and some ointment on the wound. When she wakes up, give her the medicine." I tried to put a cheery tone into my voice. *Keep up the illusion.* The words flashed in my brain, long-buried from years earlier.

It had been drilled into each of us as we assisted Forrester with his project. "Keep up the illusion with Project Collusion" was the catchy phrase printed in bold across each of our assignment sheets. Forrester's work was the least scientific, in my opinion, and the most dangerous, also my opinion. While Rita, Metz, Kupper, Sean, Holtz, and myself all work in labs with our materials and motherboards, our methyl groups and our machines, Forrester worked with the mind. I looked down on his work as pseudo-science. I underestimated him.

On the days that we had titrates dripping or regressions running on our computers, we were instructed to go and assist Forrester with his work. He needed people to play the role of lab assistant or lead scientist or government official. I just thought his ego demanded an audience.

The first weeks in the Bunker flew by like a blur. I was scheduled to attend forced social interactions to ensure that I was acclimating and fitting in. The administrative team followed up regularly to make sure I was happy, social, not getting too deep into my work that I would isolate myself. But I didn't want to spend all this time at mixers and taking tours of different parts of the facility that I would probably never need to know about. Sure, the infirmary and gym were helpful, but I didn't care about the meditation lounge and the test kitchen.

I was getting along well with the lab techs in my division. I was spending time with Metz as he helped me with his formula. I lived on the far end of the residential floor; room blocks were assigned based on when you joined the project. Metz had been one of the first, so his room was near the beginning of the hallway. It was a prime location: close to the elevator and a minimal commute each day. I was so far down the hallway, I thought that I was going to hear the sounds of water above my head, sure that there was no way the island was long enough to support a hallway that length.

As I walked idly back to my bunk one day, Sean told me that Forrester needed more help for his current project. I got roped into my first experience with Project Collusion. I arrived in time to see Rita in a tailored gray suit, her hair tamed and pinned back tightly into a bun. She was wearing glasses, which

I had never seen her use before. The badge on her blazer read "NSA." She turned tightly and opened the door to a room I had never seen.

Sean pushed me into an opening just next to that room. This space had an entire wall constructed of a two-way mirror. Rita was standing in front of a table where six haggard men were sitting quietly, waiting for instruction.

"What's going on?" I asked, unable to take my eyes off of Rita.

"Interview number 954 of Project Collusion," Forrester announced plainly.

"Why is Rita wearing an NSA badge?" I had a bad feeling about this setup. And more to the point, I could tell that the men sitting in the room with Rita were homeless. Their clothes were worn, their faces dirty. A look I would see again years later when I arrived back on land when no one had any home. But this was in the time before, and appearances were excellent indicators. Those men looked homeless; they probably were. But as I was about to learn, appearances could be incredibly deceiving.

"It's part of the illusion," Forrester shot me a harsh look. "Now, please, be quiet so we can all observe. You each need to be able to provide an account of the interview."

Sean was watching the scene before him plainly, he let out a deep sigh that I guessed resulted from boredom. There was nothing happening. Rita was standing there, quietly. The men at the table were sitting, quietly. No one was moving a muscle.

Then, about five minutes into watching absolutely nothing happen, one of the men coughed. His body shook as he tried to suppress the noise of it, but it was unmistakable. His face turned red, his curled fist approached his mouth, trying to cover it up. But he coughed.

Rita turned on her heel and approached him. She tapped him on the shoulder and he broke down in tears. The other men at the table stared straight ahead. The man who had coughed stood and Rita escorted him from the room.

Forrester moved to the corner of the room and pressed a button. The double-sided mirror turned opaque; the milieu disappeared.

"Interview number 954 complete," he announced.

"Complete?" I turned around. "But nothing happened."

"Hunter, this is your first observe and report. You'll start to notice things after a few more," Sean added, barely looking up from the notepad where he was scribbling observations.

Forrester crossed the small room and handed a notepad and pen to me. "Please write down everything that you noticed. No detail is too small." I hesitated before accepting the paper.

"Well, I didn't notice much happening, but-"

"No," Forrester cut me off. "Write it down. Your verbal recollections could alter Sean's report." I looked over to Sean as he spoke his name. The man was filling lines upon lines of the paper in front of him. He flipped over to the next sheet violently. I thought he would rip the page out of the notebook.

"Um, okay," I said as I accepted the paper. I wrote down what I had observed and some of my thoughts. I filled two paragraphs. Was there something I missed?

Sean completed his report, pages upon pages of chicken scratch that Forrester would have to decipher. "Thank you, Sean." Forrester took the papers from him and added them to a plain manila folder. Sean left the room as I finished my own short report.

"Here you go," I said to Forrester.

"That's it!?" He demanded.

"That was all I saw," I retorted. My frustration mounted. I had been waylaid on my way back to my bunk to come into a room and was given no instructions on what to do or what to look for, and now I was being criticized for my short report.

Forrester let out a sigh of disappointment. "Okay, Hunter. Let me explain a bit of what we're doing here." He went on to detail his psycho-social theories of coercion and compliance. "Those men were all brought here a month ago and told they would participate in a sleep study. They were each given a set of rules, we told them they would be enforced. While they think they are here for a sleep study, they are actually here to see how long a compliance task will be followed and to what degree.

"We told each of them that they were not to have any contact with each other for the integrity of the experiment. No talking, no passed notes, no physical contact, no eye contact. Nothing. We also told them that they were not allowed to wander around the facility because if they came in touch with someone who had a cold or flu that it would compromise our research.

"We have been doing these meetings daily for the past month. Rita has been their primary contact. Two days ago, we told them that one of them had their post-sleep blood work come back indicating that they had a cold. This meant one of them had disobeyed a rule and would be turned out of the facility, back to a life on the streets.

"We told them this two days ago, and today, for the first time, one of them coughed."

"Ok, so you picked up homeless men and offered them shelter and food in exchange for participation in your study, and now one of them has a cold. What part of this means Rita is wearing an NSA badge?" I repeated back to Forrester what he had just told me.

"Yes, that was two days ago. Rita said that she expected the guilty party to come forward. But no one did. Until today, when one of them coughed." Forrester seemed keen to repeat this observation.

"Ok, I'm still lost," this was not adding up for me. "How is this part of your compliance study?"

"Because none of them are actually sick. But one of them coughed. Maybe he had a tickle in his throat, maybe he started to believe that he was the one who had turned up a negative test result. Either way, the other men stuck to the rules. They didn't look over at him, they didn't try to help him or stop Rita from taking him away. They didn't break from the rules."

"So, the real experiment wasn't on who had potentially snuck out, it was to see if the power of suggestion would force one of them to confess?"

"Exactly!" Forrester appeared pleased with my comprehension. "We have proof of our compliance rules lasting for four weeks; this is much longer than any other -"

As Forrester explained his research to me, I couldn't help myself from interrupting. "Wait, this sounds -" I didn't want to cross the line, but there was no better word for it, "uh, unethical."

"Hmm, Milgram got that too," he smirked, as though he somehow knew I would say that. As though he had heard that many times already. He added my papers to his file along with Sean's and set it on top of a pile of similar folders.

"His work was unethical," I corrected him.

"Everyone points to his one study and calls him a monster. He did more than just the obedience study. Which, by the way, was groundbreaking! He would send students out and tell them to look up and then observers would count how many others would join in. Nothing unethical there."

I wanted to retort that anyone who walked out in front of a car while looking up would beg to differ, but I held my tongue. I needed to use logic against this man, not snark.

"I wanted to take his experiments and test them at a larger scale. See how long people will believe the command before they start to question it. If we infect someone's mind with an idea, how long until the antibodies, the white blood cells of our thoughts, start to attack it like a disease."

It was interesting. It was unique. I had to give him that. I would continue to sit in on more and more of these experiments. Each time we were told explicitly to keep up the illusion. Otherwise, months of data would be destroyed. If we saw any of the test subjects in the facility, we had to act our part. We couldn't betray the information they had been provided. We all had to make the set-up feel real to the participants. And HR and Marketing really liked the internal branding: "Keep up the illusion with Project Collusion!"

I've often wondered why Forrester didn't name his project Coercion or Compliance. Why Collusion? As the catchphrase flashed in my mind in that hovel, I realized that it was the subliminal instruction that we needed. We had to work together to maintain the facade, often without the ability to communicate or discuss a plan. We had to improvise and adapt.

As my back started to ache from crouching down low in that dirt pit, I realized that Dawes and I needed to maintain our illusion until we were out of range from Paula and her band of teenagers. We wished them luck and I reminded Paula of our deal. We needed supplies, that was the pretense I had entered the store under. I knew it would look suspicious if I didn't insist on payment, even though Dawes and I had enough rations for a few more days and a surplus with Michaels' food as well.

She escorted us back to the store and supervised as we each took an expired protein bar and an air temperature sports drink. After cramming them into our bags, Dawes and I picked up our rifles and continued down the road.

After fifty yards or so, I turned around to see the store shrinking in the distance behind us. I wasn't sure if Paula had gone back inside or had returned to her mud pit.

"Hey, we should head back up-"

"Shhhhh," Dawes cut me off.

I looked over at him. His excessive need for silence was starting to exasperate me. Humans made noise; life made noise.

"I just-" I started again before he grabbed me by the arm and brought me closer to him. He didn't speak, he just took his thumb and slid it across his throat, miming the action of a knife. I understood the gesture, but I couldn't quite understand the intensity of his fear. Perhaps it was time for him to hand over my tablet and I could up the dosage in his device.

"They could be anywhere. Listening." Dawes finally whispered. His eyes darted to the trees surrounding us from the embankments on each side of the road. His paranoia seemed to be unwarranted. But we had just learned that there were surviving humans who were traveling this way and who were taking extreme measures to remove their implants. There could indeed be an ambush ahead of us and we wouldn't know it.

He released my arm and plodded off ahead, walking in front of me for another hundred yards before he stopped and waited for me to catch up. We ascended the embankment on the north side of the road this time. Our feet were sliding into the steep dirt once more. I tried to find exposed roots to act as a foothold, to steady my climb. As Dawes reached the crest, I heard a low hum around me. It grew louder by the second. It was a sound that Dawes and I had heard many times, one of the Project Connect gliders. Designed to bring internet to remote areas via autonomous drone, the devices had been repurposed after the outbreak. They now served as a means of visual contact with the mainland. We saw everything that was happening from the camera lens of the Connect gliders. The riots, the bodies on the ground, their heat traces completely dissipated.

The name had turned out to be prophetic. Once intended to connect the world with high-quality internet access for all, the gliders had turned out to be our main source of contact with the crew on-shore. Until the supply line stopped.

I saw the t-frame of the glider approach in the sky. Painted a smokey blue, the glider was the size of a vehicle when it was on the ground, but from way down below it looked like a large bird. The color of the machine was a near-perfect match for the color of the sky that day, I lost sight of it for a moment before tracking it again. I looked up as it passed over, knowing that the crew on the ship would be watching.

When I made it to the top of the embankment, Dawes offered his hand to help me up. I appreciated the assistance and said as much before dusting myself off.

"Crew must be getting nervous to send the glider out," he commented.

"Can you blame them?" I asked in response. They would have been able to see that we had just spent an hour with another person, although they would have had no way to see the three teenagers on their monitoring devices. They probably wanted to check that we were still alive.

"No," Dawes said as he shook his head. "Alright, let's keep moving. I'd like to get a few more miles further east before dark."

I nodded my head and followed. I wanted to talk through the pieces of information that Paula had given us. I wanted to share that they had each cut out their devices. I wanted to explain my grief at their suffering because of my invention. I wanted hot food and a warm bed. I wanted the crew on board to feel secure in the fact that Dawes and I would do everything we could to get them the supplies they needed. I wanted a lot of things at that moment. But what I really needed, what I would walk straight into, was the truth.

PART TWO

The Walk Out

The world kept working as it does naturally. It appeared that even without man, the trees still grew leaves and lost them. Flowers still sprung to life, vibrant and beautiful, an affront to all the ugliness of this disaster. Birds still snuck in and out of branches, their brilliant blues and reds daring to stick out against the gray-brown of the wood.

It's spring in the Pacific Northwest. Lush. As in green and moist. The wet asphalt blocked out any other odor. Which is a relief because even after a day on foot, we're both starting to smell. I worried at the thought of walking so deliberately in the middle of the road. But we hadn't heard any motors running. It seemed that the world really had disappeared. Pushed along the side of the road were abandoned cars. The command team had worked to establish the supply line back when it all first happened. They must have cleared the road by pushing the cars off to the shoulder, leaving a direct path for our supply deliveries to come down the coast and reach the depot. The highway was all clear, with no physical barrier blocking our shipments.

The silence of the world made me nervous, the crunch of our boots the only sound. With each step, I could feel my damp socks rub up against my feet, wearing a deliberate and painful blister into the skin. Every so often, a bird would call out from the trees. Why wasn't Dawes more nervous? Had he learned this composure in his military training? Never be nervous? Or perhaps my little invention had conditioned him to stay calm. He rubbed his left arm against the side of his body as he walked. If I hadn't implanted the device myself, I might have passed over that detail. But I knew where his device was, just under the skin of his forearm. He was itching.

Instinctively, without even realizing it, my eyes glanced down at my own arm, at the place below my jacket and sweater where my scar was hidden. My implant was faded over, having inserted it beneath my skin years before anyone else had one. I never had the itch; I never had the reaction. In that way, I had an advantage over Dawes. He was the muscle, but I was the brains. And his only weakness as we walked in the wilderness was the urge to scratch.

That's just the thing that we men do; we humans do. We rank each other. We size each other up. We decide who we are better than. I had played that game well during my time in the Bunker on Ni'ihau.

It was pretty clear to me from our first interaction that Forrester was the alpha-male in the group. Or at least he was positioning himself that way. He puffed out his chest a little bit. He cut in to answer questions for other people. He had unlimited use of our free time to make us participate in his interviews. But the first time that I knew that he had a leg-up on us all was the first time that Rattray visited after I had arrived.

It was during breakfast as we all sat together, eating our eggs and bacon. As a team, we all dined together and chatted about things that we were discovering, ways that we could help each other. Holtz, Kupper, and Rita formed a tight-knit little sub-group. Metz and I often sat next to each other, sharing bits of information and making plans to meet up in one or the other's lab for additional research. Forrester usually cut in and sat between Rita and Kupper or myself and Rita. He always tried to sit next to Rita.

But on that particular morning, he didn't sit with us at all. The vacancy at our table was noticed, but no one seemed concerned. *Where could he go?* I assumed he probably slept in or headed off to his lab early. I heard footsteps approaching behind me, four feet tapping along at the same rhythm, perfectly in step. I turned to see Malcolm Rattray walking towards us, his three-piece suit replaced with a polo and khakis. I wondered at how he had made the trip without wrinkling, especially the harrowing descent down the ladder. Forrester was right next to him.

"Good morning, Team!" Rattray bellowed as he approached. His five-hundred-watt smile beamed out at each of us. For someone who would have recently taken a long flight and a helicopter ride, he was uncommonly chipper.

Each of us turned our attention to the boss, to the big man. He was the head of all R&D; he signed our paychecks. And for the purposes of our little group, he was the head of Project Capital. He made sure we all had funding.

I had only been at the Bunker for a little over a month, so I knew conceptually that he would stop by from time to time. He would meet with each of us to learn about our progress and give us information on upcoming grant deadlines. I didn't realize that these meetings would be unscheduled.

I was planning to have my first functional prototype put through the paces in our stress testing lab. I wanted to make sure it would work and function properly before moving onto the implantation testing phase. My design for the prototype was complete before I had even interviewed with Rattray, but it was Metz's chemical compound that I needed to make the thing usable.

"Good morning, sir," Metz said as he stood up, reaching his hand out to shake Malcolm's.

"Great to see you, Metz. You look like you could use some sun," he smiled, shook his hand, and gave him a friendly pat on the back. "I've got to say, we all owe you one for finding Hunter and bringing him into our little group," he looked down at me as he said this.

He was effusive, smarmy. Was this how he was in front of everyone? He seemed different, lighter than when I met him for my interview. As he spoke, my eyes dashed over to Forrester, his smile appeared to be genuine, and then the lights went out in his eyes as Rattray mentioned me. It took everything in me to not smirk and let out a brief laugh. Forrester was so obviously insecure about his position as Rattray's right-hand man. I couldn't care less, or so I told myself. I was here for one thing, and one thing only, a working device that would stop mass murder before it could happen. Being the sycophant to Malcolm was not on my agenda.

My time was scarce. I could feel the clock ticking every day. I needed to finish my solution. I needed to solve for this before the next act of violence occurred. There were shell-shocked vets coming back every day from a war that would never end. There were young men enumerating the ways that the world had hurt them, scribbling their plans into marbled notebooks. The number of good guys working to stop them were outnumbered. It all came down to a scarcity of resources. Not enough good ideas, not enough praise from the boss, not enough funding for your research. All these items we value are scarce.

I turned to finish my eggs as Rattray continued around the table and chatted with each person individually. By the time he reached me, my tray was clear. "Hunter! So glad to see you made it here safe and sound, how are you settling in?"

"Great," I said as I stood. It felt weird to talk to him if I was seated and he was standing. It strained my neck too much. "Being able to connect with Metz directly on the compound has been very helpful, sir." I nodded emphatically as I spoke. I was genuinely grateful for the acceleration of my project. In the Bunker, I could just pop-in and ask Metz a question on the liquid formula.

"That is great to hear," Rattray responded. He looked down at my empty tray. "Heading off to the lab now?"

"I would really like to if that is okay. Unless we all need to stay for a team meeting?" I wasn't sure what the protocol was here. I desperately wanted to get into the lab. But I couldn't insult my boss the first month in. I didn't want to kiss his ass, but I didn't want to be an idiot either.

"Not a problem at all, mind if I tag along?" Rattray seemed nervous, as though I might say no.

"Of course, you can!" I beamed back. I would get to start my testing on schedule. We hurried off in the direction of my lab.

"How are you liking things here, Hunter?" Rattray asked as we left the cafeteria.

"It's great so far. When I first climbed down that ladder I thought, 'what have I gotten myself into?' But this place is great. I feel like I have everything I could ever need to make this device a reality." I tried to look at him as I spoke without tripping over my own feet.

"That's the idea," Malcolm beamed with pride. This facility had been his brainchild. He wanted a location where scientists would work on their research, where their focus could be on inventing things that would make the world better. I figured that I would feel the same way once I saw my device operational. "I read your memo last week on your estimated timeline for human testing. I think you have a fair window to get the device ready for trials. But your testing window is pretty lengthy."

He was referring to the amendment I had sent in as part of my last report. We had to provide a progress report to him each week. Usually, it was "everything went as planned," but occasionally, we would need to make a note of a setback or change in plans.

When I had interviewed with Rattray and explained my research, I told him that I envisioned the device as a cranial implant that would react to adrenaline and noradrenaline in the system. But I recently realized how problematic it would be. Not just for testing; brain surgery is a tough sell when it is necessary, let alone when it is for an unproven device. During roll-out and implementation, the costs would be prohibitive. If the device needed to be replaced or recalibrated it would be another dangerous surgery for retrieval. I didn't anticipate inventing something that would be defective, but I was realistic about the lifetime of any piece of technology.

In my progress report the previous week, I had amended the timeline for testing based on my new focus of digital implantation. "I want to make sure we have both short-term and long-term studies on the device. Not just the initial implantation, but we need long-term information to confirm that it continues to work and that that the device itself does not become an issue. I would expect the standard itching at the incision site as it heals. But what if they give a friend a high-five and the device released the serum? What if they see rings on their fingernails from metal poisoning? I believe we have all variables accounted for, but-" I paused. I was confident in my solution, so I didn't want him to think I was doubting the efficacy, or self-sabotaging, or anything like that.

"But what?" He stopped and turned to face me.

"But life is chaos. Life is the unexpected. We are planning to tell someone who is angry and scared at what they could do, that they might hurt people, that we are going to make it so that can't happen. I'd like to make sure we don't trade one problem for another. I'd like to have more time to observe."

"I like your thinking, Hunter. The D.O.D. will want a viable product; they have the best interest of our veterans at heart. I know we all tend to beat up on the government and bureaucracy, but they want a solution too. You're going to stop Fort Hood from happening again, I know it. But don't let perfect be the enemy of good. Don't wait so long for perfection that someone else gets a product that works ninety-five percent of the time out into the market and your funding dries up."

I nodded as I took in his words. He was right. I needed to be cautious, but not so much so that it impeded the end goal. We continued to my lab where I unveiled the device.

Roughly the size of a dime, it was slender and smooth. The edges were rounded, to prevent excessive scarring. The serum that Metz had developed was stored in a small compartment within the device; the micro-mechanics were very intricate. The metal alloy was porous. If the adrenaline and noradrenaline in the system reached a precise level, the Cease serum would secrete from the device, rendering the subject calm, giving them back control of their faculties.

"Wow," Rattray looked at the device from the other side of the thick glass. I had it in a sterile environment. No unclean air or germs were going to corrupt my hard work. Malcolm was so close to the case that his breath fogged the container.

"This is only one of two that exist at the moment. Once we get through some stress testing this week, I'll work to have a preliminary order sent into production for lab testing here." I stared down at my creation in awe. I would stop mayhem; I would stop chaos with this one device. That kind of power will go to anyone's head. It warps what seems real and what is beyond imagination. It changes everything. And it turned out to be completely uncontrollable. What I hoped to put an end to, I enabled on a mass scale.

Rattray stayed and observed as I started the first of the stress tests. While I waited for the results to print out from the computer, he asked for information on how the team had welcomed me. I told him exactly how it was going. "Everyone has been very welcoming. Metz has been so great, really helping me learn my way around and obviously, helping with the Calm implant." I tripped over the new name for my device. It belonged to Peec and that meant that as the Project Calm product, it would be called the Calm implant forever. It wasn't a horrible name, but it wasn't the original name I had been calling it in my head forever. I had been thinking of naming it ARRI the Adrenaline Response Reduction Implant. Not as catchy.

"I'm glad that you and Metz have been able to share research," Rattray nodded as he spoke.

"I'm just glad he had the serum perfected. If I had to wait on the aerosol, I would be out of luck," I smiled as I spoke, making a light joke. Metz and I had ribbed each other about the problems he continued to run into with the aerosol formula. It was too strong in each iteration. I looked at Malcolm's face and immediately regretted my words. I had disparaged Metz in front of our boss. Instead of praising him, which had been my intent, I had insulted him.

"Well, I'm glad that Metz has been so helpful. He's the longest standing member of the team. He tends to take on the Papa Bear role when I'm not here." My words didn't seem to faze him. Malcolm shook his head slightly before continuing. "Has Forrester been able to help you get acclimated at all?"

"Um, no more than anyone else, I guess." It was such a specific question and an odd one at that. Malcolm nodded as I answered. It seemed I had said the wrong thing again, but this time I wasn't sure what.

"Have you kept him up to date on your research? I wonder if there might be a good cross over with his work." Malcolm turned to face me as he said this, I mirrored him, removing my eyes from the results that started to display on my screen. The device was withstanding a high amount of pressure.

"I could see how he might have a use for my device in his," I paused, using every bit of my self-control to not roll my eyes as I continued, "experiments. But my device isn't even ready for human testing for my purposes. I can certainly provide him with a workable device once I have completed my analysis."

Rattray nodded. "Sounds like a good plan, Hunter," he patted me on the back in a fatherly manner as he said this. I felt both respected and belittled at the same time. "Well, I'll let you get to the rest of your tests for the day. Got to go make the rounds. We'll have a team dinner tonight." I watched him walk out of the lab, his path visible to me from my little corner. Even though I knew that he was just checking in, I had an uneasy feeling that he was also trying to assess something more than the effectiveness of the device. *How were the office politics panning out? Was his second in command really doing as instructed?* All the office mumbo jumbo that I had hoped to avoid by sticking to the research side of things was alive and well on the corporate end of the spectrum (it had been there during my academic days as well).

We build these systems: organizational charts, procedures, chain of command, and we say it is to provide order. To give us the structure that we need to be able to thrive. But more often than not, these systems, erected and convoluted by humans, serve as a means to hold some higher and keep others lower. The most pervasive example of this being the workplace. Lab, cubicle, high-rise, whatever the location: it's all the same. Someone is below a certain paygrade; some people matter more. It's all so cruel how we capture each other in these snares. So, of course, when everything broke down, it revealed the worst of us. We had been feeding and nourishing that behavior for centuries, practicing our ability to marginalize someone, belittle them, shrink them down so small that we could just flick them away.

Flick them away we did. Like the gnats that landed on Dawes as we walked past the idle puddles through the woods. The standing water spawned countless bugs for us to deal with. Most of our skin was covered, but they swarmed our ears. The incessant buzzing grated on my nerves; I saw Dawes swing his hands every few minutes. Shooing them away momentarily before they returned.

We continued east, but we kept close to the embankment. Every few miles we would inch closer and peer down at the dirt and the mud. We were looking for signs of life, signs of a disturbance, anything. Would we find our supply-truck pulled off to the side of the road? Would we find the bodies of the drivers splayed out? But we saw nothing. For miles and miles, nothing out of the ordinary. It was as though that stretch of road was completely empty. It could have been one hundred years after the outbreak for the lack of life that we observed.

Why did we expect to see so much violence on land? Why were we looking over our shoulders? I had seen the footage from the first months of the outbreak. It was gruesome. The body count from the toxin was staggering, but at least those victims died quickly. The remaining population kept attacking itself, attacking each other. For food, for shelter, for power. Even with the relative calm that time had afforded, that violence was still lying just beneath the surface, ready to spring out on us.

We stopped to catch our breath and snack on one of the protein bars that we had packed. I took this time to consult my tablet and check for signs of life. Dawes took this time to relieve himself.

Dawes seemed to relax a bit with each mile that we put between us and Paula's cramped foxhole.

"The girl said something about this Reaper," I muttered as I shifted the items in my pack again.

"Yeah?" Dawes answered. I couldn't tell if he was feigning his lack of interest or if he genuinely didn't care.

"It's weird, right? We're sent here to figure out why supply lines aren't working. We're told by Chang that they suspect potential vigilante activity. This Reaper could be the person or people we're looking for."

I looked up at Dawes as I awaited his response. He took a bite of his protein bar and gnawed it around his mouth for a moment before responding.

"This Reaper is a myth. It's a story concocted to encourage hope, inspire fear, whatever these survivors need to get them through the day. They believe in it so much that they set traps in its name. They believe in it so much that they think it can save them, reset things to the way it used to be. But it'll never happen. And instead of that belief fading over time, it will only grow. We're not looking for one Reaper. We're looking for their biggest fan. We're looking for the fanatic who has taken action in their name." Dawes finished his tirade. I took it in, trying to understand where the vehemence behind his words came from.

"You've seen something like this before?" I asked, trying to mask my sarcasm. Dawes had been here just as long as I had, knew all the information about this mission that I did. Who gave him the authority to decide that the Reaper wasn't real? To dismiss my hypothesis?

"Yeah, I served in Iraq." He chucked the wrapper from his protein bar on the ground and took a large swig of water from his canteen. "People need something to believe in and in the absence of real leadership, they will follow the first thing that steps up. Religion. Warlord. Reaper. Phantom."

He started walking a few steps before turning around to face me. "Come on, let's keep going," he waved me toward him. I walked slowly, giving the two of us some space. The war might have been years earlier, but it seemed that it was fresh in Dawes' mind. I wanted to give him some room, and I also needed to mull over what he had just said.

My frame of mind had been totally different coming into this mission. Don't get exposed to the toxin. Restore the supply lines. Avoid survivors, but if they are friendly, gather clues as to what happened. Get back to the ship with a fresh supply of rations.

But Dawes saw it through a different lens. The world had been decimated. Anyone who survived the outbreak was as traumatized as any shell-shocked survivor of war. Peec had sent in their security fleet to help, but overwhelmingly, it wasn't enough. The public was abandoned.

Governments crumbled because all of the leaders died. To Dawes, we were walking through lawless land and trying not to risk any encounters with survivors because we couldn't anticipate what the apocalypse had done to them. Physically or psychologically.

Dawes' military experience gave him a whole different mindset than myself. No wonder it was so hard for me to connect with him or any of the crew. We were speaking different languages, but in the same tongue.

If only there were a common language, I thought as I followed behind him.

I first discovered that exact phrase the day I finally mustered the nerve to casually walk into Rita's lab. I had been trying to not be too aloof, but not too eager to spend time with her either. I got the sense that Forrester was either in a relationship with her or at least he was giving clear signals that he had some kind of romantic claim to her. The way he made sure to sit next to her at every meal. The defensive look he would shoot me if I spoke to her directly in his presence. The way he would monopolize her time with his thought experiments. All context clues, nothing definitive one way or the other. But I couldn't stand the thought of that smug guy with Rita. She was so sweet. In my mind, I rationalized that she was too nice, too kind. She wouldn't hurt his feelings by telling him to beg off. I decided that I could be just the Alpha Male to challenge Forrester's place.

Having successfully completed my research for the day, I took a left down the corridor of lab offices. The hallway dead-ended with Metz's lab on the left and Rita's on the right. She spent a lot of her time working with Holtz and Kupper to integrate her project with theirs, so I ran the chance of missing her. But I could just pop in to visit Metz and save face. Metz was still working on an opiate that could easily calm a crowd, or dispel a riot without loss of life. (Or at least that's what his end goal was on paper.) His project name was called Project Cease. Along the way, he had discovered new forms of narcotics, a method to irritate and then soothe the skin. And the oddest formula he developed caused a complete cessation of menses, he never divulged how he confirmed that fact, but he assured us it was indeed true. His liquid serums were spot on. But his government contract required an aerosol. That was where he kept getting tripped up. "Just waiting until this contract is done and then I'm going right to big pharma with this one," he confided in me one day. I didn't want to remind him of the clause in our contracts that said that everything developed while working for Peec, belonged to Peec.

But I couldn't worry about Metz at that moment. I held my palm to my face and did a quick breath-check. I smoothed my hair with my hands. I wanted to look good, but not too good, not like I was trying too hard.

I stuck my head in the open doorway of Rita's lab. It had the symbol for her project etched into the glass. Each of our projects had its own icon or symbol. My project, Calm, had interlocking triangles. Project Cyclops had the hieroglyphic eye. Project Connect had a cone with dashes through it, a rudimentary Wi-Fi symbol. Rita's project symbol was an ear.

I crossed the threshold into the room. There was a faint smell of lavender, a woman's touch to the office. Each workspace was illuminated in the same eerily bright white as the rest of the Bunker. White walls, floors, and ceilings with recessed lighting. But we all made the space our own. Rita had a shelf of books above her desk. Stacks of dictionaries and linguistics textbooks. And one collection of poems. *The Dream of a Common Language* by Adrienne Rich.

My eyes scanned the room to see if she was there. I saw the tall curls of her hair bobbing from the far end of the lab. She was leaning over some schematics at the last workstation. Judging by the motion of her head, I expected to see her with headphones plugged in, and I tried not to startle her as I approached. I waited until I had stepped out in front of her to wave; she looked up from her papers.

"Ah, sorry," she said as she took her earbuds out and laid them down. The faint sounds of the Cranberries continued to drift up from the table.

"No worries, I finished up my work for the day and I've been trying to meet with everyone to learn more about their projects. I know I tend to just keep my head down and get tunnel vision, so I figured I should make this effort now before I revert to my reclusive ways."

Rita laughed at my joke. "Yeah, we're all pretty much life-long loners. None of us got here by winning any awards for most popular."

Exactly! I wanted to shout. *See we know each other so well. We should go out sometime.* Years of anticipated rejection from females had taught me to not be this forward. I kept this all in my mind. Also, we were in a secure Bunker, there would be nowhere to go out to. Instead, I abruptly changed the subject as any socially awkward person would do.

"What are you working on?" I nodded towards the schematics on her workstation. There appeared to be several variations of a device across multiple pages, each marked up and annotated.

"Project Converse," Rita said. "Converse as in conversate, not the converse." She wrinkled her nose and furrowed her brow, seemingly debating if her last sentence made sense.

"I get it," I nodded and smiled. I picked up one of the schematics. A small disc, drawn to scale but magnified.

"The goal of the project was to develop a universal language. A way that we can all communicate, no matter where we are from."

"A common language?" I asked, pulling from the title of the book on her shelf.

"Yes!" she answered excitedly. She didn't realize that I had only just picked up that phrase. Encouraged, she continued. "I initially started working on an icon-based language to use universally. After four years of investing in that concept, we realized that the problem couldn't be solved by expecting humans to actually learn a new universal language. We realized that what we needed was a translator."

"Like on Star Trek?" I asked.

"Yeah, but more sophisticated than that. My project is also partially funded by the US Military, so it needs a practical combat application. What I realized is that it needed to be a wearable or implanted device that would take the sound output from the speaker and modify it so that only someone with a compatible device could understand it. No companion device, then all you hear is complete nonsense. I'm nearly finished with the prototypes."

"Hmm, *sounds* promising," I nodded as I kept my eyes focused on the schematics on the table. I wanted to look up and make eye contact, but that seemed too intense.

"Yes, except that it modifies words in the same way. If we have a soldier abroad trying to relay a message, someone listening who has an ear for languages may start to notice the linguistic patterns and crack the code. We need it to modify in a way that the code can't be cracked."

"So, that's your current roadblock?" We all had them, we all needed to get past them.

"Yep," she said. I looked up to see her nodding, a look of frustration shadowing her face.

"Good luck." I offered.

"Thanks," she gave a weak smile. The conversation had fizzled out.

"So, have you decided on the wearable or the implanted option?" I was trying to keep our chat going longer. Keep the rhythm between us humming along.

"The device is ideally implanted and uses bone conduction to transmit the correct words in the correct language to the subject. But given the needs of our investor, the US Military, it needs to be wearable, and it needs to be able to be removed or turned off. The concern with the implantable solution was, what if it can't turn off and no one around them can understand what they're saying. Could be an issue in emergency situations."

"Makes sense. Any experimental evidence or just conjecture?"

"We had some bad test runs. Helped us solve for that issue and also helped to give us the idea for an emergency off switch. Any user can switch the device off at will. That way, if they need to shout to a fellow soldier to keep them from walking into a trap or getting themselves killed, they can still do that." Rita gestured to a portion of the drawings with the tip of her pencil, indicating the kill switch.

"Hmm, but won't the person they are calling out to not hear it then?"

"What do you mean?"

"If you and I are linked with these devices, and I shut off my translator and call out to you in English and say 'Watch out!', if your device is still on, won't it be scrambled?"

"Nope." She shook her head and offered a coy smile as she answered.

"No?" I wondered at how long she had been working on this device to think of each of these scenarios.

"One of the first fail-safes we put in place: your preferred language is programmed into your device so it knows what you want to hear things relayed in. If any words from that language are picked up. they are relayed to you in that language as well. Whether the device was on or off, I would hear it the same way."

"Then why give them a kill switch option?" I inquired.

"Redundant back-ups are necessary." She shrugged off the explanation, but I was starting to understand the way the military liked their devices. Plan for the device failure first, then work back to solve for those issues before they came up. It was a clean way to operate, but I worried it would take years for me to get a device approved at this rate. I was wrong. The advances I was able to realize within the Bunker were unreal. I had the full support of the staff, and peers I could safely discuss my work with. Even with having to develop redundant systems for the government contracts, I made more progress in those first few months than I could have done in years in academia.

But redundant is how I felt on that trek with Dawes. At least he and Michaels had experience in active war zones to be able to prepare them for this kind of long slog. At different intervals Dawes would stop. Sometimes I would hear a movement in the branches or the snap of a twig and would pause at the same time as him. Those stops made sense to me. But at other times, he would freeze and I would nearly walk into him as though he were a tree. He used hand signals that I was apparently supposed to know. Michaels would have understood them.

I was there to check the readout on the tablet and make sure we weren't about to be ambushed. The expectation was that all the remaining people alive on the continent had my device implanted. We should be able to see them, and if necessary, stop them before attacking. But now we knew that they were cutting it out of their skin.

It hadn't actually taken me years to invent the device and the necessary redundancies. I had solved it much faster by leveraging Metz's failed formulas. I was productive. I was busy. I was useful. Three things I missed after a very long time on the Pricus and on the excursion to restore the supply lines.

The land Dawes and I passed through was silent and empty. Even the wildlife seemed to be scarce. Perhaps they hadn't been immune to the toxin. Sure, more than enough birds would take to the sky every now and again as we walked. But no deer or squirrels were visible. Had the locals hunted them? Surely the small population in this area wouldn't have taken out that many animals. But I reminded myself that the faraway dots on my tablet may not be the only people in the area. There could be more like Timoney who had carved into their own flesh to remove the implant.

During our silent march I kept my eyes open for any movement between the trees. I knew I had to be looking out for potential nomadic survivors, mad with rage, who might attack us. But I really just wanted to see a deer. Or a rabbit. Something to remind me that this land could still be alive. I hadn't been in a living environment for so long, cooped up in artificial cells for years.

The lush tropical paradise of The Big Island of Hawai`i was verdant and alive with color. But Ni`ihau was barren and desolate. There were no majestic wild animals on the land. There really wasn't much there at all. Only one small collection of buildings above-ground made up the only town, if you can call it that, on the island. The few locals didn't want to interact with us, so we let them be. Besides, then there would be questions to answer and entire stories to fabricate. Most of the Human Capital Project team took our occasional days off below ground. We had more that we could do in the Bunker anyways.

Game tables, unlimited buffets, everything you could get at HQ in Seattle we had in the Bunker. Except for sunlight, we couldn't get that down there. The network was restricted inside the Bunker and was non-existent outside of it. You couldn't get a signal for anything above ground. It was easy to opt to stay down-below. It seemed like the most logical choice, which of course, had been designed by Peec.

Not leaving the Bunker warped my sense of reality. Of up and down. Of right and wrong. Of truth and lies. I had my device, my clean solution, and my fail-safe. My next step was how to handle implantation.

My first idea was an outpatient procedure that would require no scalpel, no surgery. But it would require a needle thick enough for the device to pass through it. The device was light and thin, but it was as wide as the fingernail on a pinky. Can you imagine a needle as wide as your pinky finger being stuck into your forearm or leg? The thought of it was daunting, even to someone with a working knowledge of clinical procedures. It would be the least invasive, but no one would ever agree to have it implanted if they saw the gauge. Least of all the paranoid and those suffering traumata who were already likely to be extremely suspicious of the entire concept of such a device. Add in a massive medical instrument and their minds would spin into one conspiracy theory after the next.

Then I thought of sole implants. The fleshy skin at the bottom of the foot would be ideal for implantation and no one would be able to see a scalpel or needle or any sharp instrument coming at them. But my stress testing had returned some interesting data. And unless I could restrict the test subject and, ultimately, my patients to be less than one hundred pounds, the sole implant would be out. Even though the device width was a sliver of a millimeter, it would result in a slight bump on the bottom of one foot. That bump would change the patient's gait and then later develop into a lifetime of limping. It would become more and more exaggerated until the person just quit walking altogether.

Back to the drawing board. My next planned implantation site was the left hand. It passed all the theoretical tests I had set up.

The left side was ideal because the heart always leaned a little to the left, but in the case of an arm amputation, the right forearm would still do just fine. I always had to factor in amputations when designing for veteran patients; it was an eerie thought. With the size of the device, I knew I would need to write a protocol to distract the patient or shield their line of sight so that they couldn't see the procedure and they would walk out within an hour of arriving. Any ambulatory clinic could perform the procedure.

The thumb was the most ideal spot, but I didn't think I could develop devices small enough right away. In biomechanical engineering, the smaller a device, the more advanced it is. Having a plan for additional funding to improve the technology after a successful roll-out, I made a note to test digital implantation in the second round of development. I didn't know it then, but I should have never written that down. Thoughts are dangerous, but words turned out to be lethal in this case.

I wanted to stick with the theory and I proceeded with the lower forearm in mind. I was supposed to apply to test the device on a voluntary human participant. But, with our Bunker being on a secret island, I didn't have much of a population to choose from. Forrester volunteered his pool of test subjects to me, which I quickly declined. I did not want my breakthrough, my device, to have any required footnote to Forrester and his project. But eventually, I did have to rely on him. Through gritted teeth, I asked for his help.

I talked through the application process with Rattray on our weekly video chat. He explained the need to follow procedure. And then, wistfully, he mentioned that he admired the scientists who broke the rules, who were brave enough to test on themselves. He then reiterated the company's official position on following the rules. I read between the lines. I knew I would catch some flak for it, but I decided to be test subject 001.

I recorded my own implantation. It was surreal to cut into my arm and see the delay of a fraction of a second between when my skin split and the blood appeared. With a steady grip, I used the forceps to hold open the cut and slide the implant in. The entire implantation took only seconds. Steeling myself for the pain and mentally walking through each step took much, much longer. I used liquid stitches and marveled at the blue dot that appeared on one of the screens off to my right. The device activated with my body heat; the second it was inside my body it started to register on the screen. I felt joy and pride flood my system, or perhaps that was just the first wave of adrenaline quelled by the implant. Either way, it worked. And I recorded no immediate negative symptoms.

On Rattray's advice, more like his insistence, I reached out to Forrester for help with the implantation testing. I needed a control group that would think they were implanted, when they actually weren't, a control group to receive dud implants, and a third group to receive real implants. Forrester had dozens of test subjects cycling through the facility each month. I approached him the week after my own successful implantation to ask for his help. I swallowed every bit of pride that I had to do it. I expected his smug grin as he agreed to help. I expected his false modesty as he detailed how his test subjects could be of help. What I didn't expect was to learn more about the depths of his twisted studies.

"Of course, I'll help you, Hunter. That's what the team is for," he nodded and patted me on the shoulder in a patronizing manner.

"Thank you. I'll need to have a confirmed list of test subjects who have agreed to participate by the end of the week." I didn't really need them that quickly, but I wanted him to know that there was real work to be done on Project Calm, work that had deadlines and didn't stretch on forever without measurable solutions.

"Okay, I'll have to divert some of my newest recruits for that effort then. It will give me a chance to push up my Zimbardo study," he said as he made a note on his clipboard. I should have left it alone, I shouldn't have asked for more information, but the name was ringing a bell in the back of my mind.

"Zimbardo?" I asked him to clarify.

"Yes, we are recreating the Stanford Prison Study. Specifically, we are having the group that will be the stand-in for the guards wear the Cratus suit.

With the spring-loaded stilts and impenetrable rubber exterior, Rattray has a concern that the user might go on a power trip. Holtz agreed to it," he added as he registered the shock on my face.

I didn't understand how recreating two highly controversial psychological studies was groundbreaking work that belonged with our project team. I didn't see how it was solving for anything. Sure, the psychological implications of our devices needed to be checked. Yes, I needed to run placebo control groups. But to give Forrester free reign to run these kinds of experiments and then try to make it fit into the context of our other projects made no sense to me.

Working closely with Forrester to run my own control studies was grating, but a necessary evil. The rest of what he was working on, well, I didn't know how necessary it was, but it seemed excessively manipulative. It wasn't my area of expertise though, so I kept my concerns to myself. When told to assist with one of his scenarios, I followed instructions and maintained the illusion. For some reason, Forrester had been blessed by Rattray as the right-hand man, the up-and-comer, the one who could do no wrong. I didn't understand the larger plan at that moment. I didn't see it all come together until I took that shore excursion with Dawes. But I did see the corporate politics at work during my time in that Bunker. I saw the way that the management structure was designed to keep us working harder. I realized that their corporate incentives, those promotions and perks, the carrots they dangled, weren't carrots at all. They were orange rags coated in kerosene, ready to be ignited, ready to incinerate me. My career about to go up in smoke. Another casualty of quarterly profits.

Dawes showed no sign of slowing down as the sky started to indicate the first signs of nightfall. We had meandered back down to the road during the afternoon and the trees around us started to look blacker and bleaker as the light receded. The hues that were visible above the treetops faded into neutral oranges; the clouds dulled what might have been a vibrant display. I began to feel the chill in my hands and feet. The air temperature dropped quickly along with the sun.

"We should plan to make camp," I muttered to Dawes.

"Alright, sounds like a good plan," he responded without looking over at me. He turned off the road and started up the embankment. The incline was steep and the dirt was loose underfoot. For each step we took up, we slid back down. The effect was exhausting. By the time we reached the top, my legs were on fire. Dawes continued walking for another hundred feet or so. He must have had some reason for selecting this arbitrary patch of forest that looked much like the other ones we walked by. I dropped my pack at the base of a tree, as did Dawes.

He radioed into the ship.

"Pricus Capricorn, Dawes reporting for final check-in of the day," he waited for the response.

"Copy. What is your status, Dawes?" A new voice responded, another one I couldn't quite place.

"Making camp for the night. We encountered a small group of survivors earlier. Hunkered down by the gas station we passed. You would have seen it overhead from the glider."

Another pause. "How many survivors?" The voice echoed through the trees; I heard a bird take off nearby.

"Four," Dawes looked at me as he responded.

"You think they've been interfering with the supplies?" The radio emitted a brief whine, the static at the end of each transmission more piercing than ever before.

"I doubt it. Most are too weak to move around. One will probably be dead within the next forty-eight hours. We're continuing east in the morning." Dawes dismissed their speculation. If the crew on the ship had seen these survivors, they wouldn't have had to ask.

"Copy." The voice from the ship cut off. Dawes removed his finger from the button.

"We should tell them that they're cutting out their implants. And aren't you going to tell them about this Reaper?" I didn't know why Dawes wouldn't include this information. Especially considering the chilling message that unfurled when Michaels was murdered.

Dawes looked directly at me. He shook his head once and then tapped his finger on the button once more. "We'll radio in again tomorrow if we have any updates." He flipped off the switch on the radio and tucked it away.

"Why didn't you mention the Reaper? I'm starting to suspect that whoever this Reaper is, that person or persons is causing the disruption in the supply line." I couldn't believe he had failed to mention this information. Even with his explanation earlier of followers and those who would worship the Reaper, it was still an important development.

"Yeah, me too," Dawes answered, brushing off my concerns.

"So why not say anything?" I pressed him.

"Because, if we say those people were talking about the Reaper, they'll send in bombs tonight. Personally, I don't want them confusing their heat signatures with ours." He kept an even tone. It wasn't the idea that the people we met earlier might be killed that offended him. It was the idea that we might be hit instead.

"Why would they do that? We need as many survivors as possible if we ever want to rebuild society." My own words sounded naïve, even as I spoke them out loud.

"No one on that ship is thinking about rebuilding society right now. Their focus is on getting the supply line restored. Anyone who might threaten that, this Reaper or his disciples, is a potential risk."

"Disciples? Isn't that a little strong?" Images of Leonardo DaVinci's *The Last Supper* swam in my mind.

"You told me what they said, how they spoke about him. The Reaper is their savior, their protection against some rival faction of survivors." Dawes' interpretation of their words interested me. I hadn't made that connection from what Chang had said in our briefing back on the ship. Dawes turned around; he was done with this conversation. I ruminated on his theory as we moved onto our next task.

We each kept our rifles with us as we walked out to gather whatever dry branches we could find. We set about the task of setting up camp, each knowing what to do. We needed to make a fire, so that required kindling. We needed to sleep, so we cleared out rocks and found patches of ground that weren't perturbed by tree roots.

As though we had been waiting to relax, to release, the moment that we sat down in front of the fire, we began to talk. Dawes started, surprisingly.

"Michaels was a good guy," he stared directly into the flames of our small campfire as he spoke.

I nodded in agreement. I wasn't sure if I could eulogize him, it would make his death feel too real, too close. "What the hell did we get ourselves into?" That question was all I could offer.

"Someone had to do it," Dawes answered. I could tell that he interpreted my question to be about the mission at hand. I didn't correct him. That his answer could have also applied to my intended question was ominous. "I know we haven't always seen eye-to-eye, but we were the three-best suited to the task," he threw the leaf he had been wheedling into the fire.

I looked over at him, grateful for his vote of confidence. "They're all going to die if we can't get the supplies running again." I thought about all the men and women left on the ship. Imagined them sitting down to their dinner of stale rations. Were they all aware of how dangerously low the stockpile was? Was Captain Gomes debating when to tell the crew?

"They sure will. Or they'll come ashore and get attacked by this tribe of Reaper followers. If the weight of their mortality isn't enough to inspire us to get the job done, I don't know what will." Dawes leaned back and rested against the tree behind him. A twig snapped in the fire, the popping sound jolted me back into that moment, ripping me away from the vision in my mind of the ship sailing unmanned once everyone starved. I already felt the weight of so many lives on my shoulders. Now I had the crew to carry as well. The weight was unbearable, the strain too great. I wanted to tell Dawes exactly how it felt to have a soul on your conscience, but I held my tongue. We were all entitled to our own pain, comparing it did nothing. It would be like comparing two eternities, they are both different and immeasurable.

As the fire dwindled, I offered to take the first watch. Dawes accepted without hesitation and leaned back into the ground, his hat covering his face. In the blood-orange light of the embers, his body looked red. It reminded me of the flashing red lights on the day we had a security breach in the Bunker.

The white walls, floors, and ceiling had flashed from a placid and calm soft white light to a brilliant and terrifying red. I was in the Cease lab with Metz. Waiting for the test results of my first group of trial subjects, I had more time to help him out. I could either help Metz or help Forrester, so the choice was easy.

Metz had told me about his latest issue the night before at dinner. After the rest of the team cleared away and we were left with the last scraps of our dinner, he finally spoke. He had been despondent most of the evening, but he often fell into glum moods, so I didn't think much of it at first.

"They want me to reformulate it again," he mumbled the words as he picked at his food. Going back to the drawing board was part of life as a scientist. Metz had made great strides, and his liquid formula was perfect for my needs. But the aerosol that he needed to develop for his government contract had been a multi-year exercise in trial and error. He was like Sisyphus in the way he had to keep starting over. I knew it wasn't the process that frustrated him. It was the perception. Everyone else on the team had great progress to report. His liquid serum and its application in my Calm implant were old news. Metz felt that he needed something new, a win. A finished product to secure his place on the team moving forward.

I sat quietly and let him continue to speak; he had my full attention. I knew better than to talk; this was my time to listen. "Apparently, they like that they can say there is a device that can just knock people out safely, but what they want is the toxic mixture. They want to be able to kill en-masse with my device and then when the carnage wracks up, blame the manufacturer."

I let out a sigh. "Metz, that can't be true." I shook my head as I tried to contradict his words.

"It is, that's what they told me today." He looked up at me. His eyes were red. his cheeks were sallow and drooping. He had been down in this Bunker for too long. But he was also not getting any younger. The pressure to produce and leave a legacy was weighing on him.

I shook my head before responding. "Why in the world would they want us to create something lethal? The mission statement is to-"

"They don't give a damn about the mission statement!" Metz interrupted me with vigor, his voice louder than I ever heard it before. He slammed his fist on the table to emphasize his point, our trays and utensils shaking with the force. People at the other tables turned to see what the commotion was all about.

"Metz," I reached across the table to try and steady his forearm, but he tucked both his hands into his lap before I could reach him. He shook his head and pushed his lips together. The frustration on his face was kinetic, his forehead creasing, moving like the sea, his mind trying to quell the storm of emotions that he was feeling.

"Hunter," he finally said after a tense moment. "I need your help." He looked me in the eye. I could almost feel his gaze reaching out to hold me, to grasp my hands, to beg for assistance. The act of speaking that sentence was a sign of intense strength in my book. I looked up to this man; he had helped me get to this stage. To me, it was a no-brainer. Of course, I would help, and

I wouldn't ask any questions about what kind of help he needed. On the surface, I could tell myself that he needed help with the formula. But I think that I knew deep down that what he needed help with was an escape. It was the most forbidden of things on that island.

"I'll help you. We'll get to work first thing in the morning," I wanted to do something more, but I didn't know what that could even be. He would move past this moment. he would put his nose back to the grindstone. There was no way I could see him surrendering his work and giving up on it now. I was sure that his hyperbolic statements were the result of his frustrations. They certainly couldn't be based in fact.

He walked off with his tray and I returned to my food, now cold, and finished the last few bites with ungrateful effort. After years in the Bunker, it was all starting to wear on me too. The months had run together easily; time flew by without notice until you actually sat and thought about it. Everything in that facility focused on the success of the projects. Any setback amplified the pressure. You messed up and cost hundreds of thousands of dollars in research funding and put your project and the support staff at risk of being shut down. You might as well stroll the halls like a criminal doing a perp walk.

I thought about how Metz must be feeling as I walked back to my bunk. If my trials revealed that I needed to go back to the drawing board, I would be angry too. I would be frustrated with no one to take it out on except myself. My mind flooded with all the ways that my tests could go wrong. Already, the subjects were complaining of an implantation site itch. That could be a natural part of the healing process or a flaw in the implantation technique. I tried to tell myself that I didn't have to be concerned. But already my compassion for Metz had turned into a selfish introspection; I started to worry about myself. I fell asleep to a repeating loop of my test subjects scratching at their skin, leaving it red and raw, and in some cases bleeding. The nightmare didn't end when I woke up.

I headed to the cafeteria to grab a breakfast burrito to go. I had promised Metz first thing in the morning and I meant it. I didn't see Metz there, so I guessed that he was already in his lab. I made my way over there quickly, trying to eat and walk as best as I could. I arrived at the lab to the sound of chaos. A scrape of a stool against the floor. The woosh of a pile of papers as they spilled off the desk. I spotted Metz as he stood up and brushed himself off. He had a similar set up in his lab that I had in mine. He worked in the back corner so he could see anyone who entered. But his back was to me, so he didn't see me come in just yet. I saw him pull a thumb drive from his computer and put it in his pocket.

Thumb drives were strictly prohibited in the Bunker. All the data belonged to Peec and was shared and saved through a secure internal network. No one was allowed to use any external storage devices for fear that the proprietary research would escape the facility. I didn't even know how he got a thumb drive in, but he had it and was clearly using it.

"Metz?" I called out to him as he started back towards his filing cabinet.

He spun around to face me, but turned too fast. He lost his balance and tipped over.

I rushed to him, concerned for his safety. The smell of the whiskey hit me before I reached him. Metz was lachrymose, his kind eyes watered down and his mouth fumbling for stasis. Drunk. On the job, first thing in the morning, drunk.

"Are you okay?" I offered up that usual stupid question. Of course, the man wasn't okay. I should have asked if he was hurt. If he was out of his mind.

"I never wanted this. I wanted to help people. This is going to kill people. I have to stop them." His words flowed together as though they were all one.

"Metz, come on, we'll figure this out," I tried to pull him up by his arm. He couldn't support himself on his legs and slid down again.

"They're gonna kill so many people. Their vision for the world isn't what they told us. I have to stop them." I still couldn't quite fully understand what he was implying. Or why he was taking this round of redevelopment so hard. Before I could open my mouth to console him or encourage him, the alarm started screaming. The walls went cherry red like we were stuck inside of a hard candy.

A rumble of boots sounded down the hallway. Six guards filtered into the room. I lifted my hands instinctively. I knew that there were guards at the facility, but I had only ever seen one in the pillbox on my very first day. I had mostly forgotten that they were here.

In seconds they had Metz by the arms, picked him up, and started to frog march him away. The tips of his toes barely touching the ground. I could hear his screaming as they took him down the hallway and out of the Bunker, and therefore out of existence to us on the Human Capital Project.

Maybe he had divulged too much or pushed the wrong button. Maybe a security camera caught his taking the thumb drive. Later, someone told me that on his first big test, his compound had incapacitated the riot so effectively that everyone had died. I guessed that was what he had been babbling about. Poor Metz, I thought.

And what was it he was screaming as they pulled him away?

"I'm just a man!"

"Get out while you can!"

"Don't tell Dan!"

Not sure what it was, never will. But I have hindsight to inform my best guess now. In the few weeks before that shore excursion with Dawes, I thought about Metz and the mess he had invited me into. If I had never been included, then my invention wouldn't have been finished. I would have been just another civilian at the mercy of the outbreak. It might have changed everything; it might have changed nothing. I blamed Metz for a while, pointing to his introduction as I worked through my anger with Dr. Simmons. I felt betrayed by him. He had brought me in and then he had broken the rules and left me without a mentor. He made choices that put me in a bad position. But ultimately, I came to own my part in what happened. Metz didn't know when he first reached out. How could he have?

A betrayal is never just one act. It is never a single horrible decision. It is the consistent silence, the non-events. The betrayal is in the emptiness, the messages you don't receive, the support that isn't there. It makes you realize it was never genuinely there to begin with.

Dr. Simmons' soft words filtered into my dream. "But Hunter, what could you have controlled?"

My eyes snapped open.

The trees around me were black as pitch. Dawes was pacing nearby; I could hear his footsteps working their way around and around in an even and methodical circle. In between the branches of the trees above me a deep blue sky shone with the pinpricks of a thousand stars. There was no light pollution in this world. On the ship we had our lights running all evening. Even on the nights that I would brave the cold of the North Pacific, I could never see the stars above. But in this forest, I could see as many of them as my eyes could take in, except for those blocked by the branches.

I heard Dawes pacing as I started to drift back to sleep. That was when I saw a tree move. I froze. In the space between the trees and the sky, I could just make out the shape of the one that had moved. It was no tree at all, but a towering figure. With arms, not branches. With legs, not a trunk. And unmistakable, as it moved away from our little camp, were two hoses sticking out of the back. Why this figure didn't approach to introduce themselves, I didn't know. For a few moments, I expected to hear the death gurgle of Dawes, attacked in the darkness. But his steps continued without a single break or hitch.

Perhaps it had been a trick of my imagination. A phantom brought on by exhaustion and the near-sleep state of my brain. If someone wearing the Cratus suit had been nearby then surely, they would have tried to help us. They would have tried to connect. So, it must have been my imagination. I shook my head as though I could rattle the thought loose. *Those stupid tubes*, I laughed at them in the privacy of my own mind.

I had called out their vulnerability pretty late in the development. Holtz asked to practice his presentation with Sean, Kupper, Rita, and myself. Kupper and Rita would join in as they introduced the Cyclops and Converse components. The presentation went well. But I already knew the features and the purpose of the suit. Another military-funded project, the suit was designed for combat. But we knew that there were humanitarian applications that the team wanted to keep in mind. Specifically, they were thinking of search and rescue in flooded areas, the first team back in after volcanic explosions, and pandemic aid.

I knew that they had considered every function for the suit. Each ounce had to earn its weight. Too heavy and the person couldn't move, let alone make use of the suit. Too light and they risked being told to add more features. They went through the spring-loaded stilts, giving the soldier both a height and speed advantage. The built-in Converse devices in the helmets that transmitted encrypted messages. The Cyclops scanners that gave the soldier the ability to see through structures and anticipate attacks. In case an enemy released a nerve gas or other toxin, the suits came with a built-in air filtration system. Hence the tubes. Forrester had signed off that the tests subjects who wore the suits showed no greater propensity for abuse of power than had been observed in the original Stanford Prison experiment, which was somehow considered a "pass" on the psychological impact to the wearer.

After the three finished their presentation, I looked over at Sean to see if he wanted to give his feedback first. He nodded my way to let me ask the first question:

"What happens if someone pulls the tubes out?"

Holtz shook his head. "Why would someone do that?"

I stated what I thought was perfectly obvious. "An enemy gets behind the line? A scared person just attacks? Doesn't matter. What if someone pulls the tubes out?"

"It seems to be very unlikely," Holtz continued. We all knew that he couldn't pull this when he presented to the review board.

"What's your fail-safe?" I enunciated each word. Holtz let out a deep sigh.

"I really don't think it is necessary, but there is a button on the front of the suit. It can completely cut off the oxygen filtration system. It makes the suit a completely closed system. No air in, no carbon dioxide out. I've estimated that a soldier under duress would have a thirty-minute supply before they started to get light-headed. Should be enough time to subdue the attacker, restore the tubes, or make it back to safety."

I nodded, pleased with his response. Sean wasn't, though. "Okay, so if this soldier is under attack, could the attacker just hit the button and cut off their air supply? Or what if they are pinned and they can't reach it?" These were excellent contingencies. We couldn't plan for all possible outcomes, but these were likely. My initial thought was that whoever was wearing the suit would have to be careful not to pass gas and breathe in their own methane. Sean was much more practical and responsible.

"The button itself is intentionally insensitive. It would take a massive hit to cut the supply off because it should be a last resort. Your adrenaline has to be pumping, you have to be in a do or die situation. So, a hard pound on the chest would do it." Holtz answered with a crude demonstration, a manly whack on his sternum.

"And if their arms are pinned behind them?" I asked.

"They hit the deck," Holtz responded without a second thought.

"They fall on their face to activate the button?" I couldn't help but laugh at the thought, but I chided myself for not taking it seriously enough.

"That's right," Holtz nodded.

"Any other weaknesses you can think of?" Sean added.

We looked at each other and then at the team. Holtz, Rita, and Kupper were smiling tentatively. Did they have their peers' approval? They sure did. Although I still thought those tubes looked goofy. But they made the first roll-out. I had hoped they would have found a solution to remove them or better hide them for the second iteration. But the outbreak happened and all plans for the future ended.

Dawes nudged my foot, bringing me out of my restless sleep. The last images of the Bunker flickering in my mind. *Did any of them make it out? Were the admin and lab techs still toiling underground, carrying on as usual? Or were they entombed, already starved after the supplies stopped arriving?* I pushed their faces from my mind. Their souls couldn't weigh on my conscience if I was going to carry my pack another twenty miles that day.

Daybreak was starting to illuminate the sky, a dull lavender visible between the branches and trunks of the trees around us. The fire was doused and smoking, Dawes was packed and ready to head out. I stood groggily, rubbing my eyes before wiping any leaves off my clothes. The seat of my pants felt soaked through from the wet ground I had slept on. I didn't have a sleeping mat, or a sleeping bag, or any of the gear that would have made camping easier. My years in the Scouts had exposed me to a plethora of gadgets and add-ons that made camping more comfortable. But the ship didn't have such luxuries on board, which meant that we didn't have any of that to bring with us.

I wondered if the group we had encountered the day before had made it through the evening warm and dry. Surely, they had time to scavenge for the proper equipment. *Maybe we should have stayed with them the previous evening*, they seemed safe enough. But Dawes didn't trust them.

He handed me a breakfast ration bar. I ate it quickly, pacing around the campsite. My bones were chilled in the cold morning air. I knew that moving around would warm me up. Dawes must have hated all the noise I was making with my lethargic footsteps rustling the leaves, his eyes shot daggers at me as I passed him.

We didn't talk much, but we didn't need to. We had a mission to see through to the end and we had nothing else in common. We both knew that we had to continue east until we found the source of the disruption or reached our supply station. Also, because Dawes was irritated by any noise that I made, it was best to not talk.

After I finished the bar, I tucked the wrapper into my pack. Some habits die hard. Then I checked my tablet. I saw a fresh birds-eye view image from the Connect glider that passed through that morning. Based on our current pace and what the glider showed, we would walk into a decent-sized town just after midday. It was a straight shot up the road we had been walking on. No blue dots on the screen. No one there. Or at least no one who had an implant was there.

I followed Dawes as we plodded down the embankment back to the road. The silence between us gave my mind nothing else to focus on except the chill of the morning air. I could remind myself that the cool air would burn off by mid-morning and I could keep my body warm once we got moving, but nothing stopped my nose from dripping and chaffing as I wiped it on my sleeve. Of course, Dawes hated each sniffle and loud breath. I considered whistling as we walked to distract myself, but I thought the better of it.

After about seven miles, roughly two and a half hours on foot, we passed the next ghost of civilization past. We came upon a roadside billboard, the frame visible beneath the slashed canvas that used to be a colorful ad. The flaps of materials rustled idly in the errant breeze. This was the first sign of what had been lost. The trees told no stories, the asphalt revealed nothing, the abandoned cars gave no testimony. But this abandoned sign, this was a symptom of the outbreak. No one left to sell to, no one left to buy anything, no one left to maintain the advertisements. This didn't belong in this new world. Such an act of abandonment would never have been allowed in the time before. The marketing machine had to run to keep the economy churning, to increase spending, to return investments. This sign was emblematic of our society. We could see through to the frame, the facade exposed.

Up ahead, I could see more billboards and road signs starting to announce themselves on the horizon. The road dipped down, declining as it rolled into the town ahead of us. We had put the miles behind us efficiently and would be there within the next hour or so. We might just stroll on through without any trouble, or there might be an ambush before we even reached the town limits. If we kept our current pace, we would reach the supply depot by nightfall.

We continued to walk in silence, but we both had our guard up. My rifle was in my hands, not across my back. I saw Dawes head swivel as he continued to scan his periphery. We were approaching a town. And as we passed by a few more cars that had been pushed to the side of the road, we saw that one had a message sprayed over it with crude paint. "This is Reaper Country."

A shiver ran up my spine.

That tell-tale shiver, the presence of a cold-sweat, reflected all the signs of nerves kicking in. That special mix of fear and anticipation combined, inducing excitement and panic. A very human sensation, to not only feel those emotions with your mind, but to experience them manifesting physically. I marveled at the delicate balance required to make it happen. The right chemicals released at the right time. And I had been the one to master them, to control this reaction.

I had felt that raw power of conquering nature as we headed into full-scale trials on the implant back during my days in the Peec Bunker. My implantation scar had successfully healed over. I had watched several action movies and recorded my feelings the whole time. But it's hard to fake rage and anger. The device wasn't supposed to suppress all adrenaline. I wasn't going to sentence my subjects to a life without any excitement. Imagine going through life without any thrill, any anticipation. No, the device only kicked in at a certain level of adrenaline and noradrenaline. It had to be serious. You had to feel that you were in danger.

The initial results were promising. The group of Forrester's test subjects who were homeless vets did indeed have underlying anxiety and PTSD issues. They were suspicious and on edge. In the first week of visual observation after they had the implant, they appeared to be more at-ease; their shoulders relaxed. Based on the collected data, we could proceed with additional testing. But the transformation in front of my eyes was amazing. Their anxiety was gone, it would never bubble up into rage and violence.

Forrester had some ideas that he shared with me to help get the test subjects to feel that mortal terror. Would the device kick in when needed, or was this all just a placebo effect? He was very good at coming up with these fake scenarios, having crafted so many for his research. The current group testing my implant had already been through his thought experiments. Time for a new batch of recruits. More homeless men brought down into the Bunker.

It seemed wrong to exploit their vulnerable position in society. But these were the people that I most wanted to help. I wanted to keep the current generation of soldiers returning from war from realizing this same fate. I thought about all those men and women who came and went from the Bunker. Brought in, then released, but to where? What security measures were taken to make sure the location of the Bunker stayed secure? Were they at least delivered to a shelter once they left? These were all questions that I suppressed. I didn't ask because I didn't want to know the answers. Any response likely would have been insufficient. It would have been too much truth for me to handle.

So, I signed off on his plan. Fifty volunteers would get an active implant. Fifty would get a dummy implant, none of Metz's serum would be built in. The remaining fifty would be taken into an operating room, sedated, their forearms wrapped, and told that they had received the implant when in actuality nothing happened beyond a simple incision. There were overflow accommodations in the Bunker complex for these types of experiments. Just as I thought I knew the extent of the underground facility, more was revealed.

We started to do preliminary interviews with each test subject. They were told that they would receive an implanted health tracker. Measuring their footsteps, heart rate, pulse, etc. This would help us fine-tune the device before sending it to market. All of those features were built-in, but we did not disclose the primary purpose of the device. Forrester built the framework for the experiment. We would interview each participant at a baseline. Then we would introduce them to a situation. Forrester planned to put them into the isolation corridor where all his test subjects usually stayed and then throw the alarms. Isolated in their bunks, in an unknown place, this should trigger a fear response.

It was the most humane test that he proposed. He also suggested having armed soldiers file into the hallways. I vetoed that pretty quickly. Forrester also wanted us to push it further and have each subject hear gunshots that would be replayed from a recording. I also vetoed that. These men had nothing left; I didn't want to take the rest of their sanity. I just wanted to see if my device would work.

I sat and watched each preliminary interview through the two-way mirror. Forrester sat beside me, quietly observing. Having to spend so much time with him was grating on my patience. He was smug. He was too pleased about working together.

"I came here on a plane. The police officer picked me up in the park and put me on a plane." This man was one of a dozen who had received a dummy implant. His name was Greg. He had arrived at the Bunker appearing thoroughly gray, his skin pale and covered in dirt, his hair ashen and greasy, his clothes covered in layer upon layer of sweat and skin. He had been cleaned up before the implantation and had been able to maintain a much more decent appearance. Three square meals a day, a bed, a shower. It was a miracle what basic resources could do for a person. But his words still told the story of a man who was not quite right in the head. I moved to make a note of paranoid delusions.

Forrester held up his index finger. "No, that's real."

"What?" I asked, now missing the rest of the testimonial Greg was giving. I would have to watch the replay.

"There was a program a few years ago to offshore the homeless population. They were given one-way tickets from California and Oregon to Oahu." Forrester's disapproving tone told me that he did still have a conscience. I started to think that maybe he wasn't the enemy after all. He had devised actual programs like the one he had just told me about. But they were all theoretical. Who had proposed an actual solution to send the homeless to another state? It sounded barbaric and cruel.

Forrester was helping me out. I was helping those who needed it more. I thought I was helping shell-shocked vets, the highest concentration within the homeless population. It was supposed to help reduce instances of violence and death among the mentally ill. I appreciated Forrester for a split second for helping me to reach my goal. Helping people like Greg find a better way in this world.

But then I remembered that in one of Forrester's thought experiments the previous week. he had taken a group of inmates from one of the Oahu jails, all arrested on suspicion of drug-dealing. He played out a scenario where they were abducted by aliens and told that they would be given clemency in an invasion if they promised to help. It was a ridiculous scenario, but enough were strung out or fried that they believed it.

They shipped their homeless here, we shipped our drug dealers back. My brief appreciation for Forrester faded as I remembered that particular stunt. What if what he had just told me was a lie, a project?

Forrester was grinning in the corner; he delighted in his lies. These false words that were part of the experiment. He loved to see how people reacted to the things he came up with. He wanted to notice the moment when his vision implanted in their mind. He loved playing God.

After we finished for the day, I headed off to our barracks to shower and clean off the guilt of the perpetual lie from my skin. Forrester headed down the hallway towards the labs. I should have followed him. I should have been suspicious that after a day of feeling so in power over the people in the test group, that he would go looking for more ways to exert his dominance.

At that point, it was about two years into my stay in the Peec Bunker on The Forbidden Island. I had settled into a routine. Each morning I woke up a little slower, wanting more time to sleep, wanting to forestall work just a little bit longer. I still loved my job, but the monotony of life in the Bunker dulled my excitement. Each day was a carbon copy of the one before it. The only variations occurred in the margins. Today is "Team Spirit Day," wear your college alma mater proud. Today the cafeteria is serving Asian Fusion. Today you are all expected to deliver updates on your project status.

Other items stuck out, like when Forrester flipped out and threw his chair across his lab at an assistant. That day I remembered; the murmuring of gossip filled each corner of the compound. Of course, the day that Metz had been taken away. Also, the day that Malcolm showed up unannounced and demanded updated status reports and informed us all that we needed production-ready prototypes in four weeks. That one I won't soon forget. My initial concern was that the accelerated deadline would lead to mistakes, sloppy errors that could torpedo the device before it ever made it into clinical trials. But I told myself at the time that this was the price I paid for going to the private sector. Even in academia, I had felt the time crunch, the pressure to produce and publish. Peec hadn't given me carte blanche. Malcolm had stakeholders to answer to, or at least that is what I told myself. Another innocuous concern pushed down. Another piece out of place that makes this all the more disturbing when I look back on it.

Few other instances rose to the top of the pile of distinct memories from my time in the Bunker. There are a handful that are seared into my brain. The crisp edges of these scenes, these mental playbacks, have a certain tone about them. As though they are calling out a warning from the past, cautioning me, urging me to see what was so plain.

The most vivid was the day that Rita went away. I had shuffled down to breakfast, barely managing to assemble a clean outfit. My hair was unkempt, my t-shirt wrinkled beyond recognition. It was a week after Rattray had announced that new deadline and I had been spending every possible minute in my lab. I had forgotten to send my clothes for laundry. I figured I might get a visit from HR about hygiene, but I didn't mind if people thought I smelled a bit. Then maybe they would steer clear and I could get some work done. Either way, Holtz and Kupper didn't seem to mind my body odor as I joined them for breakfast. The novelty of a daily breakfast buffet had long since waned and I looked down at the pancakes on my tray as though they were thin sponges for substandard syrup, which they were. I grumbled a greeting at my colleagues and began to devour my meal. Holtz and Kupper continued their conversation.

"Has Rattray confirmed who will be taking over?" Holtz directed a question at Kupper with a mouth full of eggs.

"No, I think it would be too soon for them to have that figured out," there was an edge to Kupper's response. A strain, a stress underlying his words.

"How could she do this? We're weeks away from our deadline and she just walks?" Holtz slid his tray away as he spoke, apparently too upset to take another bite.

"Her portion of the Cratus suit is fully integrated. But you're right. If we have any issues, she won't be able to help us troubleshoot or Q.A." Kupper's words settled into my brain. My neck snapped up from my plate. I glanced at each of them.

"What are you guys talking about? What's going on with your projects?" I asked, but my brain was already processing. It was like a sense of déjà vu or precognition. Rita was gone.

"Rita resigned. Malcolm told us late last night." Holtz shook his head as he said the words. He rubbed his hand over the buzzed hair covering his head, a tick he seemed to pick up when he was nervous.

"I didn't even think we could resign based on those ironclad contracts we all had to sign," Kupper mimicked his partner.

"Did she say why?" I cut him off, my words quick and demanding.

"No, Malcolm just told us that she had resigned and would be on the first transport out this morning," Holtz explained. I jumped up from the bench, hitting my knees on the table as I did so. I didn't stop to wince or apologize for my abrupt departure. I ran as fast as I could towards the women's dormitory to see if I could reach her before she left.

I had been so engrossed in the trials for the implant that I hadn't seen much of the team except for Forrester. I couldn't remember the last time I had seen Rita. I had a schoolboy crush on her, but my work had always come first. Confronted with the idea that she was going to leave, nothing else seemed to matter anymore. I just couldn't believe or understand what I had heard.

I reached her room and stood outside panting, trying to catch my breath. The walls were bare, all the signs of her personality removed and packed away. It was just another white room now, a sterile prison cell. Rita must have heard me because she turned around immediately, jumping back.

I almost did the same. Her dark skin was slick with tears, and her right cheek was almost purple it was so dark. The bruise was thick and bloated. She must have noted the shock on my face. "It looks worse than it feels," she muttered, turning back to her suitcases.

"Holtz and Kupper just told me," I started. I had a million words flying around my brain and those are the ones that came out.

"Well then," she said, letting her words trail off.

"What happened?" I asked.

"What do you think?!" she yelled at me as she stood back from her suitcase. "What do you think?" she asked again, this time whispering it as she sunk down onto the metal bed frame. She covered her face with her hands. I could tell that a fresh wave of crying had started.

I wanted to go over and hold her, to comfort her. But I stopped myself. I could feel anger welling up inside me. I wanted to hurt whoever had done this to her. I wanted to make them pay. Maybe it was my long-repressed anger over not being able to save my own mother and sister. Maybe it was the long-simmering frustration I was feeling against one of our colleagues. Maybe a combination thereof. But I was angry and I felt a primal instinct to lash out, to protect.

"Who was it?" I demanded to know.

"It doesn't matter," she shook her head and wiped her face with her hands.

"Yes, it does." I tried to not direct my anger at her, but I wanted to know who I needed to go and pummel. I didn't care if I got kicked out too. It was as though a switch had flipped. Being the protector, being the judge and jury, and avenging Rita was now my most important mission, not the research I had dedicated my life to.

"No, it doesn't Hunter. I'm expendable. This person isn't. It's clear as day," she stood and returned to her packing.

"Was it Forrester?" I asked, finally voicing my suspicions. The way he always acted so possessive around her, the way she always tried to placate him. Had I been so blind to the signs earlier? Should I have known to step up sooner?

She still hadn't responded to my question. "Was it Forrester?" I asked again. She wouldn't look over at me. That was all the evidence I needed. I stormed out of her bunk and headed over to the labs. Instead of saying goodbye to Rita before she left for good, I had left her with a vision of me angry, hoping to avenge her. Instead of being the comfort that she needed, I was just another irate man. It didn't matter that I was marching off to knock Forrester out. It wouldn't undo whatever had happened. It wouldn't get Rita her dream job back. It wouldn't change anything. But still, that is what I did.

I flung open the door to the interview room. Forrester was already in there preparing his notes for the day. He was facing the far wall when I entered and yelled his name. As he spun around to see what was heading his way, I noticed a scratch on the left side of his face. To me, that was it. He was guilty. It wasn't even a conscious motion, my right arm drew back, I was about to hit him with all the force I had in my body.

And then everything went black.

I woke up two hours later in the infirmary. A nurse told me that I hit my head when I passed out. My device worked after all. I didn't hit Forrester, didn't get my sweet revenge. The implant had kicked in and knocked me out. I stewed with my anger for the rest of the day as I waited for my skull to stop pounding.

I thought about that thoroughly unsatisfying spell, the inability to attack, to take action, as Dawes and I stepped closer and closer to the town. The volume of cars on the side of the road grew exponentially. The road signs became more prescriptive, covered in years of grime, but still happy to announce the exact distance to the nearest fast-food franchises.

The road had started to level out. I stopped abruptly and pulled out the tablet. Dawes paused a few feet ahead once he noticed that I was no longer next to him.

"What are you doing?" he whispered across the distance. There was an edge to his voice. The crease of his forehead displayed his concern and frustration equally; his thick eyebrows now joined together.

"I'm disabling your device," I answered without looking up from the tablet. It was a few quick swipes to make the initial change and then a few more to override the system safeties. The alarms on the Pricus were likely to start going off. For all they knew, Dawes was off the grid, which could have meant that he was dead. But the way I saw it, we couldn't risk him passing out if an attack started.

This was my real fail-safe, my backdoor into the system to make sure I could turn it off if I needed to. But I knew that when I was presenting the device that I couldn't advertise that to the panel, then it wouldn't be much of a secret anymore. So, when they asked, I had told them about the other fail-safe that they had requested. A different kind of kill-switch.

About a week after Rita's departure, I was cleared to return to my trials. They were nearly complete. With Rattray's accelerated deadlines they had to be, regardless of my initial timeline. I had even less time to prepare, let alone time to miss Rita.

I practiced my presentation with Sean, Holtz, and Kupper. So, I was ready when I got the question.

"What's your fail-safe, Hunter?" Rattray asked, glancing at me above his glasses.

I had anticipated this. I had planned for a solution. I didn't like it, but I told myself that anyone who elected to have the device implanted would be fully conscious of the risks and would actually want this feature. No one wants to be a monster; no one wants to ruin lives. Deep down, no sane person wants to be a murderer. That was what I told myself.

"We have a graduated series of controls, sir." I opened up the program on the tablet and maneuvered to the correct display. There were several lines on the screen. Each with a dial that I could control with a swipe of my finger.

"I'll need a volunteer to demonstrate the first one," I said as I looked up at the review panel. Most stared back at me with vacant expressions. "Just hold the device in your palm, no surgery required," I added with a laugh. It broke the tension in the room.

Edwin Hurlbert stood up and said, "alright, I'll give it a go." I recognized him from the company website, our CEO. I was stunned that he was even at these presentations. I did my best to avoid eye contact with him through the beginning of my prepared remarks; I pretended I was just presenting to Rattray. But then Hurlbert volunteered, I tried to hide my awkward nerves. He walked around the long table to join me next to my prototype samples.

"Okay, you'll need to wear this," I said as I handed him one latex glove. "To prevent any contamination of the device. This way, I won't have to sterilize it after the demonstration."

"Not a problem at all," he said as he snapped on the glove. He seemed very pleased with himself to now be part of the demonstration. He was being a good sport. He was on stage. He was part of the performance now. He puffed out his chest and held out his hand. He seemed like the CEO who was sad to not be in the weeds anymore, like he wanted to play along as a common worker with the rest of us, but he could never go back to that way of life.

I set down the tablet and grabbed the first petri dish on my right. With forceps, I gently grabbed the implant and placed it in the palm of his hand. I found that my hands were steady, not shaking at all. I thanked my own little implant for that, having seen the spike in my adrenaline before the presentation, it had administered the correct amount of the serum to calm me down.

"Okay, ready?" I asked Hurlbert.

"Yeah," he said with a smile.

"Okay. Just know that this is purely for the purposes of demonstration. I need you to show your genuine reaction to the stimulus. You volunteered for this, and I did not select you out of the group." I wanted him to know that there were no hard feelings.

"Uh, alright," he said with noticeably less confidence.

I nodded and picked up the tablet. I touched my finger to the first dial, labeled "HEAT." I started to slowly move my finger up the line.

"Oh, that is getting very warm," he said.

"Yes, the devices have been set to heat up if the subject has multiple serum injections in a twenty-four-hour period. It tells them that they are too hot, so to speak. Our aim is that the device will be forgotten. If it is working well, the subject won't even notice it is there. They may just think that they are calmer than before. But we don't want them to forget it completely. They need this intervention to stay calm and not lash out. So, if the device is called into action multiple times, we need to remind the subject to calm down. The heat sensor is set to be warm. It should be enough to call attention to itself, without injuring someone. But for each additional system trigger after the initial warm-warning, the temperature will increase."

As I said this, I slid my finger up to the top of the line. The dial now at one hundred percent.

"Ow!" Hurlbert let out a yell before snapping his hand back. He rubbed the spot on his skin where the implant had just burned him. I dove to catch the implant before it hit the ground. I caught it in the petri dish just before it hit the floor.

I stood up; my eyes wide with disbelief. I had actually saved the device. I let out a deep sigh of relief. These prototypes were extremely expensive. I looked over at Hurlbert, expecting him to look equally relieved. But his face was blank. He continued to rub at his palm through the latex glove.

"Sorry about that," I said, realizing that I had potentially given the CEO of our entire company third-degree burns.

"Alright, Hunter." Rattray's voice called my attention back to the rest of the panel.

"As you can see, any subject who is consistently spiking their adrenaline levels is going to get a clear message to calm down before the other measures kick in." I nodded towards Hurlbert, indicating that his portion of the demonstration was done.

"Well, it certainly works and they won't soon forget that they have the device." Hurlbert continued to rub his palm as he maneuvered back to his chair. He seemed to have decided to not hold a grudge against me. "What other measures have you put in place?" he prompted me to continue.

"If we see that a subject continues to display signs of aggression, we have two more options." I approached the table with the second petri dish.

"The second warning system emits an electric shock." I tapped on the tablet again. "I won't need any volunteers for this one," I tried to break the tension with another joke. I only received weak smiles in return.

I slid the dial on the ELECTRIC gauge up. The implant began to move in the petri dish, alive with current. It danced, rattling the dish like a jumping jelly bean.

"And will this incapacitate the subject?" Patricia Gonzalez, head of North American operations for Peec, asked from the end of the table.

I turned to face her as I answered the question. "In small doses, no. But if they hit the max, yes."

"And that's what we want with these measures," Rattray interjected. "These fail-safe options will only be triggered if and when certain escalations happen. The whole point of this device is to prevent mass-murder, to prevent the kinds of attacks we've seen at Fort Hood and Sandy Hook. A person would have to be really determined to enact some violence to get their adrenaline levels up to trigger these reactions." I nodded at his words. He was helping to convince the panel for me.

"Indeed, and there are manual overrides if needed?" Hurlbert asked. He crossed his arms and waited for my response.

"Yes. We have a kill switch, sir." I pulled up the tablet in my hand and showed him and the committee the screen. The video screen behind me changed from the readout on my tablet to a camera focused in on six petri dishes in our production lab. Six bright blue lights shone on the screen, in the exact same position as the six devices they were observing. I pressed the top right corner of the screen, the big red button. Each device secreted the necessary dosage to incapacitate a person. The metal discs sitting in a puddle of liquid Cease, Metz's formula.

Each member of the committee nodded, clearly pleased with the solution. I knew I had been idealistic, but this seemed too much to me. The device would work before things got out of hand. I pictured the next potential mass shooter. Sitting in his bedroom, building himself up for an attack, ready to grab his bag and show the world what he was really about. But instead, he would take a nap. I didn't see how he would ever get out of that room, how he could remain calm enough to get anywhere on his hit list without the necessary reaction happening. But I understood why they needed the fail-safe. Technology malfunctions, humans made snap decisions that made no sense. I told myself it was a necessary precaution; this was the logical conclusion.

But that fail-safe had produced devastating effects. I had lived with the words of J. Robert Oppenheimer rattling around my brain for the last three years. I wasn't naïve enough to think that the same outcomes wouldn't repeat when Dawes and I most needed to be in control of our faculties. He seemed frustrated that I made a unilateral decision to deactivate his implant. It was very invasive of me to blatantly exert such control over his body. He seemed to calm down a bit after I reminded him that if he ran into trouble, that he would be more likely to pass out than stand his ground. And those attacking us would be devoid of such limitation if they cut out their own devices.

We continued together, taking slower, more deliberate steps. Moving our feet toe-heel, toe-heel like a feline, trying to be as quiet as possible.

The town materialized with each step. A few roadside shacks stood with faded signs for farm-fresh produce, out of stock for years. The trees gave way to more and more signs of a life abandoned. A few storefronts remained boarded and empty, appearing to have been long forgotten even before the outbreak. The embankment on either side of us receded and we were in the middle of a collection of cookie-cutter buildings. Most were only one story tall with large signs proclaiming fast and delicious food, or bargains and deals, or new designs for the season. Even small towns like this one weren't immune to franchises. One of the signs for the burger joint read: "PORTHANA FEAR YOUR REAPER" in block letters. A wind kicked up as my eyes fell on the sign, sending another shiver down my back. A feeling of déjà vu washed over me again.

"What do you think that means?" Dawes asked as we passed the words. The Reaper we had already heard enough of. But the rest didn't make much sense. Perhaps that was the name of the town.

Within a block, older masonry storefronts took over. These buildings had the carefully constructed charm of the west: dark wooden boards, carved store signs, large picture windows. Perhaps if they had more time, the commercial property owners would have finished their remodel of the town. But everyone ran out of time when the airborne toxin hit.

Up ahead, I saw a large black square in the road. As I focused on it,

I could make out the muffler and undercarriage, the wells where the tires should have been. It was an upturned vehicle with the bottom facing towards us. The charring let us know that it had been engulfed in flames. I knew at that moment that it was our supply truck. It had to be. If the vehicle had been damaged during the outbreak and ensuing riots, the cinder would have long blown or washed away. This burnout looked fresh, gritty.

I caught Dawes' eye and nodded towards it, indicating that we should look at it. That was when we heard the clicks.

An unmistakable chorus of rifles being readied.

We had checked the tablet while we had been in the safe cover of the trees; before we stepped out onto the road. The town appeared deserted based on what we could see. But we knew this was unreliable now. People had cut their arms and hands open and ripped their implants out. I thought we would eventually hit an ambush. The time had come.

I took a deep breath and lifted my hands above my head. My rifle hung around my neck, I knew better than to reposition it, even if my aim was to lay it on the ground. I couldn't know for sure if whoever was waiting for us had any ammunition, but it was a risk I wasn't willing to take.

Fortunately, Dawes and I had worked out a more comprehensive backstory in case Paula, Jack, and Rachel had already alerted this group to our arrival in the area. They seemed cut off from this community, but looks could be deceiving.

Dawes matched my action by raising his left hand; his rifle was still in his right. "We're just passing through," he hollered out into the wind. "We don't want any trouble, and we don't have anything more than one day's ration on each of us."

Silence. The wind whistled past the buildings and down the street.

I could start to make out the shapes of figures on the rooftops of the building from the corner of my eye. Their hunched shoulders leaned into their rifles. Their faces obscured by their weapons. It was like a bad cowboy western. The two of us strolling into town, the local posse holding us at gunpoint. If I hadn't been facing an execution at the hands of traumatized survivors, I might have found the situation funny. I couldn't help but notice the irony. The device that I invented to prevent people with PTSD from letting their anger manifest in gun violence had likely been implanted in each of these gunmen, and that they had potentially cut it out. The one failure I had never planned for. *Sheer human will.* The ability to withstand extreme pain in order to survive. The desire to never be controlled by another human.

But what had scared them enough to cut it out? What had spooked them? Dawes seemed to have at least acknowledged my warnings from earlier. Whether the Reaper was real or not, the people in this town believed in it. He initiated our hastily crafted story.

"We don't have any implant either," Dawes added.

At this, we heard some movement, footfalls.

The wind kicked up again. We heard more footsteps. There was either an army marching towards us or three loud guys heading our way.

In reality, it was somewhere in between. A group of six people rounded a building to our left. Five of them spread out in a line across the road. One man stepped forward. This whole situation had the feeling of a well-rehearsed scene in a play. Every one of them on their mark, playing their role. Dawes and I remained with our arms over our heads. Gravity was starting to weigh on my forearms; my shoulders were slagging a bit without my undivided attention.

Each of the men and women approaching us had a very specific mixture of exhaustion and anger that showed just how hungry they were. Their clothes were all hanging slack on them, nothing fit or snug. Their guns brandished, ready to take action. I thought again about how real the threat of gunfire was. *Had they stockpiled everything in the surrounding area? Were they running low too? Could they expect that we might only have a few rounds each?* I wasn't willing to take the bet that they were bluffing.

The man who stood out in front of the line was tall and thin, his tanned skin hidden behind a bold black beard. His dark features gave him the look of a pirate. He eyed us up and down with his head cocked back, assessing us. His Adam's apple protruded over his jacket, exposing his neck. Slung over his chest was a rifle, his arms crossed in front of his weapon. Easily within reach if he decided he didn't like us.

"That's a very dangerous thing to announce so boldly," his voice seemed to echo against the buildings.

Shit.

Had Paula meant another town up ahead on the road? Had she just imagined people walking by telling her to cut out the implant? I wanted to be able to talk to Dawes about what we should say next, but I didn't dare move or make a sound.

"It's pretty dangerous to have one," Dawes called out. I wanted to tell him that my device was not dangerous. But I knew better than to betray our plan.

The man in front of us must have appreciated the answer because he dropped his head as he let out a small laugh. "You can drop your arms," he said and he waved his hands to signal the group behind him to fall in.

I dropped my arms, my shoulders stinging from the weight of my limbs. It seemed we had passed some kind of test.

"I'm Hamden. This is my guard. Welcome to New Hope." Something about his manner and his voice reminded me of Michaels. Similar features and coloring, same thin and lean stature. I wondered if the good doctor had survived another day if he might have met a long-lost cousin.

"I'm Hunter, this is Dawes," I reached out to shake Hamden's hand. Without hesitation, he took it. I expected him to pause, to have a suspicion of outsiders. But he grabbed my hand greedily and pushed my jacket up on my forearm. He saw the thin scar from my implant and nodded.

He then grabbed Dawes' hand and found his as well.

"Forearm and not thumb, weren't we lucky?" Hamden said. He made no apologies for inspecting us so brusquely. There was a hint of anger in his voice.

"I guess we were all lucky to survive this long," I added.

Hamden raised his eyebrows and nodded his head, a silent smirk. "Some of us have luck. Some of us have help." The group behind him nodded heartily. I couldn't understand what kind of riddle he was speaking in. For a terrifying moment, I thought he could read our minds, that he knew we had been receiving rations from the supply trucks, that we had survived the outbreak from the safety of a well-equipped para-military ship. But there seemed to be a different meaning behind his words.

"Look, we don't want any trouble. We just want to pass on through," Dawes said in a calm voice.

"You come up this road?" Hamden asked, gesturing to the road behind us.

"Yep," I answered.

"You pass by Maxine's?" He asked.

This had to be some kind of test. "Yeah, we saw Paula," I answered, looking for a sign of recognition on his face. "We saw Timoney, too," I added.

Hamden's expression changed. "You did?" he seemed very interested in this fact.

"Yeah, we had some first aid items. But our antiseptic cream and penicillin are way too late for that level of infection." I tried not to sound angry. But I had a feeling that this man or one of the ones behind him had instructed Paula to have the kids cut out their implants, and that they had come back to see that it was done and recognized the first signs of Timoney's sepsis. Perhaps they were hopeful that she had somehow recovered, I couldn't tell.

Hamden cast his gaze down. He was silent for a moment before he looked back up at us. "Come on. I'll show you around. If you've only got one day's rations, you'll need a bit more."

With that, he brushed past us. Dawes and I turned to follow him, stealing a quick glance at each other. This certainly hadn't been part of the plan. But we had to go along with it.

Huh. Going along with it. Seems to be something I have gotten pretty good at.

Going along with it was how I survived the Bunker after the presentations. When I had the deadline to focus on, I could push thoughts of Rita aside. My longing could be delayed for the sake of science. I couldn't afford to let my rage for Forrester boil over. But once the device had been approved by the executive committee and was off for development, I had to learn to just go along with it. Our seating arrangements for meals had shifted when Metz was dragged away. They were altered again in Rita's absence. Holtz and Kupper sat closer to me. Forrester avoided us, or rather, he avoided me. We found a way to coexist in our metal box below the surface of a forgotten island.

A month after the final presentation, I was lazily lingering at breakfast, knowing full-well that I might risk a run-in with Forrester. There wasn't as much urgency to get to the lab, the deadline had passed, the implant was approved, and I knew I would be facing a lot of work in a few days when the first shipment of devices arrived at Walter Reed. I would be on-call for remote assistance on the initial trials. Given the extreme time difference, I was bracing for a challenge.

Holtz arrived at breakfast very late, having only managed to scrape up the last of the cold cereal before sitting down with me and Kupper.

"Did you hear the news?" Holtz asked as he began to dig into his meager breakfast.

I assumed that he was referring to the ongoing Public Relations issue that Peec was facing. A company-wide memo distributed earlier that week told us not to comment on the situation if we were approached by a reporter. The crew in the Bunker had a good laugh at that.

The issue had started several weeks earlier, just as everyone on the team was emerging from our presentation stupor. In addition to being one of the largest technology companies in the world, Peec was also the largest e-commerce retailer. Apparently, that division of Peec was taking heat from a news documentary piece that aired on primetime. The segment highlighted working conditions in the distribution centers, employees working long hours, and rushing to meet the demands of overnight delivery. They also detailed a report that Peec had a fleet of airplanes and delivery vans to rival any airline or mail service in the world. And they needed those vehicles because of their one-day delivery guarantee. People demanded their gifts and gizmos immediately, Peec was dominating that market. Well, several environmentalists had taken to the news and social media to condemn Peec for contributing to global climate change. I read the stories that were posted and they each had merit. Peec was likely one of the largest contributors of excess carbon. A press conference was held and Hurlbert said that Peec wasn't the problem. The company was meeting the demands of the people. If that led to excess, he asserted, then it was on every person who ever purchased from Peec. He highlighted the charitable giving option on every sale, the slower delivery options that hardly anyone selected, and the R&D division that was dedicated to researching solutions for humanity's greatest problems with no expectation of profitability.

His response didn't quell the media frenzy. Naturally, I assumed that Holtz was referring to this based on his question that morning.

Kupper responded, "Something else we're not allowed to mention in front of all the reporters who manage to get into our top-secret facility?"

"No, not that," Holtz managed to get out between gulps of cereal. "Forrester is out."

Both Kupper and I gave Holtz our full attention. "What do you mean, out?" I asked.

"His lab is cleared out. His bunk is empty too. The man is gone," Holtz enumerated his evidence as Kupper and I stared at him. I could have made a poorly timed joke about remaining on Survivor island as our team continued to dwindle. I was suddenly aware of the fact that Sean wasn't at breakfast either. I turned and saw him coming towards us, as if my worry has conjured him out of thin air.

"Well, good riddance," Kupper responded. None of the rest of the team had said a word against Forrester in my presence. Not before *the incident* and especially not after. I felt a tug of loyalty to Kupper and felt my shoulders ease ever so slightly. He was gone. But this news reminded me of the reality of the situation. Rita was still gone too.

We finished our breakfast without much else to discuss. The news about Forrester was the most exciting part of that day. Or it should have been. But only looking back can I see how this news coupled with the other events of that afternoon.

I was looking forward to a quiet week. The big wigs were all headed out to some boondoggle to celebrate the successful completion of several projects. Something that I was sure would be used against them in the press, given the media scrutiny on the company at that moment.

I was happy that the Calm implant had passed, but I had reservations about the roll-out plan that Rattray had pushed forward. We still didn't know what the long-term side effects could be. My lack of satisfaction, my dogged need to continue to solve for this problem was my saving grace. But I also wanted the quiet to be able to mourn the loss of Rita and Metz. Surely, they weren't gone from the Earth, at least I didn't think so at the time, but they were gone from my life. I knew then that I wanted to request a new assignment back on the mainland. I was done with the Bunker, done with the isolation. The memories of Metz and Rita were everywhere I went and the legacy of Forrester lingered as well. This den of discovery had now become a hollow prison. I had an email requesting my transfer drafted to send to Rattray. I wanted to read it through once more before I clicked "send."

I enjoyed the peace of my lab. The quiet hum of the air circulation system. The satisfying whir of the machines and the hiss as each new alloy sample was hermetically sealed for examination. I kept my lab space clean, with no errant papers or stacks of disposed samples. That wasn't my style. I needed a clear desktop to work, to think.

I poured over the subject logs, looking for anything that might stand out in the collected qualitative responses. Each test subject had a file containing all the numbers. Heart rate, blood pressure, white blood cell count, adrenaline levels. But they also had to provide open responses on their emotions, how they felt. Anything that they noticed, but hadn't been accounted for in the rest of the survey. Almost every person reported itching at the implant site. I had anticipated this immediately following the implantation. I wanted to be able to follow-up with each subject in another month to see if the itch persisted. The whole point of the device was to help people stay calm and prevent the high levels of aggravation that would lead to an outburst. A constant itch would drive a person mad. I couldn't have that; I wouldn't be satisfied with that.

I heard the glass door to the lab open as I made notes on potential solutions if the itch did persist. I preferred to work further back in the lab, away from the entrance, away from the exit. I could get lost in my work if I couldn't see people walking back and forth in the hallways. The shelves and tables obscured the entrance just enough.

I turned as I saw Malcolm, he was moving towards me quickly, as though he had been looking for me. I was genuinely surprised to see him. He had been spending a lot of time on the island with us. I expected that he would have been well on his way to the cruise for the executives. I suspected he had to deal with several inquiries about his division after the CEO's comment at the press conference. When I saw him in my lab, my first instinct was that something was wrong.

When I saw him throw up his arms and flash a smile my way, I knew I was off-base. "You're not out celebrating with your cohorts?" he asked as he reached me. The thought of celebrating weeks after the approval of the implant seemed comically ridiculous. But I let it roll.

"No, I wanted to dive back into the data. I'm not sure that the itch that was reported will fade with time. We just don't have the long-term reporting to make that assumption." I started right in on my thought process, expecting that he would be able to keep up with me.

"Hmm," he shrugged and considered my words. "You're coming to the cruise tomorrow night."

Evidently, he had something on his mind as well. His words didn't register at first and I corrected him.

"No, that's only for the head honchos. I'll be here doing what I do best."

"It wasn't a question, Hunter," Malcolm said. I turned to face him. "You're coming with us tomorrow."

The gravity of his words started to hit me. I was being invited, or instructed, to attend an event that was for the executives. Did this mean I was being groomed to take a management position? Was I being considered for a promotion? How would this be perceived by my peers?

"Oh, okay. What do I need to bring? When do we leave?" I responded with the tactical questions. Not sure how else I could or should reply.

He gave me the details. Apparently, I would need to wear a suit. Thankfully I had brought one sport jacket with me that nearly matched the one set of dress pants that I had in my wardrobe. Both sat unused for the years I had been living in the Bunker. I took quick notes on the first piece of paper I could find. After a moment Malcolm nodded, clearly displeased with my response, but his face showing that he wasn't all that surprised either. I was never good with the social cues. As he started to turn away, I called back.

"Thank you," I could hear my own voice echo slightly against all the glass surfaces in the room.

He turned. "You earned it, Hunter. I just didn't want to see you get left behind." Thinking back on his choice of words now, I realize that he didn't see me as a kid on the playground. There was more to it that I couldn't understand.

"I appreciate that. And this," I gestured to the space around me. I had a lot to owe to him. One 'thank you' wasn't going to count for all of it, but I knew it had to start somewhere. I felt a moment of guilt as I remembered the email sitting in my drafts.

"Sure thing," he turned and started out of the lab. His task complete. We scientists can be very short, but it is because we are focused. I appreciated his brevity. It left me time to mull over the implications of this change. The pieces on the chessboard were being moved. What was the next step, the next potential risk? I pondered different power moves and career opportunities. I never saw the next move coming, I never saw it at all.

Just like I never could have predicted that our hostile greeting party in New Hope, the survivor town en route to our supply depot, would decide to show us mercy.

Hamden walked with us, leaving his posse to return to their posts. He took us down the far side of the main drag and then we crossed and headed down the next road. I noticed that he crossed the street without hesitation. I stopped and looked both ways before realizing how idiotic this ingrained habit was. Who on Earth was about to come driving down that road?

Dawes stayed behind me as I walked shoulder to shoulder with Hamden. He explained that most of the people who had migrated to the area over the past year were originally from the United States. More and more groups of people had been passing through as of late.

"I don't think too many of them have been on the run, at least not the ones I've seen. Most come through and take their time, aren't looking over their shoulder. Likely they were released or the Porths abandoned their post."

I nodded, feigning comprehension at his words. Were these Porths a rival faction, an organized town in the south that threatened the peace? Certainly, enough to attract the taunts of the Reaper. We passed under the sign again: "PORTHANA FEAR YOUR REAPER."

"You think they are coming up this way because of the Reaper?" I asked.

"You've heard of the Reaper?" Hamden stopped in his tracks and asked me, his deep and dark brown eyes examining my reaction. It was clear that his momentary friendliness was a paper-thin sheath over his deeply rooted suspicion. One wrong step and Hamden would execute us.

"Rachel and Paula mentioned him," Dawes answered from behind us.

Hamden nodded.

"Yeah, we've found that more and more people have heard about the Reaper. Groups that have come through the past few months have mentioned him. They see our sign and know they are safe here." We kept walking. As we did, we passed a pile of ratty stuffed animals and candles burnt low. A curbside vigil.

"Who is that for?" I asked. It reminded me of the roadside gifts that would pop up after a mass shooting. I assumed it was a memorial.

"Offerings to the Reaper," Hamden said without hesitation. We kept walking past.

He finally led us to a storefront with a hanging sign that read, "Joe's

Furniture Outlet." The windows were covered with sheet wood stained with graffiti. "This is our community center," Hamden said as he led us into the building.

Once inside, our eyes adjusted to the dim light. A thin strip of daylight peeked through the tops of the wood. But it wasn't enough, each of the tables that lined the far wall of the store had lanterns set up. I could just make out the shape of large squares on the back wall, mattresses leaning up on their sides. The couches had been rearranged in rows. The chairs and dining room tables were pushed together. A couple dozen people were chatting, eating, playing cards. Some were sleeping in the recliners.

The store smelled horribly of body odor, but wasn't as pungent as I would have expected. Dawes stood next to me and placed his hands on his hips.

"Well, I think we have a new prime suspect in our case," he whispered so that no one else could hear him. And his suspicions were spot on with mine. The burned truck was still further up the road; we hadn't been able to get a closer look yet. But given how many people were just in this building, it seemed that Hamden and their community had many mouths to feed. The prospect of an entire truckload of rations would be tempting. But then how did they even know what was in the truck? How could our team at the supply depot be so poorly informed as to drive right through a populated town? There were more questions to be answered with each minute that passed. But I assumed Dawes and I would be able to talk through everything on our way out of town.

I assumed wrong.

Hamden had walked ahead of us and leaned over one of the tables to talk with two men and a woman. They looked over at me and Dawes with a mixture of suspicion and curiosity. I looked around the room. More people were peering over to inspect us. Some were covert, looking up over their books or out of the corners of their eyes. Others, mostly the children and teenagers, were staring at us, gaping at the sight of strangers.

It wasn't the feeling of being in a fishbowl that discomforted me. I had experienced that during my first two months on the Pricus. I contracted the common flu and faced the scorn of every member of the crew. I can still feel the eyes on me. In the mess, walking through the labs, on my way to the top deck. I was the one in quarantine. It was early on in the outbreak, so every sign of illness was treated as a potential death knell. They knew intuitively that I couldn't have anything related to the biochemical attack that decimated the population of the Earth. If I did, I would have already dropped dead, a symptom that I should have regarded with more suspicion. But the worry persisted, I saw it in the way they regarded me. Could I still carry some spore, some strain, that could wipe them all out? It didn't feel worse than any other run-of-the-mill sinus-infection, but the cough lingered for weeks.

Ninety-nine-point-five percent of the global population wiped out. It was a sobering number, so I understood why the crew had been wary of me. Standing in that adapted furniture store, I knew what it was like to have eyes follow me. I understood the fear. For the first few days, I was manic with worry that I would perish in a plastic-lined room on a boat in the middle of the ocean. I was worried that my body would be shoved over the side, wet and cold for all of eternity. But I recovered and the crew mostly stopped watching me. But some always remained a little skeptical. No, it wasn't having all those strangers look at me that made me nervous. It was their scars.

Each man, woman, and child that I observed in that room had some kind of obvious mark. Chunks of their calf muscles scooped out and healed over with a knot of scar tissue. Forearms cut up and healed over. Some missing their thumbs, amateur amputations with tell-tale signs of phantom limb symptoms. Each person here had survived the outbreak, had survived the riots and lawlessness that ensued, and each had pried my invention from their skin at great personal pain. That was never what I had wanted. My implant was supposed to help. To quell the rising panic that would spill over onto the streets. To give them a better way to cope with the fear and meaninglessness that accompanies that kind of event. The world as we all knew it had ended, everyone was running on adrenaline and making poor decisions because of it.

Had it been the implant itself that had been defective, still too itchy for the end-user? Seeing that they had cut it from different places on their bodies made me mad. I had shared with the committee that the leg and thumb were potential implantation sites. Potential. But they had mass-produced and distributed my invention without heeding my warnings. And now I saw face-to-face the consequences of my failures. All these people had worn my implant. And all of them saw fit to cut it out. It hadn't helped them. It had handicapped them. The incessant scratching. The inability to stand and fight for themselves. I had designed the device to stop the killing, to stop the violence. Not to instigate it, not to enable it.

My stomach turned to a mass of knots. I felt my head start to spin; white spots appeared on the periphery of my vision. There was no fresh air in that room. I needed to go back outside, I needed to escape. Dawes must have sensed my growing panic because he gently touched my shoulder. "I think the bathroom is outside, Hunter," he said loud enough for those around us to hear. It was the cover I needed to be able to walk outside and around the corner of the building, behind the dumpster, and start retching. Nothing came up except for the sound of my throat fighting against my stomach. Did Dawes know just how disturbed I was by the sight of the pain inflicted by my own invention? Did he suspect?

Was he just as disgusted at me as I was with myself? What would Dr. Simmons say? Let it all out Hunter, just let it all out. She would have meant my thoughts and emotions, not my rehydrated breakfast.

It took a few minutes to compose myself. To steady my breath. I took off my pack and grabbed the water. I drank down the rest of the warm liquid, the taste of the plastic bottle masked the bile in my mouth, so it was an improvement, but only a slight one.

If anyone from the town was watching me, I didn't notice. I stuffed my empty water bottle back into my bag and stomped back into the storefront. In my absence, Hamden had moved closer to Dawes again, and I caught part of their conversation.

"Huh, so you were deployed when it happened?" I heard Hamden ask.

Shit.

"Yeah," Dawes answered, nodding his head. This was not part of any story that we had rehearsed. And based on the way Hamden was rubbing his chin as he considered Dawes' story, I could tell that he wasn't buying any of it.

"Hey," I interjected as soon as I was close enough to get their attention.

"Feeling better?" Dawes asked.

"Yeah, those berries we found must have been poisonous or something," I didn't want to admit the real reason that I got sick. I didn't want Hamden to know how shocked I was.

"Well, let's make sure we set you up with some extra rations so you don't have to chance it again." From the recesses of the room, a squat woman waddled towards us. Her steely gray hair framed her face, wrinkled and aged prematurely. Her almond-shaped eyes twinkled. In spite of the pain she had lived through, she was kind and sweet. In each hand she had three packets of MREs, the Peec logo stamped on the front. Dawes and I each accepted our portion from her. For a moment, I felt safe, comforted by her sweet appearance. Her grandmotherly look and the overwhelmingly kind gesture.

"We don't have-," I started, but she held up her hand to stop me. Hamden nodded at her, indicating that she had done the right thing.

"You don't want payment for these provisions?" Dawes asked.

"What currency could you pay with? Foods gonna run out eventually. Sure, it'll be that much faster now, but we all got to go at some point. I'd like to die without your starving on my conscience." I had anticipated an elderly quaver in her voice, but instead, it was clear and smooth. Familiar in a way that seemed unlikely. I also knew that while this woman may feel a moral imperative to help others, Hamden was potentially using this gesture as a way to build trust. In the few moments we had spent with him, it was clear that he was a leader and a strategist. I thought that he would see the advantages of recruiting two able-bodied men to stay and help protect the town.

I nodded and tried to discretely put the rations in my pack without exposing that the bags we were just handed were identical to the ones that we already had. It was such a kind exchange, but it didn't fully distract me from the damning evidence. They were living off of the food supply that they intercepted from our ship. This was it. This was the point of interruption. Hamden and the town needed to eat; I couldn't blame them for what they did. But the phrase, "yeah, you and what army?" rang through my mind. Dawes and I could do nothing but wait to get well out of range before reporting this into the ship. As it was, I expected that the crew of the Pricus was already in panic mode as Dawes' implant had been disabled. I could feel a cold sweat gathering on my hairline.

"If you're not feeling well, you should really sit down," Hamden signaled to the empty chairs next to the men and women he had been chatting with when I ran out. I nodded and Dawes and I followed him to the table.

I noticed that none of the people in this room were eating. How low was their own store of ransacked supplies? Were we stealing food out of their mouths? Likely all of the easily gathered food from local stores had been expended. With a community this large, the local game would be quickly exhausted. This group was just as close to starvation as the crew on the Pricus.

We all sat down just as the man on the far corner stood up. He was barely any taller standing up than he was sitting down. His dark skin was peppered with even darker freckles. It made me think of my sister's freckles; the first time I had let my memory float an image of her for years. "Ah, I'm Jim," he said shaking our hands before he left. If there was a signal passed between Hamden and Jim, I didn't notice it, but I'm sure now that there had been.

Hamden introduced the man and woman who remained at the table as Rick and Suze. They appeared to be hunched over at the same angle, their posture nearly identical, although their features were distinct. They smiled at us, Suze more genuinely than Rick. The lantern at the end of the table cast shadows, keeping half of their expressions in the dark. We must have looked just as odd and menacing to them in the limited light.

"So, Hamden says you boys have been walking up this way from the south." Suze started right in with the questions. I had only seen Hamden exchange a few words with them when we first entered. I wondered what gossip network had already been churning, spreading the news of our arrival through the town.

"Yes, we're headed due north, but we've been traveling inland for the past day or so," I responded. This was the story that Dawes and I had prepared. His fake backstory of being deployed at the time of the outbreak was further back than anything we had discussed. It occurred to me at that moment, as I thought about his story, he was stationed on the Pricus at the time of the outbreak. He had been on deployment with the Peec Security Force. But we couldn't say that to these people.

"Well, we're glad you made it here. The forests seem mostly clear in this area, but we know some of them are still springing ambushes on people further south."

"Who is springing ambushes?" Dawes asked, leaning in. I would have asked the exact same question.

"The Porths," Rick answered before taking a sip of coffee from a worn mug.

I nodded as though I recognized the name.

"But they don't bother you up this way anymore?" I asked, trying to see if I could gather any more context clues.

"No, no, no, no," Rick shook his head from side to side. A smile crept onto his face. "Not since the Reaper came through here almost-" he stopped and looked at Hamden. "Well, that must have been about a year ago, right?"

"Thereabouts," Hamden answered. He was leaning far back into his folding chair, his neck resting on the top of the seatback. "But we know the Reaper was responsible for the earlier attack too."

"Yeah, about two years ago, we had a break-in at the community library. Nobody really ventured out much. Most of the people you see in this room were hidden in their own second-floor spaces around town. We didn't have much of a way of getting in touch with each other," Rick started.

"But that's what we had to do to survive," Suze added. To me, this made the most sense. Even though they didn't need to stay in isolation a year after the outbreak.

"So, one night, we hear a commotion. That's nothing new. The Porths would come through at will and break into a storefront, smash things, if they found anyone, they would take 'em or kill 'em. Brutal beasts," Rick shook his head at the memory. "So, we hear the noise outside," he started again.

"Or Rick and I heard it, I've asked others and several said they didn't hear anything until the yelling started." Suze corrected him.

"Right, so we hear the noise outside. And maybe twenty minutes later we start hearing their yell. That high-pitched shrill sound they all make," Rick started motioning with his hand, as though waiting for myself or Dawes to chime in with our impression of this sound. But it was a sound we hadn't heard.

"So, I peered out the window and see two of 'em going at it. I mean really fighting each other," Suze started.

"Well, I'd never seen anything like it. Porth on Porth. This was unheard of." Rick shook his head; the thought still so unbelievable to him.

"And it was odd enough that it was an extra one coming into town to patrol, but that's another story," Hamden added.

"Right you are. But these Porths are going at it, so I headed downstairs to get a better look," Rick continued before being interrupted.

"And I followed him because I didn't want to be upstairs alone if something happened to him," Suze carried on. "But by the time we got to the window downstairs and looked through, the one was standing over the other, it had killed the other one." Suze's eyes grew wide with shock, as though she was seeing it all again for the first time in her mind.

"Well, at this point, I'm spooked because this one is lethal and in a bad mood. But I don't dare move to call attention to myself. Even the small part of the window we could see through, it's still a viewpoint. And then it just it ran off." Rick snapped his fingers, as though that would demonstrate the speed of what they saw. *It*, I mulled over this word.

In my mind, I had pictured two people dueling in this tale. But it wasn't until Dawes asked for more information that I realized that I had the mental image all wrong.

"So, that was it. They had some infighting and then no more trouble from this group?" Dawes asked.

"Oh no, two days later, this place was crawling with 'em," Suze answered with a look of disgust on her face. "They were everywhere. We thought for sure they were going to firebomb us or drag us all out into the streets to execute us. I was half shocked that they didn't use their little triggers to knock us dead," she gestured to her forearm, concealed under a thin sweater.

"Because they could have, you know, stunned us with those little devices. We didn't wise up to cut 'em out until a few months after this," Rick jumped back in. "It was scary, we thought this was it. One of them had turned on the other and now everyone in our little town was going to pay for it."

"It didn't help that we strung up the dead one from the light pole," Hamden cut in. The thought of such an act was barbaric, but if this community had been living under the fear of this rival group, who was I to judge?

"Yeah, they really didn't like that," Rick nodded emphatically at Hamden, shooting him a look of disapproval.

"Well, there were about a dozen of 'em that day. And it was a bad day. The streets were washed in mud. It was pouring down rain. Not the kind we usually get around here. Usually, the rain is soft and slow. But that day, it was just coming down really hard." Suze was using her hands to emphasize just how hard it was raining.

"Which is how the Reaper snuck back in," Rick told us. The couple fell silent for just a moment, just a beat. The first break in their conjoined tale since they started. The pause had an effect on me. I felt my stomach drop again.

"It must have known to wait for the rain to hide itself, but all we heard were the yells. Those fiendish yells as one-by-one the Porths dropped," Rick pointed with his finger motioning downward, indicating that each of these enemies fell and didn't get back up.

"And those suits they wear were heavy, so the sound when they fell was loud too," Suze popped in. This comment triggered both Dawes and me to turn our necks at the same time. *Suits? Like the Cratus suits?* I silently asked myself, knowing better than to actually say those words out loud. My mind started to work hard to think through what other suits they could be referring to.

"But the way it moved. It was like a shadow. I've never seen anything like it. How something so big and scary could be so silent and nimble. Just cut them all down, one after another." Rick finished to catch his breath, the words taking all of his energy to relay the story.

"Who did, who cut them down?" Dawes demanded.

"The Reaper." Suze leaned in and whispered. "We saw it from across the street," she pointed towards the front of the store, to the boarded-up window.

"And did the Reaper see you?" I jumped in.

"Yes, yes, he looked right at me and then just took off." She spoke the words with reverence in her tone.

"Just like that. He didn't come after you too?" Dawes clarified.

"No, it was like he had done what he needed to and then just turned and left." Suze shrugged at this comment.

At that moment, Rick looked down at his coffee mug and frowned. "You want a refill, honey?" he asked. Suze nodded and they both got up and left the table with their empty mugs.

"It was nice to meet you both," I waved as they walked away.

"So that's why the Porths don't come around here no more, we've got the protection of the Reaper." Hamden sat up as he spoke, catching our attention.

I nodded, acknowledging his words.

From the other side of the room, I heard a commotion. Hamden popped up and headed over to a pair of teenagers who had spilled a canister of sugar and were frantically trying to clean it up. I was grateful that Hamden stepped away from us for a moment. I turned to Dawes and caught his eye as

Hamden continued on his way, waiting until he was out of earshot to speak. "Okay, so it seems like whoever this Reaper is has been the one interrupting our supply line, but doing it for the sake of this town."

"Or the people here are still acting out in the name of the Reaper. We also need to check out this group they call the Porths," Dawes responded in a low voice. "We restore the supply lines, that group could cut it off again. We need to isolate both."

"Dawes? Seriously?" I asked him, waiting for all the pieces of the puzzle to click for him.

"What? This group was terrorizing this town from the sounds of it." Dawes dismissed my questions, but I kept at it. He had to see.

"Those suits they described were the Cratus suits. From *Project Cratus*," I emphasized the full code name to help him realize. I could see the understanding dawn on him, changing the expression on his face.

He let out a sigh. "Yeah, sounds like it," Dawes had his thinking face on, his brow furrowed like he was trying to push a cement block through his ear canal. "So that does just leave the Reaper, or his followers."

"But the people around here seem to like what the Reaper is doing. We take the Reaper out; we may get another vigilante on our hands," I worked through the potential ramifications out loud, trying to think through to the best solution.

"Everyone wants to eat. But we have people on that boat who have no other resources. Here they could hunt game, farm. Out there, we've got nobody." Dawes was resolute. I understood what was at stake. I didn't need a lecture on that. But I wanted him to understand how futile our mission was. Even if we succeeded and restored supply lines, they could just be shut down again the next week.

I saw Hamden heading back over to us, walking up behind Dawes. I changed the topic abruptly so that he wouldn't overhear anything.

"We probably need to get a move on if we want to make camp up in the woods tonight," I looked past Dawes and directed my comments to Hamden.

I was ready to get out of that cramped storefront. Just as I had been ready to get out of the Bunker. A cruise with the Peec executives as a reward for hard work. Sure, I wasn't much of a social guy. I didn't like to schmooze, but I liked the feeling of being in the in-crowd. Something that had eluded me my entire life.

Malcolm and I were picked up in a helicopter with some of the other big-wigs. This was a nice ride, the same fancy model that had taken me from the Big Island so long ago. A sleek commercial model with smooth leather seats and faux wood paneling, not the utilitarian ones I would soon grow used to on the Pricus. It was my first time leaving The Forbidden Island in over two years. Just as strange and barren as it had been when I had first landed, I marveled at how such an immense operation could remain hidden beneath the surface. The miles of hallway that I had learned by memory were all buried below the ground. As the helicopter climbed vertically, the island looked smaller and smaller, almost comically tiny.

I looked out over the vast open ocean as we headed north. The sun was still high in the sky after our journey that lasted several hours. Each of the executives seated near me was glued to their smartphones. Answering emails, buzzing and chirping and straining their necks as they concentrated on their devices. I was suddenly very grateful that my smartphone had been confiscated before I left for the Bunker years earlier. It was freeing to be without it.

After staring out at the ocean for so long, I thought I was hallucinating when I saw a stark white shape on the horizon. A luxury cruise liner, smaller than the big tourist ships, but still much bigger than a yacht, appeared before us. Below, I saw another helicopter departing. Our pilot positioned us to land, seemingly one of many arrivals that day.

As we touched down, the pilot instructed us to take precautions as we exited the aircraft. He fully powered down and then told us it was clear to grab our bags and leave. Some of the executives seemed ruffled at the idea of handling their own bag for the ten feet it would take them to reach the men dressed as bellhops on the landing pad.

I took my duffel without complaint and waited for everyone else to leave before me. I knew my place in the pecking order.

"Hello and welcome to Peec at Sea!" one of the bellhops announced. A waiter stood nearby with a tray of champagne flutes.

Rattray was next to me, waiting to hand off his bag. "Peec at Sea?" I asked him in a sarcastic tone.

"Gotta love our marketing department," he said back as he grabbed a glass of champagne.

I was fully prepared to walk my own bag down to my room, but Rattray nodded to indicate that I should hand my bag off to the gentleman. I did as I was instructed, just trying to blend in and not call attention to myself. I was out of my league with the big-wigs. They were suave. They were wealthy. They were above my paygrade.

I stuck close to Malcolm. As it turned out, our rooms were situated near each other on the same corridor. "Let's meet up around five for cocktails in the main lounge. Hurlbert and Gonzalez will be there. It will be good for you to get some face time with them."

I wanted to remind him that I had met them before, during my presentation. Maybe they didn't remember me; they would have seen many projects during their visit. I didn't correct Malcolm. I nodded and entered my room so that I could have a panic attack in private. Hurlbert and Gonzalez? What in the world would I ever have to say to them? As I started to imagine all of the possible bone-headed things that I might say, I felt a cool calmness float over me, like spring water from a gentle waterfall. I smiled at the knowledge that my own device was helping me out.

I sat on the bed and flipped through the premium movie channels for a bit. I just wanted some background noise as I hung up my jacket and slacks. I didn't like these formal occasions. I knew I would have to make small talk and I felt horrible doing it. I was better at chatting with my type of people: scientists and engineers. At one time, Hurlbert and Gonzalez would have fit those descriptors, but they had been in management for too long. They had played office politics; they knew how to survive. Forrester would have been perfect for this. He had played the game for years. But he had been ejected from the Bunker. He might as well have dropped off the face of the planet as far as the corporate ladder was concerned.

I couldn't help but wonder if Malcolm was disappointed that he was left with me as the representative for the Projects. Metz had been dragged out kicking and screaming. Rita had been asked to leave, and then not twenty-four hours earlier Forrester was escorted from the Bunker. I guess that left me. But I owed a lot to Malcolm. He had taken a chance on me, had funded my research, helped to push my device through the trial screenings, and was ensuring that the first shipment of prototypes would arrive at Walter Reed within the next few days. My vision was about to become a reality because of him.

As the sun started to sink low, I dressed. I slicked back my hair and put on my infrequently used cologne. Checking my reflection in the mirror, I felt more confident that I could survive this. It was a booze cruise; it was a celebration of the team's success. How bad could it be? All I had to do was drink the free champagne, make small talk, leave with a good impression. Not too much to ask.

I headed up the carpeted staircase in the main atrium of the ship. A dazzling chandelier floated down, changing colors and twinkling to the beat of the piano music being broadcast through the ship.

I headed over to the bar where Rattray was standing with some of the others from the executive team. I saw them huddled in their close group. All in tuxedos with black satin cummerbunds. All of them had wisps of hair remaining on their head, but it was still oiled and slicked back. It made them look like well-preened birds, like ravens. At that moment, I amused myself with the mental connection, that a grouping of birds has a distinct name. For ravens, a grouping is a "conspiracy" or an "unkindness." I should have connected the dots then that those men were indeed conspiring to do something unkind.

I ordered a bourbon on the rocks and joined them silently. They expanded and allowed me to stand shoulder-to-shoulder with them for a few moments before the CEO of the company, Edwin Hurlbert, turned towards me. A decade older than Rattray, but with far fewer fine lines around his eyes, Hurlbert had perfected his corporate image. His jet-black hair had the look of a hundred-dollar haircut, his stance was relaxed, but still commanding. "So, Hunter, we're so glad you could join us. You must be enjoying some time outside of that Bunker you've been toiling in."

I nodded my head, "Yes, sir. This has already been such an amazing trip. Thank you for inviting me."

"Well, we're happy you could make it. Your Calm Implant is going to do a lot of good for the world," he lifted his glass towards mine.

"Yes, sir. That's the plan," I nodded and took a sip of my drink.

"Hunter's device has already shown great promise," Rattray cut in. I appreciated him; I had no idea what else to even say.

"Excellent, any case studies you can share with us?" Hurlbert asked. He looked directly at me, the rest of the men in the group stopped chattering and turned their attention to us. They were waiting; they wanted a good story. But how could I reveal the results of a test patient without breaking confidentiality? How could I detail their medical history and why the implant was so effective without turning their ears for at least an hour? I needed a pithy anecdote. He didn't want a drawn-out case study; he wanted a party joke.

"Uh, well," I stammered, searching for something to share. And then, the simplest one just spilled out. "It certainly helped me out when I got nervous about having dinner with you all tonight. Calmed my nerves right away," I let out a small laugh. Would they appreciate my self-deprecating humor? Would Rattray throw me off the boat for embarrassing him?

I knew my answer right away. Hurlbert's eyes lit up like a kid in a candy store. "You don't say?" His eyes glanced down at my arm for a moment and then back up to meet my eyes. "That's remarkable! When we're done with our government contract, we can take this thing to market. Imagine if you could shake off those anxieties with ease. It would be so much easier to just communicate with people, say what you mean!" He clapped me on the back with his broad open palm. The jolt of it caused me to spill a little bit of my drink.

Pleased with my answer, Hurlbert turned his attention to one of the other men in our circle. Rattray nodded his approval. I hid behind my glass, realizing too late that the alcohol went straight to my head. When the group turned to the dining room about fifteen minutes later, I couldn't have been more relieved. We all filed through the atrium. I had no idea where we were going, but I just followed the men in front of me. I let my gaze wander. This was the first time I had ever been on a cruise ship. The surfaces all sparkled, every shining detail stood out.

And then, a movement from above caught my eye. Balanced on a metal hoop was a woman, spinning from her white silk cloth. It was extravagant and over the top. I thought for a moment that the bourbon was making me see things, but she was really there. Was anyone else even looking up at her? What did we all look like to her? The woman dangling from the ceiling in a golden bodysuit, her hair warped into whimsical buns. How did she see us? Upside down, way below her, drinking, dining, and scrambling like mice. I have to think that she had a name like Juniper, or Willow, or Zephyr.

Something that evokes soft winds and sweet scents. Surely, nothing as pedestrian as Sarah, or Lindsay, or Meghan.

How long did she spin around for? Was she up there the whole evening? Did she sense the trouble and decide to stay on her hoop to please us, or did her humanity kick in, causing her to flee? I don't think I saw her after that night. Certainly not after I evacuated. But perhaps I did. I couldn't see the features on her face easily from the deck.

Did she think of us as fun-loving scientists, getting a much-deserved celebration? Or as spoiled over-achievers, making her spin and twist for our base entertainment? Had this always been her dream? It's easy to focus on her. She was ornamental, a moving decoration. The people that were real to me, whose names I knew, whose dreams I encouraged, I cannot think of them. I've walled them off in my memory. They live behind a water-tight bulkhead, gasping for the oxygen that is quickly dwindling. They scrape at the door, but I refuse to open it. My aerialist, she guards that door, distracts me from going past her. She keeps me from those memories and she keeps them from me. Twirling, floating on a suspended hoop in my demented head.

I spent most of the evening quietly sipping on champagne, accepting a new glass each time it was offered. I tried to be invisible at the dinner table, afraid that my thoughts were written large across my face. *I want to leave all this.* The attention, being invited to join in was nice. But it was a temporary high. I had grown so frustrated and disillusioned with my research that I couldn't think of spending any more time with the team, let alone the big wigs who had been the ones to corrupt my vision. I didn't want their recognition or the benefit of being on this luxury celebration trip. They were the ones who had sent Rita away.

I saw each of them in the low light of the table, the glass window behind them overlooking the ocean that was as black as the night around us. Their jowls jiggling as they laughed too deeply, ate too quickly. Their glasses continuing to fill and empty with liquor. They were celebrating mightily. It seemed excessive to me. Our projects had been approved, but we were all still months away from a full roll-out. I had done the numbers in my mind. It had been six weeks, so some prototypes were likely ready for their first shipments. I did the math.

For the first time in my life, I calculated wrong. To be fair, I didn't have all the information. They had started production months before our presentations. They had something up their cufflinked sleeves. I just didn't know what yet.

It felt as though that dinner went on forever. Rattray was next to me, but didn't speak the entire meal. His eyes were fixed on the window, as though he were expecting to see a light in the distance from a far-off ship. Or perhaps he was expecting something else. Every so often, I looked to try and catch what was so fascinating. But I saw nothing. Until, just after midnight, a small light began to form in the distance. One yellow circle piercing the veil of darkness. It was as though he had been expecting it. When I noticed the dot, I caught him checking his wristwatch in my peripheral vision. Was this light, this approaching vessel expected? Was it late or right on time?

In my fading memory, the vision in my mind flickers, as though the boat had somehow lurched, the smooth fiberglass sliding to one side, lolling in the ocean. In reality, the ride was smooth, but my mind embellishes for dramatic effect.

The mind tends to do that.

Play tricks on you. Enhance certain memories. Distort them. Make them more prominent.

Thinking back on that encounter with Hamden and his community, I wonder now if that happened as well. Were the people in the town really all that kind? Or has my mind just emphasized their kinder gestures as a contrast to what happened next?

In all, Dawes and I had been in the town for an hour. We had been received with suspicion, but had quickly gained enough trust to be given time to rest our feet. We had enough information to be able to radio back to the Pricus our concern about the Reaper, and the fact that this town seemed to relish the death of a dozen of our soldiers in Cratus suits and had given them an unusual nickname.

Dawes and I stood to shake hands with Hamden. He told us we would be welcome back any time if we found the terrain too rugged as we headed further Northeast. We refilled our water jugs and heaved our packs back on. I continued to play my part, knowing that we would need to wait until we were well clear of the town before discussing anything we had just learned.

We headed out of the storefront and back onto the road as a light misty rain accelerated. It was almost as though the rain had been waiting for us to step outside before really ramping up. We started up the street, picking up where we had been escorted off our route. The rain was sort of a haze, a mist that lingered in the air. We could barely see a few feet in front of us, everything beyond that was milky white.

We had gone maybe fifty feet when I heard something behind us. Not the rush of feet as the community guard headed for cover in the rain. Not the slosh of water running into the sewer. No, this was the sound of two resolute and heavy feet planting themselves.

I turned and saw only the same rain behind us that I had seen in front of us. But then my eyes could make out a darker shape, a large creature looming in the mist.

Architects

PART THREE

Civil Unrest

"Hunter, you're needed in the aft conference room," I recognized Rattray's voice over the intercom system. I had tried to rest in my elegant cabin on Peec at Sea. The ship had come to a dead stop and the waves hitting against it did nothing to lull me to sleep. Instead, my stomach was churning. Something had happened on land, only I didn't know what. I wanted to know more. I wanted to get home to the comfort of my small confined room in the Bunker. I wanted to wake up and realize that this had all been a dream. But Rattray's voice pulled me back to the reality that I found myself in. I had only expected to be here for one night, so I put back on the clothes I had arrived in and headed up to the main atrium once more.

I pushed past the groups of wait staff chatting in the hallways, forming in small clumps as they worried over what was happening on land. I caught a few words as I brushed past them. "No, I haven't heard anything." "I can't get a signal at all." "My feeds are frozen."

The worry was evident in their voices, the anxiety permeating the air. The televisions in the atrium were displaying the rainbow color blocks that indicated that the transmission was dead. No news was coming in. But no one had bothered to shut off the screens. A few of the corporate wives, still in their gowns, their make-up starting to droop and smear, huddled on the plush couches by the main bar.

The night before, our dinner had been interrupted by an urgent call that the executives had to attend to. Their hasty departure did not go unnoticed. Then a few panicked announcements. Everyone was to go to their cabins immediately. Further instructions would be provided by the crew in due time. I plopped down on the spacious double bed in my cabin, a luxurious delicacy compared to my bunk, and flipped on the television. No news, no movies, no sports. Nothing. My head had been heavy with champagne and I dozed off.

That morning there had been an announcement that we could all go to the main dining room for breakfast. I didn't go. I hadn't left my cabin at all until Rattray had called for me over the intercom.

I tried not to let the panic of the people around me get to my head. I pushed past them, walking the length of the ship as quickly as I could without breaking into a sprint.

As I approached the end of the ship, the length of the hallway running out, I noticed a set of doors to my right. They were guarded by two tall and muscular men in inexpensive suits. The guard on the left nodded at me once and turned to open the door. I expected a cacophony of sound to pour out from the room. Panicked words hollered across the table, new reports blaring on the television. But instead, all I heard was the click of the door latch releasing. The room was eerily silent.

Grim faces hung from each person seated around the long table. Shoulders hunched forward, as though their loose bow ties were being pulled, weighing their necks down towards the surface of the table. The hum of the ship gently coasting above the waves permeated the air, filling in the corners where there should have been any other noise.

I hesitated for a moment, taking in the somber scene before clearing my throat. Rattray popped his head up and looked over in my direction. He removed his glasses to rub his eyes and then stood to greet me. He handled me, maneuvering us over to a coffee cart on the far end of the room.

The windows that made up the far wall of the room started to change color. The brilliant blue of the sky started to darken as clouds passed over the sun. There were balled up pieces of paper in the waste bin next to the coffee cart. Evidence of a long evening's brainstorm and the physical proof that they had been trying to find some solutions. The words were practically illegible from the penmanship and crumpled papers. A few words stuck out in my mind. Biochemical. Toxin. Quarantine. Control. Those ones made sense. Some of the others didn't. Words I had never seen before, I assumed in another language given the multi-national team assembled in that room.

"How much have you heard?" Rattray whispered the question to me, capturing my attention. Instead of pouring himself more coffee, he stuck his hands in his pockets, careful not to touch anything.

"I know something has happened onshore, but I don't know any details." I could read his response; his face was too tired to betray any other expression at that time.

"There's been an outbreak. Some kind of weaponized disease released in a biochemical attack. Appears to be airborne, so it's spreading fast. There have already been fatalities." He spoke quickly. As though getting it over with was going to help. I started to process what he was saying. An outbreak. A deliberate attack. Fatalities.

"When did this happen?" That was the first logical question that popped into my mind. The rest were panicked and jumbled. That one at least made sense.

Rattray sighed and took his hands out of his pockets so that he could pour himself some coffee. I thought it was a sigh of despair, of accepting that this was our reality now. I thought.

"It seems to have started last night. We have been getting reports all morning of mass deaths, some people dropping dead where they stood. As you can imagine, there is a mass panic among those who haven't succumb to the toxin." He poured his coffee slowly before adding the ominous word: "yet."

I took a deep breath. My mind jumped into solution mode. There had to be something we could do. In that room, we had the head of R&D for our company as well as the smartest business leaders in a century. They had built Peec from a small startup to the largest company in the world. Surely, someone here would be smart enough to propose a solution. It seemed that was why they called me in.

Rattray motioned for me to join him at the table. As he walked up the rest of the exhausted faces looked over.

There was Edwin Hurlbert, the founder and CEO of Peec. Patricia Gonzalez, Head of North American operations. Claude Marrullier, former head of European Operations, current CFO. Nancy Gannett. Andy LoPresti. Richard Whimbly. And several faces that I didn't recognize. But they were in this room, so they had to be important. And now I was in this room.

"Team, this is Hunter. He heads up Project Calm," Rattray placed his left hand on my shoulder as he spoke. I nodded and silently waited for instructions.

"Calm? We could all use a little calm right now," Hurlbert gave a half-hearted smile. Everyone around the table groaned in agreement.

"I'm here to help in whatever way I can," I added.

"You're the only one from the Human Capital Project on board, aside from Malcolm," Hurlbert gestured to my right. "He thinks that the developments that your team has made could help in this situation." His statement was an invitation to expound on the possibilities.

I started to spin out as much as I could.

"Okay, so if we have a biochemical attack, our first order should be to focus on preventing another one," I began.

"D.O.D. and D.H.S. are already on it," Gonzalez chimed in.

"Good," I nodded, trying to call up my confidence once more to continue. "In the meantime, we need to identify the toxin, so we know what we are working with. Any theories?"

"It is killing people too quickly. We're going to need tissue samples from the victims so that we can analyze them," Marrullier responded.

That made sense. To have impacted this many people so quickly, we didn't have any symptoms to work from. But how had we not had any warning? Weren't the C.I.A., or N.S.A., or someone supposed to be tracking these things? And a biotoxin that could kill that quickly. It seemed to be a nightmare scenario.

My mind flashed on Metz being dragged away. The intensifying discussion pulled me back into the moment; the severity of the situation needed my attention. The men and women at the table looked at me, expecting me to deliver something to them. "Well, then it had to be a coordinated attack with the same biological agent being released in multiple cities at the same time to be this widespread-," I started.

"We have a team working on that angle." Hurlbert cut me off. "But the damage is done, now we have survivors who are panicking."

"Then the Cratus suit is our best solution. We likely won't have enough produced for every remaining person, but if we can get our first responders geared up, we can make their jobs a bit easier." Everyone around the table began to write notes on the pads of paper in front of them. Emboldened, I continued.

"If fatalities continue, we may have issues with utilities and infrastructure. We can't help with electricity or water, but our Connect gliders can provide short-range internet access. Help people get information on loved ones, report any new attacks." Another whispered round of notes.

"What about the riots?" Marrullier asked. This was the ugly part of what the project could do. Almost all of our projects had military applications. The Cease canisters popped into mind and I mentioned them right away. I hadn't noticed, but Malcolm had slipped away from the table and returned with a new chair for me. I sat down and continued to answer questions and provide suggestions for the next hour. We had covered all of our immediate thoughts and concerns about what was happening on land. We finally worked our way around to quarantine and that's when the true potential of Peec revealed itself to us.

"We think the people that are off-grid are self-quarantined, staying inside to avoid any potential exposure," Gonzalez announced.

"Okay, until they decide to come into town and see what's doing," Marrullier shot back.

"They won't make it to town with the blockades."

"Oh, because people who live off-grid love it when a government official tells them what they can or can't do." Hurlbert gestured with his arms, growing more frustrated with each passing second.

"That's a generalization," Malcolm added.

"And a US-based stereotype," I backed him up.

"He's right. This is a pandemic. How do we reach people living in rural China to tell them to seal their windows, to don masks? To tell them to stay indoors without exposing them to any particulates in the air?" Marrullier put the problem to the team.

The idea hit me with force. I spun around and directed my idea at Malcolm. "Connect! The gliders. Could we retrofit some kind of flier or communication device?"

"Hmmm," he pondered the suggestion. "That could work."

"But where do we target?" Gonzalez threw out another potential issue to solve for.

"We can use Atlas," I added.

"You mean Project Cartograph?" Malcolm corrected me. I had to keep myself from rolling my eyes. Always the insistence on the internal project name. This was no time for our corporate jargon. The branding for the global mapping system was botched on roll-out. No one wanted to "cartograph" their directions for a road trip. Too many syllables. The free service was amazing and no one was using it because of the name. So, Peec rebranded it to "Atlas." It was effectively a map of every road in the world. Peec had teams around the globe drive in retrofitted vans with three hundred and sixty-degree cameras to document their excursions. They knew every street, back road, private property, abandoned rental, and footpath.

"Yes," I answered before launching into my explanation. "We have a visual record of every boulevard, dust road, fire trail, and path across the globe. We can already tell which areas are rural and target the Connect gliders to drop information at each residence." It all fell into place. It appeared that we had every necessary resource that the globe needed in this time of crisis. World leaders faxed in their authorizations, some carte blanche: just fix it. That's what they wanted. Stop the spread. Dispose of the rioters, quell the panic, and make sure the surviving population doesn't continue to pick each other off.

But who would be brave enough to face these frantic survivors? The Cratus suit was the solution. An impenetrable body armor. Every soldier was instructed on how best to use the suits. They were intimidating. They were designed for war. But on such short notice, we couldn't change them to look more pleasing. They would stay as-is, black and menacing as they were. And though it was best not to scare anyone they were helping, all communications between those wearing the suits remained encrypted with Rita's invention. No time to take it out.

Right from that command center, we worked out the solution. Me and the heads of the company, or I thought. They had already worked it out months earlier, maybe years earlier. But they were just following the simple command from Forrester's catchy slogan. They were keeping up the illusion for me.

And then, Hurlbert suggested the next step. "If we have to stop people from panicking, for their own good, we have a solution for that. Don't we?" He looked at Rattray and then to me.

My device.

If everyone on land had it implanted, then those who were panicking would be put to sleep, dream through the madness, skip the horrors of survival. I pictured the worried mothers and children suddenly resting on their couches. The looters and those trying to exploit the situation would doze through it too. Anyone worried about another attack would trigger the response, they would sleep where they were.

But no one had the device implanted. The first production batch for extended human testing was set to arrive at Walter-Reed… I checked the date on my watch. It should have arrived that day. There were some devices available, but who would be able to track them down? And even then, the priority on land was to isolate the healthy in air-tight locations and stop the next attack.

"It could have helped if we had been a few years earlier," I shook my head. This would have been my one chance to help, to see my device stop the pain and suffering going on. This could have saved lives.

"What do you mean?" Malcolm asked.

"I mean, we have maybe a thousand devices created, but they were due to be delivered today. My guess is that they were lost in the melee. We can't divert resources to finding them right now." I shook my head.

"Hunter, we need every possible solution right now. This problem is more than just the disease. We have people out there who are terrified and acting on pure adrenaline. They aren't thinking rationally. They can't think clearly. This is precisely what you designed this implant for. We're gonna find your devices and get them to as many people as soon as we can." The confidence in Malcolm's words struck me. A thousand lives saved, spared from the hysteria of the pandemic. Malcolm gave me a quick pat on the shoulder, I met his eyes and he gave a nod of approval. A silent 'well-done.'

But I didn't know at the time that it wasn't just a thousand devices that they would disperse. And that they didn't need to retrieve them. The order never went out to Walter Reed. Instead, the devices were shipped to every Peec regional office around the globe. Each arriving days before the outbreak.

In the days that passed in that conference room, more solutions were presented that made use of Peec projects. It made sense to me at the time. We were working with what we knew was available. Our company had developed this technology. Of course, we were finding an application for it.

The Cratus suits were discussed at length. Generals from Peec's private security force on the ground in different cities were patched into our conference room on Peec at Sea. In their briefing on the outbreak, I stepped in for Holtz and detailed the uses and weaknesses of the Cratus suit. I told them that if anyone attacked a soldier they would need to drop to the deck and remain still. If they pulled out the tubes on the oxygen filters, they had to immediately press the button on the front of the suit to shut off the flow of air. The soldiers would still have a limited supply in the suit, but they wouldn't be exposed to any airborne pathogens. Dropping down face first would allow them to hit the button and cut the airflow leaving them with a two-hour supply of oxygen. (Holtz had increased the capacity in time for his presentation.) The fail-safe that Holtz had designed would be a lifesaver to many soldiers.

Auxiliary troops were briefed as well. I told them about the functions of the suit, the Converse translators that would keep them all in communication with each other, the Cyclops camera that would give them additional visuals. And then I told them that before putting the suit on each of them would have a Calm device implanted in their arm. Those with forearm tattoos would have their implant placed in their thumbs. If there were any objections to this, they didn't voice them. I couldn't see their reactions, so perhaps they had just swallowed their objections and followed orders as all good soldiers do. I explained that it was for their benefit. The implant would help them stay calm, in case of potential infection. What I didn't tell them was that Marrullier and Hurlbert also worried about their mercenary force defecting. I knew that a secondary reason for my implant was in case any of them deserted. But I didn't hesitate for one moment. I had the ear of our CEO and the executives. I was helping in a time of crisis. I was getting dopamine hit after dopamine hit as I received praise from my boss and his bosses.

I had been taken in by the entire scene presented to me. I accepted the information as it was reported. I had no reason to question that it could be a fabrication. Who would make something like this up? I don't know the exact moment when I figured out that it was all a ruse. I think bits of me knew it, select synapses in my brain were aware that it was a lie. But it had been reinforced so well. And by the time I was ordered back on land three years later, I needed to believe it. I had built a theory that there had indeed been a terror attack using a biological weapon, but I worried that it had been orchestrated by Peec.

It wasn't until that afternoon when Dawes and I stepped out into the main street of New Hope, the survivor settlement in the North Country on our way to the supply depot, that I realized just how wrong I had been.

The rain was a constant hush, a light whispered sound on the back of my neck, straining my hearing, getting my eardrums used to the pattern, becoming white noise, lulling my mind into thinking that everything was okay, but keeping me on my toes all at the same time.

The figure appeared in the shadow of that mist. Barely a shade darker than the gray of the rain at first, but becoming clearer as it stomped forward. Each footfall reverberated in the dirt beneath our boots. The silt turning into mud conducted the impact of the approaching beast. Too tall to be a man, too slow to be a machine. Whatever it was, it seemed to delight in this taunting march towards us. In all the outside noise, I managed to catch the sound of metal on metal. Doors were latched, structures were locked up tight. The town braced for what was about to happen.

It must have been ten feet away when Dawes and I could both see it clearly. He let out a stifled, "what the-" before it moved.

The thing jumped before I could sound an alarm by screaming. A shrill yell, a fiendish holler, came from the direction it had jumped. It was demonic and sounded like those prerecorded monster sounds you would hear in an amusement park, pushed up against a dying speaker as it gave its last warbles of noise. That sound was terrifyingly familiar. Maybe these folks were right to revere this creature.

The Reaper had arrived.

I dove to my left, acting on instinct. I hit the dirt hard, the curb of the sidewalk jamming my shoulder. With no time to hesitate or whimper, I scrambled on all fours towards the boarded-up law offices behind me. I crawled on my knees to the door and tried to open it. Locked.

This had all happened in the span of a second, maybe less. I was acting on pure instinct, pure adrenaline. This was flight or fight and I was trying to fly away as fast as I could. I attempted the door again and it wouldn't budge. Rational thought was hard to summon at that moment.

I heard the screaming of the monster once more and turned. My back was pressed up against the door, an old habit. A human fallacy, that if your back was covered that you were safe. The sight that greeted me confirmed that I was not.

The creature had crossed the distance between where it had been stalking us and where Dawes stood, shocked into stillness. I could see the fear on

Dawes' face. His eyes were wide with panic. His right hand shook as he slowly tried to reach around for his rifle. Of course, the creature saw this. He was moving too slow; his movement was delayed by absolute terror. I knew he was feeling it because I was too.

In my memory, this entire attack felt like it took minutes, maybe even half an hour. Every drop of rain hitting the ground is pronounced. The mist collecting and then dripping from my nose and chin were a frozen ocean daring my teeth to chatter. The gritty dirt under toe is broken down into individual molecules, each one too loud, about to betray my location. I watched from a few feet away, hiding in plain sight on the sidewalk. I was sure that whatever was about to happen to Dawes would be repeated on me.

The creature towered over Dawes. In the mist, I could make out the back of the monster. Tentacles rose up from its back, added appendages that could strangle Dawes. I blinked. No, it wasn't a set of tentacles. It was a large box with tubes leading from the torso to the head. I blinked hard, sure that the moisture in the air had blurred my vision. It wasn't possible. But my attention was shifted away from this thought as the monster raised its arm before cutting into Dawes. In one organic motion, the attacker had split Dawes in half. I heard two thuds as one half of his body hit the ground and then the next. My eyes snapped shut, but it was too late. I had already seen the spray of the blood, heard the wet sound of organs being ripped open.

The Reaper stood over his work, satisfied in the swift murder. Then, very slowly, it turned its head towards me. Without reminding my legs to stand tall, they crumpled under the fear. I slid down the length of the locked door, hoping that someone was about to open it and pull me in. I wanted to pound on the door, but I didn't dare turn my back on the creature.

It stared at me. I stared at it. I thought that if I blinked that it would be on me in half a second, pouncing on me as it had Dawes. But instead, it turned and continued on its way. Disappearing into the mist just moments before the rain let up.

I couldn't believe what had just happened. My circumstances had changed suddenly. I seemed to have been spared, once again. The last time I felt this mix of emotions was the morning that Rattray told me I was going to be one of the people airlifted off the cruise ship.

"We're being transferred today." The news was delivered as Malcolm entered the conference room that had become our command center on the luxury ship. The hardwood table and comfortable chairs had been helpful and the view of the water was spectacular. But the room wasn't soundproof. (There had been wild gossip spread throughout the ship quickly about what was happening on land.) We needed an actual command center. We needed a war-room. Secure, equipped with live video feeds, and probably some actual military leaders who had successfully managed quarantines and not just a bunch of nerds who happened to be out at sea when the attack happened.

My neck was stiff from hunching over the latest reports and falling asleep at the conference table every night since the outbreak occurred. I had ventured back to my cabin once to shower and found the chaos of the passengers around me too much to handle. If this was bad, I couldn't imagine what it was like on land. I cracked my neck and rolled my shoulders before I responded. "Where are we going?"

In the first few hours, after the news had settled in, I assumed I would be heading back to Ni'ihau to continue developing a more sophisticated device.

Malcolm handed me a cup of coffee, delaying his response. Suddenly, my mind flashed on the possibility that we would be dropped off in Seattle or Vancouver. Both cities were easily a day's journey from our current location. We could dock and step foot into a warzone based on the reports we were getting from the mainland. With each millisecond that he waited to respond, I pictured what we would find. How quickly each of us would succumb to the disease? Which of us would be left alive, forced to fight for our survival as gas lines went unattended and exploded, or carbon monoxide leaked from homes, or everyday scrapes and cuts festered untreated?

"They're airlifting us," he gestured with his hand to the empty chairs at the table, indicating that those who had retreated to their cabins were included, "to the nearest Peec vessel in range. The Pricus Capricorn."

I looked at him, expecting further elaboration. He misread my expression. "Yeah, they really take this P.C. thing too far. It's a ridiculous name-"

"No, that's not what I'm confused about," I interrupted. I could have explained the mythological origins of the name, but I focused instead on the most pressing question. "How does Peec, a technology company, have a ship in the middle of the North Pacific?"

"We have high-value assets around the world. In terms of our facilities, our technology, our R&D," he nodded towards me as he said the last. "Of course, Peec has security forces to protect their investments. All ex-military, all well-trained, and completely clandestine." His explanation made sense. All of the reasons I had heard throughout my time at Peec fit. There were logical reasons for each of these things to exist. Only now, looking back, I can see their plan all clearly laid out.

I packed my overnight bag that had only contained a few items, but had somehow managed to migrate across the nooks and crannies of my cabin over the course of a week. I wasn't sure what to expect. Definitely not the luxury cabin I had on Peec at Sea. As the Pricus Capricorn came into view that afternoon, I knew that I needed to drastically lower my expectations. The vessel looked like a military ship, gun-metal gray with utilitarian turrets and weapons on the deck. The helicopter that picked us up was nothing like the luxury aircraft we had taken a few days earlier, this was a loud, no-frills chopper.

I was pleased that my stomach had survived the journey. Until we landed on the deck and my legs wobbled. The sea was timid, but the ship was still rocking. I was shown my cabin, the one that would begin to feel like a prison cell. I was instructed to drop my bag and head up to the bridge for a meeting with Captain Gomes. Rattray and I were given the basic overview of when to show up for meals and to keep out of any area that wasn't specifically to be used for this crisis. We were then shown into a command center that had been set up. Unlike the one we had established on the cruise liner, this room had no windows, no ventilation, and no light except for the computer screens and monitors on the walls.

We set to work, but we continued to be interrupted as new team members arrived. Most were pulled from the private security staff, arriving from other locations around the world. But two men finally walked into the room that Rattray and I recognized. Two of my team members from Ni'ihau.

It was our first night on the Pricus Capricorn. It was the first of many late nights on board. Everyone from the Peec R&D team was required to stay in the command center, a claustrophobic room covered with monitors and flashing sensors, until the mission was complete. Holtz and Kupper had been airlifted to the ship earlier that day. When I asked about the rest of the team, they shook their heads. I pressed for more information.

Holtz glanced up at me with a pained look on his face. "They had each of us isolated in our bunks. A few of the guards had recently come back from their week of shore leave. We think that when the hatch was opened, the toxin must have leaked in. Everyone else is gone." He looked just below my eyes as he spoke, unable to meet my gaze.

"Gone?" I whispered the question, not intending for it to actually leave my mouth.

"One of the guards survived and put on a Cratus suit and checked each bunk. We were the only two still breathing," Kupper cut in. His tone made it clear that he didn't want to discuss it any further.

I felt my spirit whither in that narrow hallway as they clamored past. I stared off at nothing, my eyes looking at the gray bulkhead, but not seeing it. I pictured Rita, sweet Rita who had so much life. She was smiling in my mind, excited to announce another new breakthrough. She was alive and well in my memory. Until a gray vision of her lying stiff invaded my mind, eroding my real memories with this false and terrifying one. Where had she gone when she left the Bunker and had she survived out there?

After Holtz and Kupper dropped their duffels in their new bunks, their even more cramped cabins, they came back out into the hallway, breaking my trance. We all went back up to the command center and busied ourselves with stopping the madness, quelling the destruction.

A group of Peec security officers, retired military who had signed on to a private contract with the company before the outbreak, was trying to hold a quarantine line in Sioux City. Civilians continued to push against the barricades, trying to escape. The outbreak had decimated the military and national guard. It fell to our relatively small private fleet to provide support.

The current cabinet secretary, who was still alive in some bunker and had executive authority as the rest of the government went silent, had signed off on our private force acting in lieu of the national guard. The team had simple orders - no one crosses the line. They were given clear directions that until we could confirm that there would be no further attacks, they all had to stay within the quarantine zone or risk additional fatalities. Of course, people didn't want to remain sealed in their homes, gas masks at the ready. No one wanted to be told that they had to stay put in a time of crisis.

There had already been violent insurrections across the country. People ramming trucks through barricades. Soldiers being attacked left and right.

Why so much violence? Why so much fear? In a time of mass panic and confusion, why so much anger? Because it was always there. In the great "civilized" before, it was always just behind our view. We had laws to stop the violence, we had rules to hold back the rage, but it was there all along. That's why the rates of sexual assault were so high; it just couldn't be contained. All that hatred and evil. Bubbling just beneath the surface, barely containing our savagery. All of this evil was unleashed upon the world when the outbreak happened. Well, of course, it was. A descendent of Cain had something to do with it; that evil just can't be helped.

Equipped with the most advanced technology the Human Capital Project had developed, the team on the ground in Iowa did their best. Wearing the thick Cratus suits, each was outfitted with the Cyclops cameras that were feeding our monitors on the ship. We could see the heat imaging of people approaching the line, their figures crouching behind abandoned vehicles that were just outlines on our screens. But we had no tracking mechanism on the actual suit. Therefore, each of the soldiers had the Calm device implanted earlier that day. I could see all of them lit up as bright blue dots on my monitor. Their adrenaline started to increase steadily as the hoard of detainees approached the line. It was my job to make sure they stayed alert and awake. If their adrenaline spiked too high and triggered a reaction, they would pass out, leaving the rest of our minimal team in a bind.

On the screens, we could see two figures. They appeared to be male, huddling together, working on something. One of the team members on the ground radioed in. "I think they're getting ready to attack," his words delayed, an echo of the original words spoken, just barely audible. The garbled nonsense of the Converse translator built into the suits was a premonition, a cue for us that they were about to send through a message.

Kupper was monitoring the feeds of his Cyclops cameras. "I think they're about to launch something at our team," he said, looking over at Rattray. We could all see the swift motions on the screen. Rattray stared straight ahead. "Sir?" Kupper asked, trying to call his attention to the situation at hand.

"Release the canisters," Malcolm said in a definitive tone. Captain Gomes stood by, observing. On this ship, he was in command, but this was a ground operation and Rattray was the man in charge in that regard.

The team on the ground had been equipped with multiple canisters of the aerosol gas that Metz had developed. The Cease serum. Did they know that he had expressed his concerns about the aerosol formula? Did they know that they might very well kill every person approaching them instead of just knocking them out?

We could see the canisters fly across the screen, landing just in front of the approaching rioters. The Cyclops cameras gave us full visibility as the gas released. Each figure on the screen stopped and sank to the ground. It was clear that some had fallen hard, the sound of their heads hitting against concrete or steel filtered through the speakers.

This was the first of several such exercises. It happened again and again across the world. Each day brought new horrors until suddenly there just weren't enough people left. Within two weeks, the number of remaining groups dwindled. Reports came in that the airborne toxin claimed more and more of the population every day. Even in the remote areas.

On the eighth evening, Rattray interrupted our attention from the live video feeds being sent in from the Connect gliders. "Hunter, Kupper, Holtz." The three of us huddled in the corner with Malcolm.

"Uh, you guys have all seen how things are going out there," he kept his focus on his shoes as he spoke. We each nodded solemnly. "We're not able to stop these attacks. We estimate only less than one percent of the population will remain in the next forty-eight hours." I felt the words hit me square in the chest, a blow to my vital organs. I swallowed hard, my best defense to steel myself against this news. Any hope that I had that anyone I once knew on land survived was washed out.

Holtz and Kupper were quiet as well.

"Hunter, it's time for us to issue the order," Malcolm looked at me, his eyes commanding my attention. Back on Peec at Sea, I had agreed to the remaining security force receiving the implant. It seemed so impractical to try and implant it on the surviving population. They needed to hunker down and seal their homes against the toxin.

Malcolm pressed on as I mulled over the implications. "There are so few people left; we need to ensure that they survive or else we are done for as a species. We need to stop the madness-,"

"Oh, and rounding them up and forcing them to have a device that will control their adrenaline response implanted will help?" I shot back.

"It will keep them calm!" Malcolm thundered at me. We were all exhausted, all on edge. We had all lost someone, lost everyone. I wanted to help, but the fear in my mind had reinforced my most basic instinct, to rely on data. There was no data here.

Holtz finally spoke. "Hunter, at this point, it can't hurt." I looked over and saw the defeat written across his face. This was a last-ditch effort. I gave a silent assent, a nod, a single movement that gave Malcolm the all-clear from me. Why he even needed it, I didn't know. He was in charge; he could have given the order at any point with or without my approval. Perhaps he already had. Perhaps with this, he could wash his hands of the guilt for this particular action.

With this decision, a full-scale operation was launched. Our team on the ground was redirected to find any of the remaining survivors and bring them in for implantation. It was like a well-organized capture and release program. Only these weren't endangered sea turtles or bald-eagles. These were people. I saw some of the footage, the people running for cover. I couldn't stand to look at it. I threw myself into my task on board: making sure every last person on the Pricus had an implant.

I teamed up with Dr. Michaels and he observed the first few implantations before he started to tackle them on his own. There were over three hundred people on the ship at that time, all of them were ordered to report for implantation. We needed to be efficient and get our work done.

It took us one week to process everyone on the Pricus. Some of the crew rotated out for supply runs to shore, so we had to work around their schedules. Michaels and I developed a decent rapport, but I could tell he had the same concerns that I did. The device was untested. We were rushing the roll-out. He didn't say anything to me directly, but I could tell by the way he spoke to me that he didn't approve. Did he sense my own concerns and that they mirrored his? I certainly never voiced them to him.

We worked quietly, handling each small procedure and connecting at the end of the day on what, if any, issues arose. We had decided at the outset that we would be the last to have the procedure done, our dexterity would be impacted while the incision healed.

On that last day, I swabbed Dr. Michaels' arm and prepped the disc. After syncing it to the main system, I instructed him to look in the opposite direction. The procedure was quick, he was bandaged within minutes. When I told him he was done, he looked over at me. There was something in his eyes.

Perhaps after a week of working together, he had sensed my underlying resentment. My angst over the way my invention was being used.

"Good work this week," he told me. These four words communicated much more than their surface meaning.

"Thanks, you too," I responded as I turned to place the instruments in the sterilization tank.

"So, who is going to do your implant?" I was glad that my back was to him when he asked this.

"I'll do it myself," I said as I moved about the lab, prepping my own procedure.

"Are you sure?" I could hear the suspicion in his voice.

"Yeah, I implanted myself with the first one back when we were still in the testing phase," I turned and explained to him, without making eye contact.

"So, why do you need a new one?" He jumped to the most logical conclusion right away. I was partially frustrated at how quickly he reached the next question, but he was a smart guy.

"It was a dud," I lied. "Testing the reaction to the metal," I added. I wasn't even sure where these words had come from. Where the lies had started to form. But they were pouring out. I didn't need a new implant. I already had one. I could have just said that, but instead, I deviated from the plan. And instead of sweating all the lies I was telling, I was calm during this entire exchange.

"Oh, okay," Dr. Michaels added as he headed towards the exit. "I'm sorry you have to do this," he added before he slipped out of sight. I felt guilty for deceiving him. He had been more welcoming to us researchers than the rest of the Pricus crew. He was a man of science himself, but he was also under contract to protect Peec research at all costs. He hadn't seen what I had seen. He didn't know just how bad it was out there.

As I prepped my arm for the retrieval and located a null implant, I let my thoughts go over all that I had witnessed. I had kept a few of the dud implants with me, not sure why I had brought them on that executive cruise in the first place, but it proved to be fortuitous.

It was too easy to make the switch. I deactivated the device in my arm and then immediately activated the new one, the one that would function as a tracker alone because it had no serum in it. If things went south, I wanted to retain full control of my body.

The procedure took slightly longer this time, I had to retrieve the device, and some scar tissue had grown around it. I slipped in the dud, secured the incision, and wrapped my arm in gauze. I didn't have any specific evidence that Malcolm or Captain Gomes might one day try to use my own device against me. But I had seen Metz dragged away. I had seen Rita banished. I had seen the fighting on the streets. I trusted my instinct.

That day in the survivor colony of New Hope, I realized that I had been right to make that switch. If I had a live implant in my arm, I surely would have been knocked out from the surge of adrenaline in my system.

I could have sat there, my back flat against the door frame, for an hour or a day. I remained so still, trying to stay unseen, hoping that the person in that suit wasn't about to double-back and kill me.

Dawes and I had just been attacked by one of our own people. That suit was issued to the Peec security team. I knew some soldiers on the mainland had been reported as AWOL. I figured a few made a run for it, trying to find their families. I didn't blame them. But I never expected this. One of our own men had - what? Gone mad? Snapped after months of non-stop death?

But that couldn't be right. All of our people had been implanted with the Calm device. The level of adrenaline required to kill someone like that should have knocked them out long before they got to that point. *Unless...* Unless the safeties had been taken off. Unless someone on the ship had given an override and commanded that soldier to kill Dawes. Or, another thought crossed my mind, the person in the suit had no implant at all. I looked to my left and right, sensing that they must be right behind me. But no. No one was there.

The only other option was that one of our soldiers had been killed and the suit was stolen by one of the many crazed and stupefied survivors. That had to be it. I recalled what Lieutenant Chang had referenced in our briefing, the raid on the headquarters two and a half years earlier. Was that the vigilante who had slaughtered so many of our team?

That would explain how they had the suit. That would explain why they didn't have any reaction to their spiked hormones. In all of the studies that I had done, there was no record of anyone having a completely flat response to violence. Even the most twisted sociopath had some raised adrenaline and noradrenaline when they killed and immediately after. We had studied their brain scans and blood levels as they recounted their killings, their body readings mimicked what they had experienced in the moment. Just like with Thomas Clifton, even though he claimed to be in a trance, an altered state, when he mowed down a group of people, his body still reacted.

I had pictured Thomas Clifton as the man in that suit, the man who killed Dawes. He was the most evil person I had ever encountered. Perhaps he had somehow survived the outbreak. Perhaps he recognized me from a brief interview a decade ago. Perhaps it wasn't him at all.

I stared into Dawes' vacant and lifeless eyes, still wide with terror. I sat there while he was murdered. I stayed crouched and hidden and did nothing to help him. I cowered in the shadows. If only his final expression had been one of disgust, I could probably stand to have him look at me, the scared man that I am.

I took a deep breath, trying to prepare myself to stand, to move from that spot. That's when I heard two distinct footsteps approaching from around the corner of the building. Someone was coming for me.

Those footsteps were like a tell-tale heart. Reminding me of the sound of my own steps as I marched to my cabin on the Pricus a few months earlier. The blare of the overboard drill unable to drown them out. The overboard drill is exactly what it sounds like. It's like a fire drill, only instead of there being a fire in the engine room, this was a security protocol for when someone tipped over the railings and was swallowed by the sea. It wasn't an immediate drill. The implant in their arm usually took some time to register the temperature drop. Only once or twice was there a false alarm. Usually, the drill was the death knell. The bell tolling for a lost soul.

One by one, each of us had started to lose our sense of what was real. We could compartmentalize and just think of this as another bunker, another station to do our research. Only there was no research to be done. We monitored how our inventions were applied in the real world. How did the Cratus suit perform when a group of survivors tried to run past the quarantine line? How did the Connect gliders do on their daily sweep? Our counterparts on land reported strong connectivity signals, but the cameras on the gliders picked up images of bodies lying dead and exposed. How did the devices perform when a group of people came across an ambush of survivors? I watched the reports come in along with Holtz and Kupper.

We kept each other strong for a while. But soon, Holtz began to end each evening with the same question: "I wonder if my Mom and Dad survived?" It was a question for no one, because no one had the answer. Until he started to ask Malcolm if he could pilot one of the Connect gliders over their house in Iowa. And then he asked me if I could look up if they had an implant. He became focused on knowing their fate. Until one day, the overboard drill sounded. Holtz had jumped.

Kupper didn't take much longer. The footage from the Cyclops cameras in the Cratus suits was disturbing. His cameras didn't invent the violence, they just reported it. But he was the one responsible for sorting through the records to pull out anything of interest. The carnage became too much. The people assigned to wear the suits began to relish the power it gave them. Unstoppable, they were the alpha predator in a world gone mad. Kupper jumped too.

Soon it was just me and Malcolm Rattray left of the original Peec R&D team on the ship. Until that morning, about three months ago, when the overboard alarm sounded. We had started to lose some of the security crew one by one. Rattray wasn't part of the security team and had no official rank on the ship, but he was commonly accepted to be the second in command. On the ship, Captain Gomes' orders were followed. But Rattray had the captain's ear. He was the top person from corporate on board. In the time before, he would have been the one to make sure our paychecks got signed. I think someone in the mainland bunker was still pushing that button. But money didn't matter anymore. Somehow, Rattray's corporate power still did.

I had seen him that morning. I had taken to running laps around the ship to keep from going stir crazy. Early spring in the North Pacific was brutal, but I couldn't stand to be cooped up all day inside. I need the fresh air in my lungs, the pounding of my feet on the deck, the burn of the freezing water spraying against my exposed cheeks. Rattray had flagged me down as I rounded the corner facing the stern. I slowed as I approached. He had been looking out over the railing, deep in thought, staring at the harsh waves.

"It's freezing out here," I called out as I approached him.

"You're out here," he retorted quickly.

I shrugged, the layers I had borrowed kept me insulated and sweating. "I'm moving, staying warm."

"Yeah, I had to get some fresh air." He looked back out at the waves. I noticed something in his eyes. Something new in his expression that I hadn't seen before. Was it worry? Concern? Remorse? He had always been the boldly confident leader, the boss, the enigmatic and detached but affable mentor.

"Everything okay?" I asked. It was the worst question to ask anyone on board. *No, nothing was okay.* We were all stuck in an indefinite quarantine at sea. The rations were bland. The quarters were cramped. There was a lack of females. But he knew what I meant. Was everything as it had been yesterday? Was everything at the same level of suck?

Malcolm opened his mouth as if to speak and then shut it again before he looked over at me.

Later that morning, as the overboard alarm rang out, I knew it would be him. I knew he was the one missing.

In some small part of my mind, I half expected Rattray to be the creature approaching me in this bleak town. Coming up from behind me, ready to enact his own form of vengeance. But that was just the guilt playing tricks on me. I had mustered the courage to turn and face whoever was behind me.

Slowly, deliberately I moved my neck, aiming my vision at the surprise that awaited me. Instead of almost seven feet of vulcanized rubber and impenetrable black, I saw faded cargo pants and fraying tennis shoes. Instead of a faceless enemy, I saw Hamden. His rail-thin frame towered over me, looking down as I sat crouched on the ground. His expression was grim. He had just witnessed the same grotesque scene. Dawes sliced open by a stranger in a bodysuit, left to bleed out in the street.

I stood up tentatively, checking that my knees weren't about to give out. I knew the next words out of my mouth needed to be from the Hunter that had just put on a front to this town, not the real me. I couldn't let anything slip. One mistake and I would join Dawes.

"What was that thing?" I asked as I brushed off the dust from my pants. I looked up at Hamden and his gaze startled me. The warm and generous man I had only just met with had turned ice cold. His jaw was fixed, his eyes penetrating my own.

"It's time for you to leave," he said with a harsh tone.

"What?" I couldn't even put together a full question. I turned around in time to see two men dragging the pieces of Dawes away, his gore staining the street red.

"We trust the Reaper. Reaper decided your man had to go, that means you do too," Hamden spoke in clear and precise words, I could see his nostrils flaring, the anger obvious.

"That thing was the Reaper?" Based on the descriptions, I had suspected that it was someone in a Cratus suit. *'One of their kind, sent to help us.'* But then shouldn't they know that me and Dawes were also "their kind." Unless it was the vigilante, in which case, why wasn't I dead too?

Hamden pushed me up against the red brick exterior of the storefront. "Don't disrespect the Reaper," he snarled in my face. I understand now how such a kind and mild-mannered person had come to lead this community. He used his force sparingly, but I was on the wrong end of it.

"I didn't mean any disrespect. I just, -" I couldn't put my thoughts together. Dr. Simmons would tell me to take a deep breath right about now. To center myself. "I just saw my only friend get murdered, and now you're saying that the Reaper you were telling me about, your protector, is the one who did it?"

Hamden released me, pushing himself back from me as if disgusted. "That's exactly what I'm saying. Reaper has never done us wrong. If your man isn't right by the Reaper, then neither are you."

I couldn't believe it. I looked to my left and right, around Hamden, and saw members of the community, the same faces that had just been smiling and carefree, looking at me with mixed emotions of fear and disgust.

"But, but-" I stammered. "The Reaper didn't come after me," I tried to appeal to some sense of logic.

"And that's why you're still alive. We don't question the Reaper. But you aren't welcome here anymore." He took another step back, waiting for me to move on. I grabbed my bag from the ground, caked in a soft layer of wet grit from the brief rain.

The town was silent as I turned to head east down the main through-street. I could feel the eyes of every person out on the sidewalks and peering through the windows at me. My feet scraping the asphalt was the only sound I could hear. I kept expecting to hear the click of a rifle before oblivion, but it never came.

The Reaper had killed Dawes. Whether it sprung the trap or its many followers had, I also considered it responsible for Michaels' death. It was counter to my mission, but it was becoming obvious that the greatest threat on land was this Reaper. While I couldn't prove it yet, I felt certain that it had caused the disruption in our supply lines, not anyone in the town. Whatever this Reaper was, I knew that I had a new mission. Beyond making it back to the ship alive, beyond ensuring that the crew would receive rations before they starved, I had to find this phantom. I had to meet the Reaper.

The rejection by the people of New Hope wasn't anything that chaffed me too much. For months on the Pricus, I felt like a pariah. I just wished the crew would see me as something else. I felt like an outsider trapped on this vessel. I felt so isolated even though I was free to interact with anyone on board. It was tough to think of the Pricus as my new home; nothing about it felt like one.

It was an extension of where I had been before, where I had been hoping to escape from.

People only ever see what they want to. Or what their brain has already told them is there. It is a fatal flaw at times, but it can also help. You think something good will happen. You find the positive in the outcome of your day. You tell yourself that you can leave at any time, and you feel free, regardless of how tightly they bolt the doors shut and how many miles away the shoreline is.

One day, about a year into our stay on the Pricus, I walked into the infirmary. The glum mood on the ship had permeated this sterile space as well. "What's up, Doc?" I asked as I gently rapped on the door.

Dr. Michaels turned around, a slight smile on his face for a brief moment. His job was somber, grim. He seemed to appreciate the levity I brought with me, trying to inoculate against the oppressive weight of survivorship. Michaels reached for the next vile on his tray. The waste bin was piling high with empties, the tiny glass bottles forming a rounded peak that could cascade in a vaccine avalanche with one swift sway of the ship.

Dr. Jordan Michaels gestured with his hand to the doctor's table in front of him before returning to the task of drawing the serum into a clean needle. I sat down as instructed, the paper between me and the cushioned table crinkling loudly. Michaels swabbed the skin on my shoulder and pushed the needle in quickly.

No, "you'll feel a pinch." No, "this might hurt."

I could see in his eyes that he was exhausted. We had received a bulk shipment of the vaccine that had been developed by whichever remaining team members on land had been left alive. We were told that the super toxin had been a mutation of several known pathogens. This injection would inoculate us should it be dispersed again. Seeing the vials had signaled to everyone on board that the attack had been real. The shipment we had received had been the largest, or so I heard. There was a plan to mobilize a foot campaign to get more of the troops out to disperse the vaccine. But we had all seen the video footage. Those left alive were paranoid and scared.

The outbreak had driven people mad; people aren't meant to survive this kind of thing.

"Okay, you may feel some irritation. If you start to present any symptoms, see me immediately," the doctor spoke these words from memory. He wasn't giving me instructions; he was reciting what he had already said over and over.

"Symptoms? Like dropping dead?" I was sarcastic; it was not the right time.

Jordan spun and faced me. His eyes widened at the audacity of my words. "Yeah," he said and turned back around to complete his task.

I hadn't meant to offend him, but so far, all I knew of this biochemical agent was that it acted too fast to present any symptoms. The footage we had seen featured streets littered with bodies. The rest of our observations were of the survivors running, trying to break away, attacking each other, avoiding implantation.

"Sorry," I said softly as I left the infirmary. I heard the click of another vile dropping on top of the pile in the waste bin.

My one potential ally on the crew now seemed like a dead-end. That was back when Holtz and Kupper were still alive. When Malcolm was still on board. Even then, I knew I would be the last one standing. Even then, I knew the vaccine was a sham. A dose of saline that would keep up the illusion.

I just hadn't yet allowed that thought to bubble up to the top of my mind. I didn't let it take hold.

Maybe it was the persistent worry that had warped my brain, turning every sound and scratch into a confirmation of my impending doom. My nascent guilt, repressed and suffocated, finally given the oxygen it needed to thrive and empty itself across my thoughts.

I thought about that feeling of being an outsider as I ran, alone, through the woods. Trying to get as far away from New Hope as I could. I needed to call the ship. But I worried that if I was followed, it would be the last thing I ever did.

I scrambled up a hill and into the trees after I passed through the final remnants of the town. Scattered gravel driveways forked out from the road, but the forest was dense in between each lane. I tripped over my feet, looking behind me, looking around me, never looking where I was going.

I scrambled up a hill and into the trees after I passed through the final remnants of the town. Scattered gravel driveways forked out from the road, but the forest was dense in between each lane. I tripped over my feet, looking behind me, looking around me, never looking where I was going.

After I felt sufficiently far away and sure that no one was following me, I paused for a moment. Bent over, I held one hand against a nearby tree to steady myself. I knew in my mind that I should radio this into the ship. They had probably seen Dawes' implant blink out on the screen, had seen mine take off an hour later. Every moment that I didn't call it in, they would surely worry about me. Had I only barely survived? How could the last scientist standing successfully complete this mission? Or worse, perhaps they thought that I had some share of the guilt. Being the last one of a group to survive either indicates uncommon luck or unfathomable malice.

I swung my pack off my back and opened the flap. As I reached in, I remembered that the radio was in Dawes' bag. He had taken it the day before and kept it.

"Dammit!" I barked, sending a bird in a nearby tree flying.

Maybe that was how that thing knew to go after Dawes. And now that town of paranoid Reaper worshippers had the radio. Would they try to call the ship? Connecting with the Pricus and other survivors who were about to starve could bring about some compassion from Hamden. But once they realized that it was our supply truck that had been torched in their town, how long would it take for them to storm the hills looking for me?

I shook my head and put my pack back on. It was time to keep moving. The sky turned purple. I walked until it was too dark to see anything underfoot. Too dark to try to find kindling. Too dark to use my wilderness skills to build a fire. So, I sat on the wet ground and shivered.

I hoped that the next morning would reveal these fears to be futile. *I need to sleep; without it, I will be useless on my feet.* But sleep has been the elusive soothing peace that I have been without for some time now; if it doesn't come to me tonight, then perhaps tomorrow. Instead of fighting the insomnia, I looked up and tried to decipher the shapes of the leaves in the darkness and scour the sky for any eyes.

I barely slept that night, each sound of the forest that used to be my favorite lullaby turned against my auditory senses. Is anyone following me? Is anything lurking in the shadows, waiting to devour me? I felt my chest heaving up and down as I gasped for air, the panic constricting my throat. Each gulp of air only made the moment more real, the gravity of my predicament more acute.

What would Dr. Simmons tell me? Heck, even she would just give me a sedative at this point.

The night was rough. I had read a study once that a person who was sleep-deprived was more impaired than a person who was drunk and was technically more reckless behind the wheel. Perhaps that exhaustion, the lack of rest for my brain, impaired the next decisions that I made.

I should have tramped back down to the road and headed east another few miles to find our supply depot. I could see that it was close from the map on my tablet. I should have confirmed that the people inside the depot were still alive. Found a way to radio the Pricus. But all the "shoulds" in my mind were weak; their hold was growing slack. My mind was working in the background, pulling pieces of information together. Helping me to see something that I was missing. Only forty-eight hours separated me and the ship, the crew, and the home that I had known for three years. But it felt like a lifetime away. I finally had time to think unobstructed.

I found myself relishing in the silence of the woods. Many men before me have taken to this refuge to find solace, transcendentalism, and quiet stillness. My footsteps were soft. But every so often, they let out a squelch as they hit the mud. The twigs and leaves surrounding me insulated and muffled my human movements. Perhaps I should have always aimed for a life in nature. I felt truly alone, finally able to connect with the Earth. My exhausted mind was straying into the unseen, wholly unfocused from my mission. I was already a dead man walking, I had reasoned. The part of my soul that yearned for completion forced the bonds of worldly worries off of me.

But it didn't stay that way for long. As I started to get a move on, the reality of my situation dawned on me. I was alone in the woods; I was on my own time and my own path. If the people in that town had firebombed the supply truck, surely, they would have thought to backtrack and destroy the depot after raiding it. And if it wasn't the people of the town that did it, then surely their superhuman Reaper did.

I trudged forward, but I kept to the trees. The sun had broken free from the clouds that had plagued the skies the previous two days. The yellow and green leaves were illuminated, shining down on me. Maybe it was the sunshine. Maybe it was the warmth in the air that had been absent from the previous days. It could have been the general mania that ensued from so much time isolated and at sea. Whatever the reason, I think I always wanted to do what I did. I think it was in me from the first moment I stepped foot into that pillbox and descended into the Bunker. A human need, a primordial urge to run, to escape.

I pulled the tablet out of my front pouch and navigated to the screen. One dot, bright blue and blinking. Me. I tapped on the dot and a series of controls appeared. Then I did what only I knew how to do. The beauty of building a thing is that you know how to destroy it. I had built a backdoor into the code for the system. Just in case something happened that I didn't approve of. It turned out that many things had happened that I didn't approve of, for years actually. I typed in the necessary codes and deactivated my implant. No more blue dot.

My dud was fully offline now, no way to track my location anymore. It never had any serum, but it had all the other functionality, allowing me to hide in plain sight. I expected to feel something inside my forearm. A snap, a cooling sensation, anything. But I felt nothing. I dropped the tablet on the ground in front of me and smashed the screen. My boot hit the surface and I heard a crack. I stomped it again and again for good measure. Taking out all of my frustration on the machine, when I really wanted to take it out on the man. I wanted to scream and yell and protest, but I knew that I was to blame for what my invention had become.

After my tantrum, I kept walking. Leaving that ugliness behind me.

Thicket, everything was a thicket now. Lawns, playgrounds, fields, clearings. All thicket, and no scratch. The meadow felt like an inevitability. I had marched so consistently through rough brambles and trees for hours, deliberately not following a path. Until I walked into an open meadow.

I marveled at the beauty of the wild land. The flowers sprouting up boldly, proclaiming that color could still exist in a world without human eyes gazing upon them. It took me a few steps to recognize that the meadow wasn't natural. It was a clearing leading up to a house camouflaged in the trees. As I recognized the structure for what it was, I stopped in my tracks. My final footfall snapped a twig. I heard the fabric of my pants swish against each other, the leaves underfoot rustling as I came to a stop.

In the distance was a thin copse of trees. The sun shone brightly through the leaves. It was a serene moment. Until I realized that it was afternoon, and I was heading east. The sun was behind me. But the glint of light coming through the trees was in front of me. In a flash, my mind reset. I could see now that it was a reflection. The copse was actually a collection of pylons acting as stilts for a raised house. The entire side facing me was glass and inlaid wood. The structure was the perfect camouflage. Hiding in plain sight.

I approached it with renewed energy. Perhaps this house would be the ideal hideaway. I could just stay here and pretend that the world hadn't gone mad. The closer I got to the house, the quicker I walked. Images of lush bedspreads filled my mind. A house this big surely had multiple bedrooms, each with large beds and down comforters. After almost three years of living in cramped cabins and two nights sleeping on the ground, the one thing that I wanted most was a peaceful sleep. I could put down my pack, lock the door behind me, and sink into a high thread count cloud.

I passed under the stilts that kept the house perched above me. A staircase revealed itself on the northeast corner of the property. Laid with thick planks of wood, a long continuous branch sanded and glazed as the railing, these stairs were the most amazing sight I could have hoped to see.

Until my eyes caught what was just beneath them. A small pool of mud, light gray and sticky, with a slick of something black on top. There were strange slices in the mud; not footmarks, but something heavy had been set in the mud or cut through it. My own pace slowed, my excitement dissipated, and my guard went up. I pulled my rifle off my back and held it up on my shoulder.

Once I was upon the puddle, I squatted down, keeping my eyes on the stairs and doing a sweep around me before examining the mud. I tried to tell myself that it was just my own paranoia. That it was good to be worried and take anything out of place seriously. But then I noticed that the black liquid on top of the mud wasn't black at all but deep, deep red. It was blood. I saw a few spots along the stairs now, bright red strokes against the pale wood.

It was fresh, still wet. It shone in the sunlight, as bright as a fire engine. Someone here was injured or hurt. I knew it might be too late to help them, but I had to try. I marched up the stairs, checking my surroundings as I went. With each deliberate step, I tried to think of what I could do once inside.

I reached the landing and saw the trail of blood stop just before the entrance. A screen door shielded a green one. Propped up against the door frame was something I had seen once before. During the Cratus suit rehearsal presentation, Holtz had previewed a rifle that would match the scale of the suits. Not only in style and color, but the weapon would be longer and would naturally slip into the extended arms of the suit. It had a built-in glow light and a camera on the mount that would feed directly into the Cyclops camera in the suit. I looked at it for a good long moment, trying to piece together my thoughts.

In the days that I had been on land, I had felt as though a fog had receded from my brain. My thoughts while on the ship had deteriorated. They were frantic and fragmented. One thread shooting off to the next and the next before I could even process what was happening. I never had enough attention to see a thought all the way through. But now, standing on those stairs, the only sounds those of the birds flitting from branch to branch, I could think clearly.

The mud, scraped.

The blood, trailed.

The rifle, Cratus.

This house wouldn't be vacant. And the person in it wouldn't be injured. No. This was the den of the Reaper.

I took a deep breath. I had been spared the previous day, perhaps I would be safe once again. I knew the suit; I knew its one weakness was the tubing on the back. I rested my rifle, standard-issue, next to the highly engineered one by the doorframe. While in the suit, this person wouldn't be stopped by any bullets I could fire.

I pressed the release and heard the latch unhook on the screen door. I turned the knob on the green one. I took my first tentative step inside.

The entrance was dark, my eyes adjusting to the interior lighting. The far wall was completely glass, letting the natural light of day flood into the house. My eyes would accommodate soon, but in that first instance, I couldn't make out what was directly beside me, or behind me.

With a quick succession of moves and maneuvers that I have only been able to identify with my mental playback of the attack, I was on my back, my wrist and thumb held at an impossibly painful angle.

"Just who the hell do you think you are?" This jarring voice spat the accusation at me. In spite of the anger and pain, that voice, the first human voice I had heard all day, was a beautiful beacon of hope. She laid one boot on my chest, keeping me down.

"I'm so sorry. I've been walking for so long. I haven't seen anyone else." I couldn't believe the words as I said them. I hadn't ever articulated that desperate fear to myself before that moment. More suspicion and fear would follow. Especially since I was worried that the Reaper who had murdered my colleague the day before would be here. On my back, I stared up at the person above me. Her features were starting to come into focus. Olive skin, pale from lack of sunlight. Her long hair was pulled back, but two locks escaped and framed her face as she peered down at me. There was a fire in her green eyes that told me that she was serious. Despite her thin frame, she was clearly strong and determined and at that moment she was ready to attack an intruder, me.

"I might be the last person you ever see if you don't give me some answers." The grip on my hand strengthened, pain shot through my arm. The boot on top of my chest began to press down.

"Hunter, my name is Hunter," I spat the words out as quickly as I could.

"And are you hunting for strays?" Her pointed question implied a deeply held conspiracy theory. Her eyes narrowed as she examined my response.

"No, I'm out of work as it were. Just on my own." My small joke about being out of work must have disarmed her for a moment. With a flicker, her hand went from potentially ripping off my thumb to gripping my palm and pulling me up to my feet.

"And you?" I inquired as I began to rub my arm. There was something slightly manic about her. Like a person gone mad, she had the look in her eyes of someone who would sing a song at the top of their lungs while sitting single-seater on a roller coaster. As she spoke, I realized that perhaps she was the one to unleash it all.

Her strength and quick movements, the scrapes in the mud, and the blood on the stairs. Maybe she wasn't an intended victim, maybe she was the culprit. Perhaps, she was the Reaper. Perhaps, she let out the demons that eventually infiltrated Peec and helped devise this plan. Or perhaps, she was the last thing left: hope. I suspected all of this the instant that she spoke her name: "Pandora."

"Pandora," I repeated, taking time to process all of the information in my mind. I had, of course, assumed that whoever was using the Cratus suit and posing as the demigod Reaper to the local survivors, was a man. Being flipped over almost immediately after walking in had jolted me and confused my thoughts. Before I turned the doorknob, I was convinced that I would find a gruesome scene where the Reaper had murdered yet another survivor. Or perhaps the beast would be waiting to attack me.

But I hadn't expected this. She was petite, her upper body drowning in a thick sweater that drooped to her knees. But the lean muscle of her neck and the strength that she exhibited told me that the comfortable outfit was not to be conflated with weakness.

"Yes," she answered plainly. "What the hell are you doing here?"

"I've been walking for days. I saw a beautiful house and started to daydream of down comforters and stacks of pillows." I was oversharing. I was prattling on nervously. "Can you blame me?"

"No," she responded. "I guess it's fair to assume that any house you come across is vacant, but this is my residence, so you'll have to find somewhere else to stay." Pandora crossed her arms.

I nodded. I could just turn around and leave, but my real mission was to uncover what was stopping the supplies. And if she was the Reaper, then she was my mission. All that inspired sleep-deprived self-talk about freedom had dissipated as I thought of the crew of the Pricus slowly starving. I could feel that I was close to solving something and that old habit of seeing things through to the end, of following orders and completing tasks assigned by the boss, it reared its ugly head. "Well, Pandora, I get that now," I rubbed my arm for added effect. If I could stay even a few moments longer, I could gather some clues.

"Sorry about that," she added in a clipped tone. "You understand why I had to-"

"Pin me down and nearly rip off my hand?" I interrupted her. "Sure." I offered a smile to show that I meant no ill will.

"Do you have any water? I can give you some before you head on your way," she sounded annoyed at the offer that she extended.

"Yeah, you have running water?" I was shocked that she had utilities.

"This place was off-grid before, had a catchment system set up as well as full solar," she turned and started towards the far side of the grand room that we were in. Now that I could see everything and I wasn't in danger of being ripped apart, I could inspect the interior. The room was a completely open floor plan with a kitchen and dining area on the near side of the house, against a wall that was entirely wood panels. The living area was spread open, facing the windowed wall with a perfect view of the glen below.

Whoever had designed this place had an eye for the small touches. There were lamps and decorative pieces throughout the area. The dining table had two planks of wood separated by an inlaid piece of glass, resembling a river.

"This place is very nice, Pandora," I said as I looked over the set-up.

"I searched for the right house for weeks," she said as she filled up a plastic burp at her sink. "And you can call me Dora," she kept her focus on the task at hand as she spoke.

"Dora," I repeated. "I don't have a good nickname; I've always just been Hunter."

She nodded, acknowledging my comment. This woman was not chatty or curious about me. She walked over and handed me the plastic burp filled with water. "You can attach this to your pack," she said and walked over to the window. I recalled my training from Eagle scouts and attached the burp to my bag and slung it back over my shoulder. I made a sloshing sound with each step I took towards Dora.

"Thank you," I said, hoping to get her attention.

"It's late in the day, you could head out now and make it a few miles before nightfall, or you could stay here." I was shocked that she had changed her tune so quickly. She spun to face me. "But if you stay here, I have strict rules that you need to follow. I haven't survived this long and worked this hard just to have some drifter slit my throat in the middle of the night."

Her accusation was jarring. This was what I had expected though. Anyone left alive would be suspicious of each other. Resources were incredibly scarce. She seemed to be speaking from experience. Something in her hard gaze, the scar on her ear, and her overall cool manner, told me that she had survived in ways that others didn't have to. But I was equally suspicious of her offer. Why demand I leave one minute, then offer me a place to stay the next? If she was the Reaper, then she had spared my life the day before, was this a trap?

"I'm not looking to hurt anyone, Dora. I'm just trying to-" I paused. I needed a plausible story. I needed a fast lie. I needed to say something, or this woman would not let me leave at all. I suspected that she would prefer to eliminate me than risk my leaving and coming back to rob her. "Survive. I'm trying to survive."

My response certainly didn't offend her, but it didn't endear me to her either.

"More people have been filtering up this way over the past few weeks. I don't like new faces. I don't like company. That's how I survive. You stay, and you owe me your word that you tell no one else that I'm here." The daylight pouring in behind her left her face mostly in the shadows. But I could still see the mistrust in her eyes.

I didn't know what else to do other than accept her offer. If I refused, she could kill me before I reached the door.

"I'll show you around; you can crash now to get your rest if you like." She moved towards the hallway off the great room. I followed her tentatively. She pointed out a bathroom on the right. A closet with linens on the left.

Ahead she pointed to a door and gave me a simple instruction.

"Don't go in that room," she tried to keep her voice calm and level, as though this were a nonchalant proclamation. Or did she know that saying it that exact way would pique my curiosity?

"Why not?" I had to ask. I had to know. I couldn't just let that statement go unquestioned. It seemed to please her that I responded as she anticipated.

"I caught one of *them*." I saw her shoulders shrug as she said it, still facing away from me, pulling me ever-forward through this house of shadows and sunlight. She didn't turn to look at my reaction. Was I aghast, was I perplexed, was I threatened? This was my first inkling that something was amiss. Everyone I had met along my journey had been terrified by the things they called Porths.

Dead.

That had to be it, whoever was behind that door wearing the Cratus suit was dead. So maybe she wasn't the Reaper, but had captured another Peec soldier instead.

Did she kill them? Did she starve them? Did she lock them away and torture them? A shiver ran down my spine as I began to think that perhaps she was a black widow spider pulling me further and further into her trap.

My mind flashed on the thick tracks of mud as I rounded the stilts towards the entrance. The puddle of fresh mud tinged with red. I had thought that whoever was inside might be injured, but I only then realized that Dora was very much healthy. The blood wasn't hers. She had flipped me, disarmed me in seconds. She had been training here in isolation. The clues had been leading me here the entire time.

I had no doubt in my mind now. She was the Reaper. And the Reaper wasn't a figment of any imagination. It was real, and it was Dora. The thing behind the door was just the suit, empty and dripping with Dawes' blood.

In the few moments that it took me to process this information, she realized that I was no longer following behind her.

"Come on," she nodded forward.

As I processed this revelation, I remembered the last time I thought I had it all figured out. My mind went back to the ship a few months earlier. To that last moment with Malcolm at the stern of the Pricus Capricorn. He had looked me in the eye and asked if I was proud of my work.

"What do you mean?" I was still naive, still under the illusion.

"Do you think what we've done, what we've worked on, has it helped humanity?" I couldn't tell if his eyes were misting because of the harsh frigid wind or something else. I processed his question and with it the futility of it all. There wasn't much of humanity left to help. Our inventions helped to make the apocalypse more manageable for a select group of survivors.

"I think we're all doing the best we can," was all I could offer. I didn't want to unlock the trap doors of emotion that I had secured in order to survive.

"Hunter," he waited for me to meet his eyes. "We did this," he whispered.

At first, I thought he was referring to our bleak life on the Pricus, the suicides. Sure, we could have pushed to go back to Ni'ihau. "I'm sure if we wanted to go back to the island-" I started.

"No, not this. Not this existence on the ship." He shook his head. "We're responsible for what necessitated it. We did this," he repeated the words. Was he drunk, had he found some security member making a toilet brew to imbibe in?

"I don't understand," was all I could offer. But my brain was already flashing on all the pieces. The global offices, the suits, the gliders, the riots, the canisters, the death.

"We did this, we made it happen," he nodded as he said it. I thought of the command center on the captain's bridge. I took a step back from him. I couldn't possibly fathom the depths of planning and coordination that would have gone into the release of a biotoxin that killed people en masse. How could they know who would and wouldn't survive? What was the point of it? To cull the population? They clearly overshot. My mind was running in overdrive. I wanted to turn and run, but it would bring me back around to him again in a few moments. There was no escape.

I looked at Malcolm. I had spent years trusting him, thinking that underneath the dynamic of boss and employee that there was a respect for each other, a friendship. We had survived this together; we had made it. But he had caused it. We had caused it.

"Hunter-" he said. But as he spoke my name, I felt a rage that had been building within me break through. I had lost everything. Everyone had lost everything. This was a living hell. To have nowhere to go that was safe. Not at sea, not on land. I was angry at what he was confessing. But moreover, I was mad at him for telling me. He had broken the illusion, he had confessed. I had no anonymous terrorist to hate, no nameless fate to spite. My anger had a face to blame now, my grief had a person to punish. The dud device in my arm could do nothing to quell the rage. And with that, I pushed him overboard. He was gone before I could even process what I was doing and I ran away. The winds were strong that day and the spray leaping up onto the deck was thick. I finished my run only slightly later than usual.

When the overboard alarm rang fifteen minutes later, I knew it would be him.

But it wasn't until I pictured the Cratus suit in Pandora's spare room that I put it all together. It hadn't been an outbreak after all. The survivors I'd encountered hadn't been afraid of any pathogen or aerosol attack. They were afraid of the suit, the potential for who or what could have been inside. The illusion had been the invasion for those on land. And it had been an outbreak for those of us at sea.

I wanted to punch the wall, but I didn't dare let on to her that I had any violence in me. All the anger that I had channeled into pushing Rattray overboard surged once more. But I swallowed it. I pressed it down. It would do nothing to help me now. Nothing to restore what had been done.

I pictured the suit, the husk of a monster prone on the clean bedspread. It wouldn't have been unfamiliar to me after all. I had seen the initial drawings and the beta versions. I had seen the prototypes and the renderings, the molds, and the first wearable versions. This was Project Cratus.

The monsters that everyone has been afraid of were never monsters, they were people.

The outbreak, not an outbreak at all. My mind had been teetering on that knowledge, keeping my weight on this side of the fulcrum for so long, but now I had gone over. I had tipped and there was no path to unknowing it.

In my moment of realization, I knew I had to keep my anger down. Because without understanding how, I knew she was aware of what was in the suit. Dora knows. So, she either knowingly killed a person, or she killed a living being and later learned the truth. Whether she was attacked or thwarting a future bout, she was lethal. She had to get that suit and become the Reaper somehow, and death had been the way.

How much did she know and when? How could I ask her without showing my hand? Because the only way that I could know is if I was part of it all. The projects, the torture, the tracking, the ruse, the suit. It all fit into place now. We were never working on individual projects. We were each handed one piece of a complex puzzle, each doing our part blindly, a cog in the machine that would consume the world. And now that I am on this side of knowledge, I have to ask myself if I didn't really know about it all along. Was I keeping the truth suppressed within my brain, not wanting to know, not wanting to find out?

And then, like a truck slamming into a pedestrian, a flood of connections occurred in my mind. The sign in the town from the day before. "PORTHANA FEAR YOUR REAPER." It wasn't the reference to the Reaper that had sparked recognition. It was the word Porthana. I had seen it before. I had seen it written twice before. But I didn't know what it meant. I assumed it was another project because of the phrase: "Porthana Corporeal." Written on Rattray's whiteboard when I first interviewed. Scribbled on the discarded papers in the conference room on Peec at Sea. Another Peec project, another code name that I knew nothing about. Until now.

It wasn't a mistake that they had failed to correct. It wasn't that the suit was unusual and gave the wearer added height and unusual speech because of Project Converse. It was designed specifically to create this illusion, to fuel this mass coverup. Peec wasn't trying to make the world better, it was trying to redesign the world on its own terms. To do that they needed a clean slate. To clean the slate without showing the blood on their hands, they needed a scapegoat. Porthana Corporeal.

"Hunter," I heard her voice from the end of the hallway. She expected me to follow her. Had she read my thoughts?

I stepped carefully down the hallway, each step exact and measured. I tried to not be too covert, to sneak up on her. That would do me no good to startle her. But I didn't want to let out any creaks or whines as I walked over the floorboards.

Looking out the broad window that opened up onto the clearing, I understood now how she had seen me coming. I had walked through there not even thirty minutes earlier. It was like another lifetime though. It was another before time, and now was the after.

She turned to face me as I crossed to stand near her. Suspicion underscored her eyes, the piercing green inspecting me. It felt like her eyes were more invasive than the Cyclops cameras, able to see everything physical and mental, able to read my thoughts. But of course, she couldn't read my thoughts. She was just a human. But she was also a demigod to the surrounding population. Even if they didn't know her identity, they worshipped the Reaper. The one who was freeing them from the grip of their 'captors.' The one who liberated food supplies to feed them.

"Who are these people?" she demanded. Her words broke my stream of thought. What people?

My eyes flipped over to the scene in the meadow. "I don't know!" I stared out at the group. Would Dora think that I had been a scout for this group, a runner who would bring a posse to ransack her sanctuary?

Dora shot a suspicious look at me. Did she think that I led them here? But she would have seen the look of shock on my face as well. And as the Reaper she had seen me in town the day before, she had to know that I wasn't with them. But she couldn't admit that.

I didn't recognize any of them from the town that I had fled from. Their faces were sweat and soil stained. Their clothes hung from their bones. Instead of filing out from one corner of the thicket, they marched shoulder to shoulder, streaming through the trees in a long line.

Knowing how society had devolved, having been chased out of the nearest town myself only a day earlier, my first thoughts were those of fear. Were they here to steal whatever resources were available, asserting that they would take no prisoners? Would they raid and plunder, nomadic pirates looking to take anything they could? Even with Dora's strength and speed and my one rifle, we would be outmanned and from the look of the weapons on this group, severely outgunned.

As they marched forward, a shorter woman at the back collapsed. One moment she was walking along, placing each foot purposefully in front of her like the rest. The next, she withered to the ground. Like all the people I had seen collapse at the release of the Cease aerosol, she fell hard.

The rest of her group turned and ran to her. Their intimidating march interrupted by this emergency. I backed away from the window and ran towards the door.

"Hunter!" Dora bellowed after me. "They cannot come in here!"

I heard her shouting continue as I dashed outside and down the steps, nearly slipping on the blood spots on the stairs. My pack slammed into my back with each step, the water in the burp sloshing violently and announcing my approach.

One of the men in the group who came to the woman's rescue looked up at me. He raised a gun and an eyebrow.

"Don't shoot! I can help!" I hollered, trying to forestall any attack. I had no idea what was wrong with the woman who collapsed. I had no idea if I could help her. But I really, really, didn't want to get shot.

"Stop where you are!" The man shouted. His face was chiseled with acne scars hidden behind a patch of blonde beard. His head was covered in a cap, but his pointed ears stuck out, red from the chill in the air. The other people in his group were starting to turn around to face me.

I slowed to a walk with my hands out in front of me.

"I'm just passing through. I saw what happened, I figured I should come and try to help." I spoke through labored breaths, the sprint from the house to this portion of the clearing had winded me. Despite all that running I did in the freezing cold on the North Pacific, I was still exhausted from the weight of my pack.

"Yeah, maybe you want to help her, or maybe you're the one that set the trap she walked into," a woman who was crouched low to the ground called out. She had a wide face with dark features, her copper skin wrinkled from sun exposure and worry.

"Trap?" I asked. I had passed through this clearing with no problem. Then I remembered my paranoid and violent greeting party, Dora.

I inched forward slowly, trying to get a look at the problem. In my mind, I was screaming at myself that I could be of no help. But it's just human instinct. When you see someone in need, you run to help them. But from their perspective, I could still understand that the timing could appear suspicious.

The haggard man and the crouching woman kept their eyes on me as the others in their group tended to the injured woman. Everything else, everyone else was quiet as she moaned in pain. I finally had a moment to stand still. I didn't dare move another inch until the man lowered his shotgun. The smell of this hoard started to sting my nostrils. The heat of their pack made the air more humid. Everything about being on the outside of the group was jarring. Had I been accepted in their group, I would be contributing to the smell, not aware of it. I would be adding to the thermic effect of the group, not impacted by it.

I heard the soft thumping of footsteps behind me. I turned slightly and saw Dora running toward us in a zig-zag pattern. The man with the scars and the gun adjusted his aim a bit as she approached. But she didn't stop when he trained the weapon on her. She kept running and then fell to her knees when she reached the woman who was crouching on the ground.

"Here, let me help her," Dora demanded. She set down a clear plastic bin next to her on the ground.

"We've got this!" A voice from inside the cluster shouted.

"Oh, and you have sterile bandages to ensure she won't get gangrene or sepsis?" Dora did not relent.

Two people, a man and a teenage girl, whose backs were blocking Dora from the wounded woman turned around. "You do?" the man asked with incredulity. He had thin spectacles that appeared bent and smudged. How unfortunate to have limited eyesight in this world, one where survival is not a sure thing. The teenage girl hid her almond eyes behind a thick swoop of bangs. Her body was swallowed whole by layers of coats and scarves. It appeared that she was wearing every article of clothing that she owned.

"Yes, now let me through," Dora persisted, unlatching the plastic bin. From the red cross on top, I could tell that it was a first-aid kit. The man with the scars lowered his gun, observing the scene unfolding before him.

"Where did you get that?" I asked, my voice carrying before I realized that I had expressed my thought aloud.

"An outdoor outfitter a few towns over," Dora answered without looking up from her patient. The woman's left pant leg was pushed up, exposing the wire trap that cut into her calf muscle. Her leg was bloody and dirty, the skin hairy and chaffed. In a quick motion, Dora plucked a pocket knife from her waistband and cut the wire off the woman's leg.

She let out a cry of relief as the wire dropped to the ground. "That's not the worst of it," Dora muttered under her breath. "What's her name?" She demanded an answer.

"Wendy," said the man with the acne scars. Dora looked up at him for a moment before returning her gaze to Wendy. I watched in awe as Dora selected from the supplies in her kit.

"Wendy, my name is Dora," she said plainly, the first calm words she had uttered since she arrived on the scene. "This is going to hurt." Dora lifted out a squeeze-bottle filled with a clear liquid. At first, I thought it would have been distilled water. Wendy's screams of pain and the odor on the breeze confirmed that it was peroxide. The thick wound that curved around Wendy's leg was sizzling, bubbling under the liquid.

"You can hate me later," Dora said as she ripped open a sterile wrap and bound Wendy's leg. She worked the gauze around and around several times before tying it closed. "You'll need to keep this clean and keep off that leg for at least a day." Dora reached back into the kit and grabbed a dozen individually wrapped packets. "Have her take one of these a day until it heals to prevent infection."

She handed the packets to the woman who had first accused me of setting the trap. "Dora, we can't take all of this. You'll be left with no pills for yourself." She looked over at the empty compartment in the first aid kit.

"Don't worry about me, I've got my own supplies," Dora answered. But her words were cut off by the man.

"Aida, this isn't the time to be humble. We'll take the pills."

The woman who had stared me down, Aida, softened her expression. She looked back at Dora and held out her hands for the medicine.

Dora stood to signify that her work was done. "Thank you, Dora," the man with the acne scars extended his hand, the one that wasn't holding a very large shotgun.

"It's nothing," Dora said. I knew it had been her trap that had been triggered, but I didn't want to give her away. She hesitated a moment before extending her own hand. They shook briefly before falling away. Any doubts that I had about the outbreak facade had been completely shattered. No one who survived an extremely contagious airborne disease would ever shake hands so casually.

"I'm Norman. We're just passing through the area. We saw a community a little while back and headed into the mountains to avoid them. We've found that most little towns don't like a big influx of new people. We're just trying to find a place to rest and make a new home."

"I'm Hunter," I offered my hand to the man as well. We shook hands and then he helped Aida to her feet. The pleasantries were exchanged. "What happened to your old home, if I might ask?"

"We didn't stick around to find out," Aida cut in before Norman could speak.

A curious look broke out across Dora's face, her brow stitched together. The teenage girl who had blocked Dora's path stood up. She appeared to be on the verge of tears, her lips trembling as she spoke.

"They just left," I could hear the mixed fear and relief.

"Megumi!" Aida chided her.

"They did. They were just gone. We figured it was a sign that they were about to destroy the town." She covered her face with her hands.

I looked over quickly, searching Dora's expression. We, more than anyone else in this little group, knew what this meant. The survivors who believed that they had truly lived through an extra-terrestrial invasion knew that one of two outcomes were possible. Either the Porthana had taken exactly what they needed and had vacated, or they fled ahead of an attack. But me and Dora, the two that knew the truth, we were sure that this action only continued the ruse. The great con. Perhaps some areas would be attacked by night only to miraculously have a human contingent fight back at the eleventh hour, carefully orchestrated by Peec. This was the end of the first act of the grand plan to bring about a new world order.

We helped Wendy stand up. The man with the glasses, Aaron, and Norman carried her as she limped on her healthy leg with the wounded one bent so it wouldn't strike the ground. The group followed Dora and me as we headed back towards the house. Thankfully, no more traps were set off.

As we neared the pylons that supported the elevated structure, I looked over at Dora. Would she let all of these strangers into her home? Her home with an empty Cratus suit sprawled out across one of the beds?

I felt the tension building with each step forward, waiting for Dora to make some kind of proclamation. Would she let them all in after she had given me so much grief? Did she feel guilty for the injury since she surely laid the trap that ensnared Wendy?

"That town that you skirted around," Dora started, breaking the silence. "They are very territorial, it's good that you decided not to pass through."

Norman, who was further back from the rest of his group as he shared Wendy's weight with Aaron, called out. "Oh yeah, this was much better."

"They worship one of *them*," Dora snapped back. I heard Aida and

Megumi gasp. Three of the others in their party began to murmur.

"It's true. They call it the Reaper," I added.

"I've heard about the Reaper," Megumi added. She pulled her right hand to her mouth as she said it, biting at a nail that was already ripped and jagged.

"You have?" Aida asked.

"Yes, it's one of them, but it protects us," Megumi protested. I tried to watch Dora from the corner of my eye to see if she reacted to this. Did her ears perk up at the mention of the Reaper? Did her neck snap to attention? No, instead she kept her head down as she focused on the steps in front of her, as though she was trying to ignore what Megumi had just said.

"You can all make camp out here tonight, but I'll ask that you move on in the morning. I don't want to attract any attention with this many people here," Dora announced abruptly. *Hmm, changing topics so quickly?* I thought.

Norman nodded silently before answering her. "I can understand that. But what's to stop us?" His tone shifted drastically. There was a menace to his words. And he was right. His group against Dora, or against Dora and me. They would have us outnumbered.

Softly, barely above a whisper, Dora responded. "Because none of us are looking for trouble." Her face was pinched into a painful expression, reacting to the implication of violence hurt her. I had seen what she was capable of. She had drop-kicked me and nearly ripped off my hand less than an hour earlier. But perhaps there were demons she was battling, guilt she was fighting.

We had all reached the shaded protection underneath the house. Dora paused for a moment before continuing on towards the steps. We all watched her walk away in silence. We heard her boots hit against the wood steps and the door slam shut. Our eyes traced her path through the house as we heard her muffled footsteps overhead.

After a moment of gazing up at the underbelly of the house, I adjusted my gaze and saw that Norman and his group were all looking at me. I was an outsider to them. I was an outsider to Dora. I was an outsider in this entire mess of a world.

The depth of the long deception weighed on me as Norman's group began to set up their camp for the night. They fell into casual conversation with each other. I resigned myself to a far corner of the space below the house, but I could still hear them chattering as they rolled out their mats and gathered kindling for their fire. This group genuinely believed that they had survived an alien invasion. That beings from another galaxy went out of their way to decimate our population and then, what?

It almost seems too outrageous to know that so many were willing to believe the lie. But if you consider that so many people died, do you just get a remaining population that isn't as skeptical? As humans, we believe what we see. As a man of science, I always required evidence to make any important conclusions, but I was human in so many day-to-day decisions. My mother had never poisoned me once in my life, I had reason to believe that wouldn't change, so I ate every meal she prepared without hesitation. I believed that the Bunker had solid air filtration because it would be criminal and pointless to suffocate us.

Forrester had asked us to act as an audience for his mock presentation, back before he attacked Rita and I tried to attack him. I had so many questions to ask to poke holes in his research. But his didn't appear to have life or death consequences. He would create theories that would continue to be studied in psychology and sociology classes for decades. He didn't have to get anything approved by a panel of medical experts or have the safety of troops on his conscience.

When he delivered his presentation, he told us about how the experiments were set up, the insistence that all team members maintain the illusion no matter what to ensure that the results were not contaminated. He went over his findings. That people believe what they are told. A figure of authority is believed almost instantly. A person who appears to have less authority is believed when there are several context clues that could back them up.

I listened to him, thoroughly unenthused. I was waiting for him to stop talking so I could pepper him with questions. He prepared for his conclusion; my ears perked up so I could raise my hand the second he finished speaking.

"In light of all the information presented and the research findings, I have a final question for each of you to consider before I open up the floor for inquiries." He paused for effect, his years of prep-school debate team showing through. "How do you know that you aren't all currently subjects in a larger experiment for Project Collusion?"

I stopped myself before I raised my arm and considered his words for a moment. It was just a suspenseful ending; it was a dramatic trick to close his speech. That was what I told myself. But as I prepared my fire that evening in the woods off the coast of what had once been British Colombia, Forrester's question didn't seem all that dramatic anymore. If anything, it was prophetic. Perhaps he had been trying to tell us something that day.

Holtz had been the first to ask him a question, it was one we all had to prepare for. "What is your fail-safe?"

"Not necessary," Forrester said before calling on Kupper, who also had his hand raised.

"Uh, no, you need to answer Holtz first," Kupper redirected.

"There is no technology involved here. No device that could malfunction. No fail-safe needed," Forrester shrugged as though this question was a complete waste of his time.

"You're working with the most flawed technology in the world, the human mind. Our rational thought can be manipulated, which you've demonstrated through your findings. What will you do if a subject takes the experiment too far?" I jumped in.

"That wouldn't happen," Forrester sounded annoyed as he answered, starting to rub his temples as though he was getting a headache.

"But it could," Rita added. "Do you have a safe word or some kind of code to give people so that they know to stand down?" She tried to help him along. His eyes flickered with anger, betrayal.

"No," he answered coolly.

"Well, you're instructing people to maintain the illusion, have you considered a time when they would need to drop it?" Holtz jumped back in.

"That's not necessary and I sat through each of your presentations and provided solid feedback to help each of you improve. If you're not going to help me do the same then you can just leave!" He shouted and smacked his hand against the podium in front of him. In the tense silence that followed, only Kupper stood to leave. Forrester stormed out of the room before any of us could say another word.

This was the root of the whole problem. Forrester's blind belief that his work was without flaw, his pride. He had no fail-safe. His illusion had gone too far. At the outset, he knew what was real and what was fake, but it soon spiraled out of his control. His illusion had extended far beyond the scope of his original experiments. He had dreamed of large-scale coercion; the executives at Peec made it happen. There was no way to put that evil back in the box once it came out, once someone signed off and appropriated the budget.

It wasn't as though I was put in a situation where I was asked to electrocute someone. Or play the role of a prison guard. I wasn't asked to compromise my morality on a daily basis. I was allowed to produce a device to help people and I did that. I was given an accelerated deadline for production, nothing out of the ordinary there. If I look back, it all adds up to this. But at that moment, no one could have seen how it was orchestrated. No one could have spotted the trend. Even the puppet masters, the executives, the grand architects of this plan only knew their part. So perhaps the most devious experiment in human history wasn't conducted by Milgram or Zimbardo. It was the daily churn of Corporate America, the command and control culture, the persistent need for innovation in tech.

It is too much to put it all on Forrester. His work was distorted. It was taken by Peec and expanded beyond what he could have ever imagined. It was well out of his control before that presentation rehearsal. It was likely that the grand plan had been constructed long before I ever stepped foot in that Bunker.

The futility of this realization made me feel empty. Nothing I could have done would have stopped it, but I still felt inept at my inability to see it all sooner. I expected my own brain to work better than that, to be sharper and more skeptical. But it was no match for the grand collusion.

As the din of conversation picked up around the glen, I slunk back into my silent corner. My thoughts were alive with new connections. With all I had seen, I had my own actions to contemplate. But I also realized now that I had been compliant with the ultimate mission. Forrester's research project. Not named Compliance or Coercion. It was named Collusion. The wordless agreement, the race to the bottom. No one had instructed me today that I needed to maintain the farce of an alien invasion. No one tapped me on the shoulder and whispered in my ear what to say. The instructions were provided years ago. *Keep up the illusion, with Project Collusion.* And I had done just that.

As that terrifying thought drifted into my mind, so did another long-forgotten conversation. Metz. He had been right all along. The plan was to use his formula to kill people.

Peec, their name was a misnomer. They had intended nothing of the kind. They wanted the opposite of peace. They wanted destruction. And we had handed it to them. These inventions for good, these plans to help the world, were manipulated. Metz had been right to try and run, to escape. But by that point, it was too late. They already had the formula. Rattray already had exactly what he needed.

I brooded over these dark thoughts for some time until I felt that I was being watched. Sure enough, I looked up and saw Dora staring at me. Her hard stare was arresting; her face completely placid and calm, but her eyes shone with anger. Could she see into my mind, see the guilt on my face?

Or did she hold everyone with the same regard? Surely, she didn't survive this long and retain demigod status without taking a hard stance on not trusting outsiders.

It took me a moment to respond to her presence with a smile. I had been truly and deeply engulfed in my memory. She sat down by my minuscule fire, inviting herself to join me. Not that I could or would object, but it was still a bold move.

She looked over at Norman's group as they all sat and chattered among themselves. "So, you're really not part of their tribe?" She asked with a pessimistic tone.

"Nope," I shook my head once and raised my eyebrows. I missed a lot of things about the way the world was. Air conditioning, cheeseburgers, plumbing. But what I missed the most was being trusted at my word. In this world, I had to prove everything over and over again.

"Well, the timing was just suspicious," she added, offering this as her apology for not believing me.

"But it shouldn't have been since you saw me back in town yesterday," the words left my mouth before I could stop them. It was time to drop the ruse.

She stared at me for a moment. I suspected that she was preparing what she would say next.

"I did," she finally said after a prolonged silence. I looked up and caught her staring into the dim firelight. I expected that she was deep in thought, but then she spoke in a voice that was no louder than a whisper. "But you are one of *them*," she added. It wasn't a question; it was a statement of fact. The way that she emphasized the word, I knew what she meant.

"I'll keep your secret if you keep mine," I responded and waited for her to meet my eye. "How did you figure it out?"

"The way you're wounded, it's not the same as us. We survived an invasion. We survived mutilation and enslavement. You don't have the same wounds as us," she shook her head. "But you are wounded." She narrowed her eyes, as though she could see through me. "Also, you showed up on the viewfinder differently with the mask on."

I smiled, thinking that Kupper must have coded the original team differently. It had saved my life.

I waited a moment to let it spill. "I used to work for Peec," in just those words I communicated so much. The prestige of the brand, the multinational conglomerate, the household name. "I worked in R&D. My life's work was to stop mass shootings from happening. And they took the technology I built, and they used it against humanity." I let the words sit there for a moment. She didn't answer. "They told us it was an outbreak, a biochemical terrorist attack. Some horribly mutated toxins released into the air. That people were in a panic about when the next attack might be." She looked up at me as I spoke. "They said our technology could help to quell the riots. To give people a chance at survival." I leaned my head back, the weight of the knowledge bearing down on me. "I guess I was important enough to develop a top-secret technology, but not important enough to know the whole truth." Saying the words out loud, putting them into the air gave me a brief moment of relief. I didn't entirely trust Dora, but when she was the Reaper, she could have slaughtered me and she didn't. Perhaps that was what made me think I could tell her.

"If you had known the truth, would you have stopped it?" Her voice was sharp.

"I don't know if I could have believed it if someone told me," I saw Rattray's body splashing into the ocean in my mind as I said those words. "This was too deep, too well planned. I was a cog in the machine. I could have easily been replaced."

"But would you have tried to stop it?" she demanded, her voice growing louder.

"Of course," I answered.

"So, what are you going to do now?" she asked.

"I'm not going to disclose the location of the vigilante Reaper who killed at least a dozen of our security force, interrupted the supply lines going out to our ship offshore thereby starving a ship of over one hundred people, and I'm guessing," I paused here, waiting for her to look at me, daring her to call my bluff, "the same person who destroyed our regional headquarters and killed another dozen or so of our executive committee two years ago."

She looked straight at me. I wanted her to say something. Admit it. Tell me how it happened. How could one person do all this? How could I help her?

"I'm not going to say a thing, because I wish I had done it myself," I let the anger that had been building for days start to release. It felt good to feel this rage again; it felt right to be able to put my resolve into this emotion.

"So, what? We each say nothing?" she asked.

"Pretty much," I replied. "Besides, I know the weaknesses of each of the technologies they used against the population."

With that, I saw something that I thought was impossible, something that I thought would never happen. A smile spread across Dora's face.

Before dawn broke the next morning, I woke to the thunder of helicopters in the distance. It seemed that the noise had roused Norman's group as well, I heard them stirring in their tents.

I had slept for most of the night; the relative protection of the group gave me some comfort. The relief of telling Dora what I knew alleviated some deep-seated anxiety. But all that fear and worry came flooding back as soon as I identified that sound.

I jolted up, my neck stiff from another night of resting on my bulky pack. Norman was already moving to the center of the meadow, peering for a better view.

"Is that our boys, you think?" Norman called out, to who I wasn't sure. He seemed to think it was the military, after three dormant years, flying in. We were deep in the woods of Canada. His accent was distinctly American. I didn't bother to point out these facts. Aida joined him, her hand pressed to her brow, as though it would magnify her view of the sky as she looked for the helicopter as well.

Aaron, Megumi, and Wendy were all looking out at their companions.

I was busy trying to calculate in my mind the time it would take for the crew of the Pricus to see Dawes' implant go dead, to see mine go dead, and then try to scramble another rescue mission. Roz would need to fly out with the few people left who had the tactical skills. They would need to send more people this time.

But it wasn't just one helicopter in the sky. We saw two more fly over us, heading west towards the town. They weren't flying out from the ship.

"Come on, let's get packed up," Norman turned back to his group and they began to gather their belongings.

"Where are you going?" I asked. They all looked over, seeming to have forgotten that I was there.

"Looks like those choppers are headed to that town we passed yesterday. If the cavalry has arrived, then we want to be there to find out what happens next." Wendy and Aaron nodded, signaling that their thoughts mirrored that of Norman's. Had they all talked about this dream scenario, of the day that some authority would come to save them?

"What if it's a trap?" I asked. Aida looked over at me with a look of revulsion.

"You must have had it bad if you think that way," she nodded and then resumed her packing.

I turned quickly, running up the stairs. I pounded on the door. "Dora! Dora!"

I could hear the group below making their preparations. A few moments later, Dora opened the door, visibly annoyed at my waking her.

"What?" If looks could kill, I would have been mortally wounded on that landing.

"Didn't you hear the helicopters fly overhead?" I assumed this would say enough to get her to take action.

"And?" Dora shrugged her shoulders.

"And now Norman and his group want to hike back into town because they think they are being rescued from the evil Porthana." I was wide awake and gesturing emphatically. Her body language may have indicated her indifference, but I noticed a twitch in her cheekbone. She was worried. She was trying to figure out what this all meant.

"Well, you said you would try to help people if you could," was all she said. She gestured with her hand, inviting me to go on and leave with Norman and his group.

"If Peec is coming to 'help the town,' I'm sure their first order of business will be to find the Reaper and eliminate it. If you come with us, you can leave that identity behind." I tried to get her to see this as an opportunity. If Peec was coming out of hiding, then they would be everywhere.

"So, what? Do we just pretend like this didn't happen, like the same people coming to help us rebuild aren't the ones who did this to us all?" Dora thundered at me, the rage that she kept at bay spilling over.

"You think I don't want to take some vigilante justice? I'm indignant too!" I was sure that our voices were carrying.

"You think I want justice? I want out of all of this!" Dora was quick to come back. I could see her leaning as though she was about to slam the door. I reached out my hand to stop it.

"Then do something, tell them before they all settle into another trap!"

"And do what? Ruin the small amount of sanity they've been able to reclaim? Come on! Think Hunter! Before all of this, when a bomb went off and killed people, what did we do? We said 'thoughts and prayers' and moved on. So now we're all just doing the same things again. Moving on. They'll move on. I'll move on." Dora's anger was seething beneath her frown and her eyes glowed with hatred.

"So what? You're just going to stay here in the wilderness and be the crazy woman with conspiracy theories in the woods?"

"Not a theory, it's the truth," Dora spoke as though that was all that mattered.

"But we're the only ones who know it!" I knew that we would never expose them, never see any vindication. The world as we knew it was gone. Those lost would never come back. There was no undoing it, no putting it back in the box.

I had a feeling that if I left, she wouldn't make it. She had spared my life, more than once. I felt the need to settle that score, to save her from what I knew would happen. "Can't you see that you won't make it on your own? Why not join in the protection of the community?"

My softer tactic didn't work. Dora shook her head at me and explained, "Because once we do that, once we form a group together, this all happens again. Little by little, betrayal starts again. I won't go." She turned and slowly closed the door. I heard the deadlock snap into place.

That was that.

I knew I would never see her again. I was disheartened by her choice to stay, but also partially relieved.

I caught up with Norman and his group as they were just working their way through the clearing. Aida and I carried Wendy in shifts with Norman and Aaron. The task slowed our progress, but we worked our way back to the main trail and then started into town.

We remained silent, each of us spending time in our heads. We all knew where we were headed, no need to discuss it. Occasionally another helicopter would fly over, giving us an excuse to look up and track it with our eyes.

Megumi walked a few paces behind us, her attention often caught by some flower or bird. Wendy would whimper each time she changed hands; she tried to stifle the pain with each movement.

As we continued further into town, the road widening, I wondered why Peec would be rolling in now. Or at all. Why? Why go to all this trouble? Why intentionally maim and murder, force our population to the brink of extinction? Why? It should be so obvious. Why do the rich and powerful do anything?

Because.

They.

Can.

No one wins this. The good guys kill all of the bad guys. The bad guys kill all of the good guys. This resurrects no one. It creates no justice and restores no balance. The time is lost, the souls are gone. So, the real solution would have been to cut and run before it ever happened. Find a yacht, hop to a remote island, and spend the days on the hot sand while the world tore itself to shreds.

I was one of the architects of this mass destruction. I was one of the mass murderers. I will head out with this group to try and help rebuild. I will burden no one else with this knowledge. It will solve nothing. Perhaps I can atone for my sins and those of my colleagues. We only wanted to make the world a better place. May our children have mercy on us when they uncover the truth.

We crossed into town around twilight, the last traces of orange fleeing behind the tall trees to the west.

With each step, I worried that a member of the town was about to call me out, to demand that I leave. It had been only two days earlier that I had been run out of town immediately after witnessing Dawes' execution.

But there seemed to be enough people and commotion that this was not going to be an issue. Large floodlights were staged on each corner, illuminating the town as though it were midday. Men and women in fatigues with the Peec logo on their backs were running back and forth. Some were securing generators, others distributing blankets and rations. All of their faces were visible, all of their actions were giving and helpful. They were 'coming to the rescue' now. Pretending that they fought off the scourge of the Porthana, when really all they did was change into a new costume.

A woman ran over to our group. "When was she injured?" the woman demanded, her pale skin chaffed red as the temperature began to descend quickly. Her fire-engine red hair was barely visible beneath a helmet.

"Yesterday," Norman grunted as he strained to keep Wendy up.

"We need a gurney!" the woman bellowed behind her, and within seconds two men ran forward with one. Wendy was whisked away, Megumi and Aaron following her closely.

Norman and Aida looked at the woman. "She'll be okay, you'll all be okay now," the Peec soldier said as she pressed her hand on Aida's arm. I saw a tear rolling down Aida's dark cheek, it sparkled for a moment in the glare of the floodlights.

"What do we do now?" Norman asked.

"Come on, we'll get you some food and have a doctor meet with each of you," the woman nodded, starting to direct Norman and Aida back into the heart of town.

"What's your name?" Aida asked.

"Megan," the woman responded as she led them away. I stood still for a moment, debating if I should follow them. I noticed that Megan had only been directing her comments at Norman and Aida. Did I look more well-adjusted, less shell-shocked? Or did she know that I had only been here for four days?

I got my answer when I heard a familiar gruff voice call out to me. "Hunter!"

I turned to see Captain Gomes about twenty yards away. I started towards him, unsure of what I was about to hear. I expected to be chastised, to be punished, to be lied to some more. Instead, I received praise.

"You did your job, Hunter," the captain said. "I'm proud of you." The words came out of his mouth much easier than I would have suspected. Hadn't this man despised me for years, looked down on me?

"I didn't get to the supply depot sir," was all I could answer. I had failed. I had even tried to run away. The guilt started to seep in.

"No, but you found these people who needed help. And most importantly," he waited for me to meet his gaze. "You maintained the illusion."

If my teeth weren't clenched with anger, my jaw might have fallen to the ground in shock. He took my stunned silence as an invitation to continue.

"You could have elucidated on your invention at any time, but you kept true to the illusion. You played your part well. More so than Rattray ever did."

I blinked, a stutter of my brain, the central processing unit of my mind working through a glitch. Of course, Captain Gomes was in on it. It seemed that everyone was. "He couldn't keep his mouth shut about it. Weeping all over to anyone who would listen. Told Simmons and she decided that she had a moral imperative to report it to me. Boy was that stupid. I would have flipped him over the ship myself if you hadn't beat me to it."

I locked eyes with the Captain. He knew. I took half a step back, the same action I took when Rattray had first confessed. It was reflex to back away from such horrifying truths.

"He couldn't be trusted. You did the right thing," he must not have seen my movement because he gave me a wink and slapped me on the back. I pushed Malcolm over because he told me that our work had killed almost the entire population of the world. He told me that my well-intentioned research and all those years forsaking any social life had been corrupted and used for evil. I didn't kill him because he broke the protocol.

Or did you? I heard Dr. Simmons' voice in my mind.

Unaware of the thoughts spiraling through my head, the Captain just kept going. "We're coming in like heroes to these people. We're finally able to fight back the Porthana and we will restore peace." He used air quotes as he said this. "We'll build this world up the way it should be."

I shook my head. "The Reaper won't let you," I said in a low voice.

The Captain stood back and crossed his arms. The twinkle in his eye shut off. His weak smile turned into a hard frown. "That Reaper is a phantom."

I wanted to look behind me. I wanted to check to see if Dora had changed her mind. I hoped that she would be standing in the middle of the road in her stolen Cratus suit, stained with dried blood, ready to give them all hell. But I didn't dare move. I didn't dare break eye contact. "Are you sure about that, Captain?"

I looked for any trace of doubt on his face. A flicker of fear, a worry that he wasn't right at all.

"I will be," he looked away from me, his body turning to face the mountain that we had all just come from. The Captain reached for his pocket and pulled out a radio.

"Go ahead, Roz," he bellowed into the device between the chirps.

I waited for whatever was going to happen next. In the distance, I could hear the helicopter coming closer. The thunder of the blades cutting through the air.

I wanted this all to just end. The deception, the lies. I wanted it to be over and for everything to be put back the way it had been. But the end of this wouldn't come. The end was not a beginning at all, and that new beginning was certainly our end.

I caught sight of the Captain's slimy smile, indicative of malicious thoughts. He was so smug. I just knew without it even being mentioned and it made me sick.

Was there time enough to out-think, out-maneuver them?

Before I could properly react, clench my fist, and swing, Roz flew overhead. The helicopter looked much the same as it had four days earlier when I saw it flying away. Only this time, there was a large cylinder hanging from the left side. A missile cut loose and Roz banked the chopper away. The popping and roar of the blazing explosion knocked us all back. The side of the mountain shuddered.

This had all been part of the plan. This had been architected long ago. This was how we would start the world anew. May our descendants forgive us.

Architects

THE END

ACKNOWLEDGMENTS

My amazing support team, family, friends, and fans have made this and all of my books possible. Thank you to my wonderful editors, Debbie and Jeff, for all of your patient guidance. Thank you to all my fans who have read each of my books and continue to ask for more.

M.K. Williams is the author of multiple books. You can follow her for more in-depth information on these books at 1mkwilliams.com. To receive updates on upcoming books, please take a moment to subscribe.

If you enjoyed this story, please consider leaving a review for Architects. Each review helps other readers discover this book. Thank you for your support.

Looking for more to read about the world of The Project Collusion Series? Read the follow-on story for more about what happened to Dora in The Dora Diaries. Visit 1mkwilliams.com/project-collusion to claim your copy today.

www.ingramcontent.com/pod-product-compliance
Lightning Source LLC
Chambersburg PA
CBHW030743110726
47900CB00008B/2427